Praise for *When in Rome . . .* by Gemma Townley

"A refreshing, funny, pacy book, it made me want to rush off to Rome and be Audrey Hepburn. I loved it!"
—SOPHIE KINSELLA, author of
Confessions of a Shopaholic

"Gemma Townley's story is infectious, sweet, charming and hysterical. She's an author after my own heart."
—SHERRIE KRANTZ, author of *The Autobiography of Vivian* and *Vivian Lives*

"As sweet and frothy as a cappuccino, this engaging *Roman Holiday*–inspired romp reveals the importance of a 'victory haircut' and the transformative powers of shopping at Gucci!"
—MELISSA DE LA CRUZ, author of *Cat's Meow* and *How to Become Famous in Two Weeks or Less*

"Like tiramisu washed down with cappuccino— seductive, and deliciously bad for you."
—REBECCA CAMPBELL, author of *Slave to Fashion*

"A delightful debut."
—*Shape*

"A bubbly debut."
—*New York Daily News*

Also by Gemma Townley

LITTLE WHITE LIES

When in Rome...

A Novel of Piazzas and Passion

Gemma Townley

BALLANTINE BOOKS · NEW YORK

When in Rome is a work of fiction. Names, characters, places, and incidents are the products of the author's imagination or are used fictitiously. Any resemblance to actual events, locales, or persons, living or dead, is entirely coincidental.

2005 Ballantine Books Mass Market Edition

Copyright © 2004 by Gemma Townley
Excerpt from *Little White Lies* by Gemma Townley copyright © 2005 by Gemma Townley

Published in the United States by Ballantine Books, an imprint of The Random House Publishing Group, a division of Random House, Inc., New York.

Ballantine and colophon are registered trademarks of Random House, Inc.

Originally published in trade paperback in the United States by Ballantine Books, an imprint of The Random House Publishing Group, a division of Random House, Inc., in 2004.

www.ballantinebooks.com

ISBN 0-345-47897-5

Printed in the United States of America

OPM   9 8 7 6 5 4 3

DEDICATION

To Maddy—for always leading the way,
and letting me come, too

ACKNOWLEDGMENTS

Huge thanks to my agent, Dorie Simmonds, and my editor, Allison Dickens, for all their support and enthusiasm; to Jennifer at the Dorie Simmonds Agency for all her work behind the scenes; to Millie for her fab photography; to Maddy and Henry for their inspiration; to Abigail for her legal brains and e-mail banter; to my parents for everything; and to Mark for everything else.

1

I have this little fantasy. I'm walking down the street, on my way somewhere really cool, when I see Mike out of the corner of my eye. I'm looking good; I've lost a few pounds and have just got back from somewhere exotic, so I've got a nice tan. I'm walking along hand in hand with Pierce Brosnan, or maybe Russell Crowe—you know, so long as he keeps his temper under control. Or even Brad Pitt. I mean, I know he's married to Jennifer Aniston and everything, but I'd only be *borrowing* him. The point is that I'm with someone gorgeous, glamorous, and obviously besotted with me. Whereas Mike is on his own and looks really lonely. His horribly thin blond girlfriend has left him and he is looking terrible. I can tell just from looking that things are not going well—he has lost his arrogant swagger and is sort of shuffling along the street. And when he claps eyes on me he suddenly sees how stupid he was to dump me. He immediately understands that things started going wrong from the moment we split up, and he realizes that he has never stopped loving me. He looks at me and smiles hopefully. Do I stop and talk to him? Do I, hell. I walk past, giving him a sympathetic smile as Pierce/Brad/Russell and I make our way to some glamorous party.

That's the way it's meant to go. That's the way I've imagined it for the past two years. Unfortunately, life doesn't always go as planned.

In reality, it's Sunday afternoon when I bump into Mike. A dreary, rainy Sunday afternoon, and David and I are on our way back from Homebase, the hardware store; my curtains have fallen down and David has offered to help me put up a new rail. We're walking along carrying this stupid iron rod thing and I'm not really looking at anything except my feet. So when a car slams to a halt next to us and drenches us with water, I go over to the driver's window and start shouting stuff about Sunday drivers and people not looking where they're going. I'm wet through and my new Jimmy Choos are ruined (I know I shouldn't have worn them, but I was watching old episodes of "Sex and the City" last night, and was inspired to turn a boring shopping trip into a glamorous expedition by wearing high, frivolous shoes). And then the car window comes down and a really sexy face looks up at me and says "Georgie?"

I mean, I'm over Mike. I really am. And I'm also completely in love with my boyfriend, David. But that doesn't mean that I've forgotten that Mike dumped me by leaving a note on the kitchen table. That after two years of running around after him, he didn't even have the decency to say good-bye. Naturally, I think he's despicable. And I'm very pleased that he never got back in touch (not even to see how I was or anything), because I have absolutely nothing to say to him. It's just that I'd like to know, you know, that things have gone downhill since we broke up. That he can't believe how stupid he was to leave me. That he hugs his pillow at night, pretending that it's me. That he would do anything to get me back. Just so I can turn him down, you understand.

The thing is, Mike's the sort of person people like me don't usually get to go out with. I mentioned Brad Pitt earlier, remember? Well, Mike's up there with him and Jude Law and Hugh Grant and Robbie Williams. He's drop-dead gorgeous. Everyone loves him. When you walk down the street with him people stare. And for two whole years he was going out with me.

So there I am in the street, with hair stuck to my face, looking at Mike sitting in some amazing car, grinning. He starts saying something about how great it is to see me, and then he sees David.

I should probably mention that David and Mike don't get on very well. Actually, they hate each other's guts—have since school. It's never been an issue—I didn't start going out with David until after Mike left, and I haven't seen Mike since. But it does make chance meetings like this a bit awkward. For a moment I kind of revel in the idea of two men staring each other out because of me, but then I start feeling a bit sorry for David. He's always been the one who did well for himself, got a proper job and everything, while Mike has been doing sod all since leaving university (he didn't do much there either by all accounts—he gets very sketchy when you ask him about his degree), and now here's Mike in a swanky BMW looking like a pop star or something, while we stand on the road feeling cold and miserable. Or is that just me?

Either way, this is not the time for conversations with Mike. I have no time to compose myself and to suddenly appear cool and successful. So I tell him we have to be getting on ("you know," I want to add, "got a couple of premieres to go to . . ."), then he winks and says "Bye, gor-geous," and he's off.

David and I stand by the road for a couple of minutes not saying anything. Like we're not quite ready to go back to our boring existence just yet.

"Come on, darling," David manages eventually. "Let's go home and have a nice cup of tea."

We get back to my flat and David puts the kettle on. David's response to any crisis is to make tea. Which is good—I mean, Mike used to go out and buy a bottle of whiskey if things didn't go his way. Tea is much better in my opinion.

I sit at the kitchen table, watching him methodically warming up the teapot (tea is important to David; it just doesn't taste the same if you don't use a pot) and adding the right amount of tea leaves. The curtain pole is leaning up against the wall and the rain is still pouring down.

"Is that the first time you've seen Mike since—"

"Yeah." I'm trying to sound uninterested, but since Mike drove off I've been going over and over our encounter in my head. What did I look like? How did I come across? Did he look single?

"You're okay?"

"Okay? Of course I am. Why shouldn't I be? Actually, I think he looked rather podgy. Don't you think?"

I want to talk about Mike, I want to discuss in minute detail everything about our meeting, to analyze every look and nuance. But I can't, not with David anyway.

"Really? I couldn't tell," says David in measured tones.

"Must be all that good living."

"Good living?"

"Oh come on—the car, his clothes. He's obviously doing well for himself," I say, as airily as I can. I hope I don't sound as bitter as I feel.

"Mike doing well for himself? More like doing well off of someone else," says David evenly as he swirls the teapot.

"You think his girlfriend is rich then?"

I haven't met or seen the girl Mike left me for. For all I know he could be on his fifth girlfriend since me, but I always picture him with the same person, and I generally imagine her to be incredibly annoying and rather stupid. All I know is that she is blond and thin. My neighbor saw her picking him up in a Mercedes when he walked out on me. He didn't remember much about her—although he described the car in detail—but I could tell from what little he told me that she was your average nightmare. Pretty. Long legs. You know the sort.

"Girlfriend, parents, friends—anyone he can get money out of." David brings over two mugs of tea and a packet of biscuits and sits down opposite me. I sometimes forget how good-looking David is—he's got a really strong face and gorgeous blue eyes that twinkle when he smiles. Maybe not quite in Mike territory, but pretty tasty all the same.

"But enough of Mike," he says very slowly. "I think right now we should forget the stupid curtains and watch a good film instead."

I sit down on the sofa with a hot cup of tea, and David walks over to the shelf to pick out a video. It's only done for show, because we always end up watching the same one.

There are two films I know by heart and back to front. One of them is *Footloose* (owing to a teenage crush on Kevin Bacon), and the other is *Roman Holiday*. I don't know exactly why, but David and I have watched it at least twenty times, and I never get bored with it—it's so sad, so funny, it's set in gorgeous Rome, and Audrey Hepburn looks just amazing. She plays a princess who has to spend all her time going round meeting people and making speeches; Gregory Peck is a cynical American journalist who's trying to make enough money to get back home. She escapes from the embassy for one night and meets him, then they spend the day together before she goes back to being a princess—having fallen in love with him of course. Oh, and he realizes who she is and decides he could get a front-page story out of it, then doesn't go through with it because he falls in love with her, too. Okay, so it's not particularly realistic, but still. The first time we watched it, we were transfixed. And right afterward, David murmured in my ear "I'm going to take you to Rome, my darling. I'm going to hire one of those scooters and I'm going to take you wherever you want to go."

I mean, how romantic is that? I have that picture in my head a lot—me being like Audrey Hepburn, floating around in pretty dresses, and David being like Gregory Peck, all manly and hard but warm in the center.

Of course we haven't actually been to Rome yet—David's always really busy with work and stuff—but we're going to go. Definitely. I actually bought some plane tickets to Rome about a year ago, as a surprise. I'd arranged with David's PA for him to have a Friday off and I was going to turn up at his office on Thursday evening and whisk him off for a long weekend. But then on the Monday before there was a huge crisis at work and he had to go to New York on short notice. I didn't actually tell him about the tickets to Rome because I didn't want him to feel bad. Still, there's always this year. David has promised me that he's going to take a proper holiday this year, so nothing's going to stop us.

I lean my head on David's shoulder as the film begins. Already I'm a European princess and he's my sexy bit of rough.

Except that David isn't quite Gregory Peck, if you know what I mean. He is solid, dependable, respectable, and generous. He's also an accountant—and I can't imagine Gregory Peck spending hours looking at boring numbers, can you? Actually, David's what you call a forensic accountant, which is perhaps a little bit nearer Gregory Peck territory. When he told me, I thought he meant he was going to be working for Scotland Yard, but he told me it isn't *that* sort of forensic. But it does sound better than numbers crunching; forensic accountants trace dodgy dealings and stuff. Like once he was working on the divorce settlement case of some really rich businessman, and his job was to track down the numerous offshore bank accounts where the husband had put all his money so he didn't have to give any of it to his wife. And another time he was investigating this drug ring that had bought up a whole load of property in London. Last year his firm even started working for the Fraud Squad, and now he gets to work with the police and secret intelligence and people like that. But that's about as much as I know. Somehow David makes exciting things like breaking drug rings sound really quite boring—lots of detailed investigations into balance sheets, and no breaking down doors and shouting "Hold it right there." I guess he's still an accountant; he just happens to be an accountant who works for the Fraud Squad and that's just not the same, is it? Not that there's anything wrong with being an accountant or anything, but they don't tend to be cool and strong, silent types. Come to think of it, they don't usually get invited to particularly good parties either. Unless you count the Accountancy Age Awards, that is, and I don't.

Mike, on the other hand, is a bit nearer the mark. He never really had a job, as such, but he is a really good DJ and record promoter (I've only heard him DJ once and he was a bit drunk, but he told me about how he could have been more famous than Pete Tong if he'd wanted to), and he's really well connected and stuff. Like, if you want to go to a gig, he can always get guest-list passes. And whenever you read an article on some new model or musician or actress, Mike always knows them. At least he did two years ago, but I can't imagine he's changed that much.

Sorry, I was talking about David, wasn't I. Okay, so David is really nice. He's "take home and meet the parents" nice. He earns quite a lot of money I think—we always go to nice restaurants and he never lets me pay unless we go to Pizza Express. He's also got a really nice flat in Putney, on the river.

I first met him at a dinner party that my old school friend Candida had "thrown." Candy is not like most of my friends—she has "chums" named Rupert or Julian and she has "soirees" instead of parties. Anyway, I was at a loose end and Candy thought a dinner party might be fun, so I dutifully bought a cheap bottle of wine, put on some lippy, and took the Tube to her Notting Hill flat.

I love going to Candy's flat, not that I've been there for ages; I kind of fell out of touch with Candy a bit before I met David again. To be honest, we never had that much in common; we used to live near each other when I was younger and we kind of stayed in touch. But her flat is gorgeous—stucco-fronted, with a huge garden that's shared with the other houses in her street. And it's huge: three bedrooms, a sitting room, and a separate dining room. I mean, who has room for a dining room when they live in London? Not me, certainly. Which is probably why I don't have dinner parties very often—or ever, actually.

As soon as I got to Candy's I realized I'd made a huge mistake. She was all dressed up in this incredible backless number, and seemed to have half forgotten that she'd invited me when I arrived. And then, after she'd introduced me to all her boarding school "chums" and I was just beginning to relax, Bridget and Ralf, one of the couples there, announced that they had just done a wine tasting course at Christie's and were going to deliver a verdict on all the wines on the table. Thinking that my £2.99 Château de somewhere in Eastern Europe would not hold its own against the expensive-looking French wine already out, I made my way to the kitchen to hide my wine at the very back of the fridge, figuring that no one cares what wine tastes like when you're on the eighth bottle. Except that someone stopped me before I could get there.

A very good-looking guy dressed in black and in Prada trainers grabbed my hand and called out really loudly "Candy, one of your guests is trying to sneak her wine out." I turned a horrible puce color. I couldn't remember his name even though we'd been introduced about five minutes ago, but decided I hated him already.

"Needs cooling," I muttered, trying to get past him.

"Rubbish," he said in his public school tones, prizing the wine from my hand. "I think it's already cold enough in Bulgaria, isn't it?"

He was laughing and I smiled thinly. Everyone in the room had stopped talking at this point and was looking awkwardly at me, not quite sure what to say. And then someone came to my defense. A rather sweet-looking bloke wearing chinos with a shirt tucked in walked over.

"Bulgaria has actually won some major prizes for its wine-making recently," he said seriously. "And 1999 was a particularly good year in some regions."

I smiled gratefully and took my bottle back from the Prada-wearing bastard who had mortified me in front of people I'd never met before. He laughed again and wandered off toward two girls who immediately kissed him and laughed loudly at everything he said. I realized that the guy in chinos was still standing next to me. "I'm David," he said. "It's very nice to meet you."

Of course, it took another two and a half years before I started seeing David. That night I ended up sleeping with the guy who was rude about my wine. He was called Mike and we left halfway through the meal because his hand was inching under my skirt and I couldn't believe that someone so gorgeous was interested in me.

David was very good about it. I bumped into him about six months after Mike left, and he asked me out to dinner. And then he asked me out again. He was so sweet! He called when he said he would. And now he's helping me put my curtains up. I mean, how nice is that?

2

It's Monday morning and I'm ten minutes late for work—because the stupid ticket machine at Shepherds Bush Tube Station refused to take my ten-pound note and not because I couldn't get out of bed this morning. I practice my excuses as I climb the escalator at Bond Street station—very toning for the bottom and thighs. (I have given up my gym membership since I read somewhere that if you always take the stairs and walk everywhere, you could do a two-hour workout every day without knowing it.)

I buy a cappuccino to make Monday morning a bit more bearable, and then decide to get Nigel one, too, working on the same principle. It doesn't seem to work. As I place the coffee on his desk, he looks up and I can see that his cheeks are slightly pink.

Nigel is my boss. He gets quite stressed when people are late, or don't do things in an orderly fashion. I know this because once he nearly cried when I messed up his desk a bit by accident. I was doing some work on one of his projects while he was away, and I'm not the most organized person if I'm completely honest. I mean, neat piles on desks—what's that all about? I like everything where I can see it, and if that means that every so often bits of paper get lost, well, that's hardly my fault, is it? When Nigel got back and realized I'd completely decimated his filing system, he started off angry, but then I swear I saw a tear in his eye. I've been trying really hard to be tidy ever since.

Nigel and I work in publishing. Usually, when I tell people what I do, I leave it at that, because then it sounds like I could be working with literary geniuses and brilliant novels. But you may as well know the truth. I work at Leary Publishing, and we produce loose-leaf handbooks and CD-ROMs for accountants. Lawyers, too, sometimes. I research new product launches and spend time talking to accountants about their business needs. So really, David and I are made for each other.

Recently, though, things have been looking up a bit. To start with, we've got a new divisional director, Guy Jackson, who keeps calling Nigel into meetings, which means he isn't breathing down my neck.

The other thing I have discovered to my amazement is that if you know a little bit about what you're working on, it's actually easier. It's not like I've been swotting up or anything, but we've kind of got this Sunday-morning ritual going where David brings me breakfast in bed and then tries to read the business section of the *Telegraph*. I ask him stupid questions about the headlines just to get his attention, and he explains each story in detail, demonstrating each point by kissing or prodding my stomach as I giggle and snuggle into his chest. This generally lasts for about ten minutes and then the newspaper gets chucked to the floor and we shag each other's brains out, spraying crumbs all over the bed linen.

But it works. Last week I actually had a conversation with Guy in the lift about risk management following Enron. I sort of dried up after telling him I thought risk management was important, but that's okay because he went into overdrive saying how great it would be to launch a CD-ROM on the very subject. Nigel was livid, of course, because he didn't think of it first, but I just explained to him that being creative is a talent and you either have it or you don't. He didn't like that very much either.

I decide to ignore Nigel's "you're late" look and head for my desk. "You just won't believe the bloody Tube," I begin, looking for a sympathetic audience in Denise, our administrative assistant. Denise, however, is on the phone with her long-suffering husband explaining that she has looked up "rising damp" on the Internet, and the work he's done over the weekend is never going to clear up the problem. Nigel clears his throat.

"I have no doubt that you have a perfectly thought-out excuse for your tardiness this morning," he begins—Why always *tardiness*? Why can't he ever just use the word *late* like normal people?—"but this is the third time in a ten-day period, and I'm afraid I'm going to have to file a report for personnel."

Nigel loves filing reports. If you ever want to get round him on something, you just write a report, with lots of figures and a few words like "strategic game plan" or "cross-fertilization." He salivates over it, files it, and you can pretty much do what you want for the rest of the day.

"So, good weekend?" I ask brightly. Nigel nods and looks a bit sheepish. I suddenly remember. "Ah! Was it this weekend?" Nigel quickly looks over to Denise to check that she can't hear. I lower my voice. "So, was it good?"

Nigel, like me, doesn't really want to be working at Leary Publishing. Actually, Nigel doesn't really want to be working in publishing at all. He kind of wants to save the world, but I'm never sure quite how he intends to do it. Nigel is a conspiracy theory nut. He thinks the government is watching us, he thinks things like the landing on the moon didn't happen, and he thinks the majority of popular culture is a ploy to take our minds off the real issues and what's actually going on. I haven't managed to establish exactly what the real issues are, but Nigel spends hours and hours in Internet chat rooms and reading bizarre newsletters that debate the latest methods "they" are using to throw us all off the scent. If you ever want to have a laugh, you just call him up and make a clicking noise down the phone. He starts thinking his phone is being tapped and he totally freaks out—sweating and everything.

So anyway, this weekend he went to a convention—of "X Files" nuts, paranoid freaks, computer nerds, and anyone else without anything to do, sitting round talking about security and freedom and stuff. I know this because two weeks ago, when creeping up on Nigel, I saw a brochure for the convention, and it was called Between Security and Freedom—Drawing the Battle Lines. Nigel only told me what it was because I threatened to tell everyone about it if he didn't.

"It was an immensely enjoyable weekend," Nigel whispers, trying to sound utterly professional but obviously full of the joys of spring. "There were people there from all over the world. The power base is growing, you know. And evidence of conspiracies is mounting up."

"Great!" I always try to extend my chats with Nigel because then I can postpone doing any work for a bit longer. Plus, if I get him thinking about security, he may forget about filing a report on my lateness. "So, meet anyone nice?"

I have a theory that Nigel is only obsessed with conspiracies because it's been so long since he last had sex. If he ever has, that is. I've never heard him take a personal call at work, and he never mentions a single friend who isn't "part of the network." He doesn't even try to talk to anyone at the Christmas party, and I don't think he's ever had a girlfriend—which means he's stuck in a bit of a catch-22. I mean, who's going to want to go out with someone who's such a freak? And if he doesn't get laid, he'll never realize that there is a whole world outside the Internet.

"It's best not to talk too much to people," says Nigel. "You never know who's listening or watching. But the network is certainly growing." He looks down as if worried he's said too much, then looks at his watch. "Georgie, I think it is time that you commenced your work. It is now nine-thirty, and as you well know, the working day begins at nine."

Denise, who has finished her phone call, rolls her eyes at me and I go back to my desk and switch on my computer.

I'm staring out the window onto the street below. It is now eleven-thirty and so far all I have managed to do is respond to a few e-mails and write the heading for a questionnaire I'm supposed to be writing. The questionnaire is meant to judge the popularity and success of Leary's latest pensions newsletter. Nigel told me on Friday that we are probably going to bin the newsletter because it's proving very expensive and we don't have enough subscribers. So what Guy wants is a report demonstrating that it was a stupid idea in the first place (it originated in the marketing department, so none of us really care if it works or not) and should be scrapped.

I type: How would you describe "Pensions Bulletin": crap, really crap, or abysmal?

I highlight the line and delete. Surely there are better things I could be spending my time on? But I suspect that whatever I turned my hand to today, I would be pretty useless. Since Saturday I have been going over and over again in my head my chance encounter with Mike. The smart car, the smart clothes, the fact that I was wearing my least flattering pair of jeans . . . and David. He was really edgy, even after watching "EastEnders" and the "Antiques Roadshow." And then he suddenly got up, made a quick phone call, and said he had to go to the office. I mean, David does sometimes work on the weekends, but to go to the office on a Sunday night has to be desperate by anyone's standards.

Really, I should be worried about David and wanting to reassure him that I'm totally over Mike. But instead I'm daydreaming about Mike. I'm imagining bumping into him again, without David, and driving off in his car.

"He is a total bastard and you are well rid of him," I type carefully, and then type it again. "You love David," I type, and highlight it in red. I picture David sitting at his desk. (I've never seen his desk, but imagine an accounting office somewhere full of Nigels in dark suits, staring at computer screens full of figures.) He's looking very serious, with those little lines above his eyes that appear when he's concentrating. I love it when David brings his laptop round to my flat on weekends and tries to work. He sits there intensely, going through e-mails and figures, and I sit there doing everything I can to divert him. I consider it a challenge when he says he has to work. Just how easy will it be for me to get his attention? Of course I always succeed pretty quickly. He pretends to get cross, then he gives me his crinkly smile and puts down the lid of his laptop with a sigh. Come to think of it, maybe that's why he ends up going to the office on a Sunday.

Suddenly the phone rings and jolts me out of my reverie. "Georgie Beauchamp" I answer on autopilot.

"You kept your name then?" Oh my God! It's Mike! Okay, stay calm.

"David and I are not married," I retort, adding a "yet" for good measure.

"You must be so happy together, so much in common," he continues.

"Is there a point to this nice little chitchat?" I sound stern, and am pleased. This is a lot better than standing in the rain without an umbrella.

"It was nice seeing you the other day."

"Well." I realize I don't have anywhere to go with this particular statement. I am certainly not ready to say it was nice seeing him, too—especially as it was very far from nice.

"I thought it would be nice to see you properly."

Properly as in without clothes? I wonder, and then get annoyed with myself. Honestly, this guy has been a complete shithead and I'm being utterly pathetic and wondering if he still fancies me.

I wonder if he does still fancy me.

"You're a shithead."

"Ah. Yes, you're right. A total shithead. But a shithead who would love to buy you a slap-up lunch if you'd let him."

"A slap-up lunch? Mike, since when are you able to cobble together enough money for that? And the car . . . surely you aren't actually a success, are you?"

Am I flirting? It feels like I'm flirting. I am a bad person.

"I can't deny it: I have money. Actually, I'm a huge success. I'm in business. Meet me and we can call it a business lunch."

Why is it that even when I'm cross with Mike he makes me smile and forget what it is that made me cross in the first place? It's always been the same: our arguments always blew over really quickly; neither of us could ever be bothered staying pissed off. David on the other hand takes things to heart much more. It took days and days to convince him that I wasn't serious when I said I would be

forced to leave him for Elvis Presley if he came back to life.
And once I turned up at his place three hours after I'd said
I would and he went absolutely mad. He actually shouted
at me for about twenty minutes about how I need to take
my safety a lot more seriously! Having said that, he was
very apologetic the next day and said it was all his fault (I
never followed the logic on that one, but who was I to dis-
agree). And the following week he got me a mobile phone
so that I could call him if I was ever late again. Nigel was
beside himself when he saw it—apparently it's some super
phone that transmits at its own special frequency and you
can only get one if you're some hotshot spy or something.
David got it from one of his clients—I suppose there are
benefits to being an accountant after all.

"So will you meet me for lunch?"

Something tells me that I should say no, but before I can
give myself time to think I find myself saying yes.

"And David won't mind?"

"David has nothing to mind. We are having a business
lunch."

"Of course we are. Okay, be at The Place at one."

"Maybe," I tease, and put the phone down. I can feel
that my cheeks are hot and I try to casually turn back to my
computer.

"So who was that then—got a new admirer have you?"
asks Denise.

"Admirer? No! No, it's just an old friend, very old—not
him, I mean we've known each other for ages; we're just,
you know, catching up over lunch, it's nothing!"

She is looking at me oddly. "I was only joking," she ven-
tures. "You're with David, aren't you?"

I turn back to my computer to get on with some work,
but my mind is buzzing. Lunch with Mike? I don't have
much time. It'll take me twenty minutes to get to the

restaurant, which means I've got about an hour to put on some makeup, and rehearse all the incredibly smart things I'm going to say about my fabulous life.

Before I can start to bullet-point the exciting things I can talk about (my new curtain rail is all I can think of right now, and I'm not sure that's really going to make Mike realize he was stupid to leave me), Nigel walks over to me.

I hate it when Nigel comes over to my desk. He kind of leans over so he can see exactly what I'm doing, which is generally surfing on the Internet or writing e-mails to my friends, and then he makes some sarcastic remark about how he's assuming I'll be staying late that evening to catch up on all my work. So whenever I see him moving in my direction, I always jump up and get to his desk before he can get to mine. One time we did actually collide, which wasn't a very pleasant experience, but I say you take the rough with the smooth.

But this time I'm too preoccupied with Mike to notice Nigel slithering over, and before I know it he's about two inches away from me. Luckily, I am at least looking at my research report. Unluckily, I have so far managed only to type the heading.

"Looks like you'll be working over lunch, if that's all you've done this morning," Nigel smirks. I smile lamely.

"Actually, Nigel, I was wondering if I could take a slightly longer lunch today." I'm trying to sound assertive, but I'm not sure it's working. We published a CD-ROM once on business communications skills and it said that to be assertive you need to look people straight in the eye and never deviate from your message. But I hate looking Nigel in the eye. He's got such thick glasses it's difficult to properly see his eyes through the glare, and he's generally got a huge spot somewhere on his face and I always end up looking at that instead.

"That will be quite impossible," says Nigel flatly. "We've got far too much work on."

Okay, this isn't going to be as easy as I thought.

"But I've got a hospital appointment at one, and I've really got to go," I wail. I've simply got to make lunch with Mike. And while it said on the CD-ROM that you should never make an excuse (that weakens your position, apparently), I'm not deviating too much from my overriding message of needing to go early.

"A hospital appointment? For what?"

I pretend to look embarrassed. "Women's stuff," I whisper.

Nigel moves back quickly.

"Very well. You may leave at twelve-thirty, but I expect you to be back at your desk by two o'clock on the dot."

Thank the Lord. I check that I've got my lipstick and mascara in my purse and go to the Ladies to get ready.

The Place is a very smart restaurant in Kensington. I have only been there once before, for a meal with my mother, who took me there to inform me that she was getting married. I didn't know about her break up from husband number three, and apparently nor did he (yet), but this didn't worry her unduly. My mother is the most unlikely man-eater. I mean, she looks her age (fifty-six), reads the *Daily Mail*, and thinks bikinis are vulgar. But she certainly knows how to make men fall at her feet. She left Dad when I was just five, and the two of us moved in with Brett, an American businessman who had a huge apartment in Grosvenor Square in London. That lasted about three years; she then decided she wanted a house and Brett preferred apartments, so that was the end of that. She met, and married, Stan, who was sweet but a bit old for my liking. (Brett and I used to go roller-skating in Hyde Park, but Stan's idea of an active day was walking over to a bench and sitting down on it. When you are eight and full of energy, sitting on a bench is not exactly a good day out.) Stan had a big house in Dulwich Village and we lived there for a good five years, until my mother met William, who owned an antiques shop in Kensington and kept giving her antiques until she agreed to move in with him. We lived above the shop in Kensington Church Street, which was great because it was the perfect place to meet boys and that's all I really cared about then. Candy lived round the corner and we soon started hanging out together (whenever she was home from her smart boarding school, which seemed to be a lot; I've never understood why the more expensive the school, the shorter the amount of time you have to stay there) with the sole intention of attracting attention from the opposite sex. My mother never married William, and the day I went off to university she told me about a new love, Stephen. Stephen became husband number three—he was in mergers and acquisitions and my mother got heavily into throwing dinner parties and being a corporate wife. Not for long, though. She came to stay with me my final year and complained that she never saw Stephen—mergers and acquisitions were too time consuming for her liking and she missed having someone around in the evenings. I think in the end she sent Stephen a fax when he was on some business trip or other telling him it was over. And then she met me for lunch, at The Place.

Mike is waiting for me at the bar, champagne bottle in hand.

"So, Mr. Business Executive," I say, accepting a glass from him and brushing his hand with mine. Accidentally? On purpose? I'm not sure. "You seem to be doing very well for yourself. Are you going to tell me where all this money is coming from, or are you going to do your usual trick of ordering everything on the menu and then asking at the end if I can put it on my credit card until your money comes through?"

"Ah, now there's a gamble for you!" Mike winks.

I let him lead me to our table, and study the menu.

"The sole is very good," Mike murmurs, picking up the wine list.

"Does this business meeting have an agenda?"

Mike looks at me quizzically, raising one eyebrow.

"I want to know why you want to see me now when you've made no effort to contact me for two years."

"Has it really been that long?"

He's doing that soppy-eyed look at me. I hate that. It always works and I end up smiling stupidly and letting him get away with whatever he's done this time.

"Yes, it bloody well has been that long."

I catch the eye of a girl a few tables away. She looks away immediately. This sort of thing happens a lot when you're out with Mike. People just stare at him. Once we were in the pub and there was this gorgeous guy in there who kept catching my eye. I was feeling pretty good about it and after a while mentioned it to Mike in an offhand sort of way. (You should always make sure your date understands how desirable you are, according to Candy. She does things like send flowers to herself, which is probably taking things a bit far, but I understand the sentiment.) Anyway, rather than looking impressed and challenging my admirer to a duel, Mike laughed, spluttering into his drink, and told me that actually the guy had been checking *him* out all evening. I mean the audacity of it! Except that when I studied the guy more closely I realized that Mike was right. It was hopeless. Not only did he get loads of female attention, but he even got more male attention than I did.

"I see," says Mike, putting his hand through his hair. He

suddenly grins at me. "Okay, well, when I saw you on Saturday, I just realized how long it's been, and I thought it would be nice to see you properly, that's all. I'm sure I must owe you lunch anyway."

"You owe me food for a year actually."

Mike raises an eyebrow. He has good eyebrows. No straggly bits, good shape. His eyes are good, too—they're soft and dark and surrounded by thick luscious eyelashes. I would kill for eyelashes like that.

"You're looking gorgeous," he says softly. You see what I mean? It's impossible to stay angry. I feel myself go red. I realize I've got to change the subject if I'm going to keep from making a fool of myself.

"Okay, so tell me about your great business deals then. What are you, an investment banker?"

Mike rolls his eyes and sits back in his chair. "An entrepreneur, my dear. I am the owner of London's coolest new record label and club promotions company."

Bastard. Only Mike could make serious money and be doing something really cool. I better not tell David.

"And you're actually staying solvent?"

"What do you think?"

The waiter comes over and refills our glasses. We order some food—I choose octopus salad to start, followed by the chicken. I'd actually prefer the sole, but I don't want to look like I'm listening to Mike's advice. When the waiter leaves we're silent for a while.

"So how are things with David?"

Does he really want to know or is he teasing me? I decide to play it straight.

"Actually, things couldn't be better. He's gorgeous. We're really happy." All of which is true, but for some reason I'm turning red again and my face is twisting into a stupid smile. Mike sits back in his chair.

"Never really saw the two of you together. Thought you could do better than an accountant. But if it works for you . . ."

How does he do that? Make an insult sound like a compliment, so that when you get angry it looks like you're overreacting. The thing is, he's got a point. I never saw myself ending up with an accountant either. It doesn't really sit with my image of myself as a girl-about-town. But there's no way I'm going to let Mike think he's hit a sore point.

"Look," I say defensively, noticing that the restaurant is getting very hot. "You have no right to say anything about David, or to ask about us being together. You left, remember, and you didn't even have the guts to tell me to my face. You are a pig and an idiot, and I don't know why I'm even here." My voice has taken on a slightly squeaky tone, so I stop talking and give him one of my best "I am really far too busy for this conversation" looks.

But Mike grins again like he's pleased with himself for getting a rise out of me, and before I can stop myself my lips start curling upward. God, he's sexy. I mean, obviously he's a total bastard, but the two aren't mutually exclusive, are they? I make myself look cross with him. The last thing I want is for him to realize that I still think he's utterly gorgeous.

The food arrives and I gratefully start to eat. Actually it's delicious. I love restaurant food. I would eat out every day and every night if I could. And when I couldn't be bothered to go out, I'd order in. I have friends who are great cooks, but all that chopping and marinating is just so boring, especially as nothing I cook ever turns out like it should. I'm only interested in the Jamie Oliver–style chuck-it-in-a-pan-and-hope-for-the-best cooking, but whenever I've tried chucking it all in, I end up with some sort of hideous, tasteless muck. I blame my mother, of course. She doesn't cook either, except for soufflé. I think she figured that as no one else can do a good soufflé, it was something worth working at. Everything else she leaves to Marks & Spencer's or Harrod's Food Hall.

I look up to see Mike watching me closely. He picks up his glass.

"To old friends?"

I hesitate. Am I really ready to forgive and forget?

"Look Georgie, I'm sorry, okay? You're right. I was a total prick. Can't we be friends again?"

Put like that I can't really say no, can I? I mean, he's admitted that he's wrong and he's even apologized. I pick up my glass, and as I take a sip Mike winks at me.

"You seem really happy. Life with an accountant obviously agrees with you. Do you think David will mind us being friends?"

"Of course David won't mind," I say, maybe a bit too quickly. Mike drains his glass.

"Well, I think we'll be needing some more champagne then!"

I consider pointing out that I've barely started my first glass, but I don't want to appear churlish. And anyway, if Mike wants to spend money on champagne, who am I to stop him?

I empty my glass as quickly as I can and Mike pours me a second glass. By the time the main course arrives with another bottle of bubbly I'm pretty drunk, and am happy to sit and listen to Mike tell me about his grand plans for world domination. Or London domination at any rate.

"I'm going to have my bands playing at every venue. Record shops are going to be full of their albums. I'm going to be on the cover of *Mixmag, Mojo, NME* . . ."

It's impressive, it really is. I mean, he is so enthusiastic about what he's doing. I'm just about to tell him how pleased I am that he's doing so well when his hand swoops down and grabs mine.

"Georgie, I've missed talking to you, y'know?"

I look at his hand. I wish someone was here to witness this. Like his bitch girlfriend or someone who will tell her. I'm not a horrible person, but having Mike put his hand on mine like that in public is quite satisfying. I notice the girl a few tables away looking at us and I shoot her a triumphant look.

"Really? Don't you talk to your girlfriend?"

Mike pauses. "I don't have a girlfriend," he says, looking at me intensely. "No one else has ever been like you."

Not like me how, I want to ask. Not like me because they are all stupid and ugly and crap in bed, or not like me because they aren't total suckers who need two glasses of champagne to forget just how callous you can be?

"I'd like to see you more." He's stroking my hand now. I shouldn't have got drunk. I'm enjoying this and I came here to remind Mike just what he's missing out on, not to let him think he can get it back whenever he wants. Think of David, I tell myself. Think of the note Mike left on the table. Think how he never even called.

"Well, I'm sure that can be arranged." I didn't mean to say that.

I look down at his hand. His tanned, soft hand. I'm just about to start stroking it when I notice his watch. Oh my God, it's already two-thirty! I meant to be back at work half an hour ago!

"Look, I've got to go." I stand up hurriedly.

"Really? You don't have to go right away, do you?"

"Yes, yes," I say irritably, pulling on my coat. Nigel is going to completely freak.

I leave. But not before giving Mike my mobile number. Just in case.

❧ 3

I get back to the office, aware that I'm just a teeny-weeny bit drunk. I gear myself up for a huge confrontation with Nigel—"You know what hospitals are like . . . I was waiting for two whole hours . . ."—but to my huge relief he isn't at his desk. According to Denise he's in a meeting with Guy.

I flick on my computer and go straight to e-mail. I have five new messages.

DAVID BRADLEY: Hi darling. Fancy an Italian tonight? Failing that, what about an Englishman?! See you later? David x

ANDREW KNIGHT: TO ALL AT LEARY: Can the person who keeps using my mugs and not washing them up please refrain from doing so? I believe I am the only Southampton supporter in the company and have two mugs in club colors. One is in the sink, dirty, and the other has disappeared. Please, GET YOUR OWN MUG!

I gaze across my desk and alight upon a red mug hidden under a pile of papers. I guiltily realize that it is indeed a Southampton mug. Next to it is a white mug with what appears to be a picture of a fluffy giraffe on it, under which is a message. I can only pick out the words *fluffles* and *love*, but I'm realizing it is probably the prize possession of someone else in the office. Not that I want to know that someone I work with is known as "fluffles" at home, but still. I resolve to be a better person in the future.

CANDIDA CRANLEY-JONES: Georgie, Mike said he bumped into you and you were looking great—I realized we haven't seen each other for months and months, let's catch up soon? I'm having the flat redecorated next week and am going to be at a loose end, so do you fancy doing something nice? I hate all my clothes at the moment, so maybe we could go shopping? Call me!

What is it with blasts from the past? First I see Mike, and now Candy, who I haven't seen for . . . well, it must be around two years if not more. I'm not sure why we lost touch really, although I think it has something to do with the fact that Candy was always telling me that I should dump Mike and I never did. I would continually cry on her shoulder when he failed to come back from some party or left me in a club while he went on somewhere, and I think she just got frustrated with me. I suppose Mike leaving me was just the final straw. I didn't know she was still in touch with him, but I guess he was her friend first, so it isn't that surprising. More to the point, this means that Mike's been talking to her about me. He's obviously been thinking about me loads. Maybe I'm looking better than I realize at the moment. I take out my compact to check myself out. One spot, deftly covered with a blob of Touch Éclat. Some faint crow's-feet appearing under my eyes, but only visible when I smile. No, I'm in okay shape. I'll need to be if I'm seeing Candy next week—Candy works on a smart fashion magazine and believes very strongly in grooming. She thinks nothing of going to the gym for an hour a day and dedicating Sunday afternoons to polishing her shoes. I'm sure she means well, it's just that after half an hour with her, I usually feel like Waynetta the Slob. I put a note in my diary to get a manicure early next week.

GUY JACKSON: Georgie, have you finished the questionnaire for Pensions Bulletin? Nigel and I are discussing our strategic plans for this business unit and he tells me that your report will be ready by 3pm. We have an exciting new project I want to discuss with you, so look forward to seeing the questionnaire.
Regards.

Shit. Shit and double shit. I haven't even started the questionnaire, unless you count my ramblings this morning, which I've deleted anyway, and I've got exactly ten minutes before Guy's going to be expecting an amazing in-depth report. I dig out the newsletter for inspiration.
Ping! Another e-mail.

MIKE MARSHALL: Hi gorgeous. Thinking about me?

I hit Reply, type "No," and send it back. After all, I'm not thinking about him. I may have been thinking about his hand resting on mine and his come-to-bed eyes on my way back to the office, and I may even have planned what I will wear next time I see him (heels, definitely; something quite fitted), but right now I'm thinking about pensions. Honest.

I open up a new document, and purposefully write "Pensions Bulletin—your views" along the top, then center and bold the words for good measure.
Ping!

MIKE MARSHALL: What do you mean "no"? You left just as things were getting interesting. I've certainly been thinking about you . . .

He's been thinking about me? Mike has been thinking about me? I flush with excitement. It's worked! My "make him realize what he's been missing" strategy has worked! He's obviously realized that success is all very well, but it's nothing compared with the love of a good woman.

I'm about to type back a flirtatious e-mail when I remember the note Mike left me: "Sorry gorgeous. You're too good for me. I need some time to get myself sorted out. Please don't hate me." If he thinks he's going to get back into my good books (let alone anything else) with one lunch, he's got another think coming. Plus, I simply don't have time for this now. I am a busy executive, and Mike will simply have to deal with that.

GEORGIE BEAUCHAMP: I mean that I am too busy to think about people who should be doing some work and not pestering me.

I turn back to my report:

Your views are of the utmost importance to Leary. Please take a few moments to fill in this questionnaire to ensure that your needs, now and in the future, are met by us.

Ping!

MIKE MARSHALL: So you would be thinking about me if you weren't so busy?

GEORGIE BEAUCHAMP: Too busy to know. Now leave me alone.

1. How regularly do you refer to Pensions Bulletin? (please tick appropriate box—monthly; weekly; daily)
2. Does Pensions Bulletin cover the subjects on which you need to be informed (always; sometimes; rarely)

Ping!

MIKE MARSHALL: I buy you lunch and this is all the gratitude I get. Anyway, if you're so busy, why are you e-mailing me back?

He's got me there. I start on question three, but feel guilty about the lunch. It couldn't have been cheap.

GEORGIE BEAUCHAMP: Thank you for the lunch. Do not read anything into the returning of e-mails. I've just been brought up to be polite, that's all. Now GO AWAY!

3. Would you prefer to receive Pensions Bulletin more or less frequently?
4. Do you consider Pensions Bulletin to be good value for money?

Ping!

MIKE MARSHALL: Well that's hardly polite, is it? I've got a good mind to talk to your mother about you. How is she, by the way?

Mike and my mother got along famously. He had flirted with her madly on the three occasions they had met and she had flirted right back. As I recall, I got in a bit of a huff.

GEORGIE BEAUCHAMP: She's busy, too.

Okay, four questions done. I need another sixteen before it will be anywhere near a proper questionnaire.

5. Do you intend to renew your subscription to Pensions Bulletin? Yes/No

6. Please circle your main area of expertise: pensions; finance; HR

7.

My inspiration has gone. I reach for the phone.

"Good afternoon, David Bradley's office." I love that. One day I want someone to answer the phone "Georgie Beauchamp's office." That would be so cool.

"Hi, it's Georgie. Is David around?"

"Hello, dear, how are you?" It's Jane, David's PA. "I'm afraid David is in a meeting—would you wait for one moment, please?" I hear muffled voices as she tells him I'm on the phone.

"Hi, darling. Look, I'm a bit tied up here at the moment. Is there a chance I can give you a call back a bit later?"

"Yeah, that's fine. I just need some information on pensions, that's all."

"Pensions?"

"Don't worry, I'll figure it out myself."

"Are you okay for tonight?"

Tonight? I can't remember making any plans for tonight, and quite honestly after all that champagne, all I can think about is slipping into a nice hot bath.

I remember the e-mail. "Oh, what, going out? Yeah, maybe. I've got a lot of work on, so it depends what time I get home. I'll give you a call later."

I can just hear people talking in hushed voices—presumably they are in David's office.

"Okay, I'll talk to you then," he says. "Bye."

I look at my watch—it's five to three. Unless Nigel is very late out of his meeting, I'm in big trouble.

I rack my brains for a good excuse. My computer could have crashed and lost the report, except I used that excuse last week. Maybe I could pretend that something is really badly wrong with me and everyone will be so sympathetic that Nigel won't dare shout at me. No, can't do that. I never lie about my health ever since I told a boy I didn't want to go out with that I had the flu and then came down with the flu the following week. I was only sixteen at the time, but it taught me a valuable lesson: don't tempt fate. Shit. Nigel's going to be furious.

Suddenly I have a brain wave.

"Denise," I hiss.

"What? Why are you whispering?"

"In case Nigel comes back. You know *Investment Analysis*?"

Denise looks at me blankly.

"That magazine they produce upstairs. We did some research on it last year."

Denise nods. Obviously the magazine has made no lasting impression on her.

"Nigel has the research file on his computer, hasn't he?"

" 'Spect so," says Denise, uncertainly.

"And you've got his passwords . . ."

Nigel's paranoia that no one can be trusted extends to us. He is convinced that everyone at Leary would like nothing better than to break into his computer and read all his stupid strategy alignment reports or whatever he has on there, and he is constantly securing his computer with streams of passwords and booby traps. Like anyone would want to break into it and read his stupid files! Apart from now, that is. Luckily our IT department got mad at him one time when they needed to access his database and couldn't get in. So now he has to tell Denise all his passwords. But he still changes them every week.

"Oh no. Nuh-uh." Denise turns away. "I am not nosing around Nigel's computer when he's due back any minute.

You're going to have to think of something else, I'm afraid."

"Please . . ."

It's three minutes to three. "Come on, Denise, you know I'd do the same for you."

"Like I'd ever need you to."

"You'd be saving my life . . ." I plead.

It works. Looking as if she would rather be fed to piranhas, Denise makes her way over to Nigel's desk.

She takes out her notepad and starts typing in all his passwords. "You know I'm not allowed to do this."

"I know, I know, but this is a real emergency."

"And what is it I'm looking for exactly?"

"Look under research. Do a search for 'Investment Analysis.' " Denise carefully types the words as I spell out *analysis*.

"Nope, can't find it."

"It must be there," I beg. "Look again. Look under . . . I dunno, try 'magazines' or something."

Still nothing.

Suddenly I have a brainwave. "Try 'strategy,' " I suggest.

"Okay, what about 'Management Strategy Review Documents'?"

"Yes!" I squeal. "I bet it's there." And indeed it is.

"You want me to e-mail the report to you?"

"I do love you, you know," I grin. "Any time you want me to take you away from all this, just say the word."

Suddenly out of the corner of my eye I see Nigel and Guy coming down the corridor.

"Quick, he's coming."

Unflustered, Denise hits a button and picks up Nigel's phone. As he turns into the office, Denise's dulcet Essex tones can be heard on the phone to an imaginary customer.

"No, absolutely, Mr. Bingham, I'll arrange that for you."

By the time Denise has carefully put the phone down and written an imaginary name and number on a bright yellow Post-it note, Nigel is hovering over his desk looking at her.

"Hi Nigel," Denise says calmly. "Your phone was ringing and I was on my way back from the Ladies, so I picked it up for you."

"Very kind of you. Anything important?"

"Oh, no, just someone wanting a sample copy of *Accounting Facts, Part Two*." Denise winks at me and takes the Post-it note back to her desk.

I race back to my desk and open the e-mail Denise has sent. The report is attached, one hundred questions ready to go. I quickly go into Edit and replace "Investment Analysis" with "Pensions Bulletin," then print it out.

"So, Georgie," Nigel turns to me. "I assume you have the Pensions Bulletin research ready for Guy?"

"Absolutely, just printing it out."

I move over to the printer, which is churning out page after page. Feeling utterly pleased with myself, I hand the report over to Guy.

He looks at it briefly. "Looks very impressive. You must have worked very hard," he says, handing it back to me. "Would you mind e-mailing it to me?"

Nigel is staring at me. "Yes, well, Georgie has had the project for a while," he says.

"Really?" replies Guy. "But we only commissioned the research last week. I think it's a great effort from your team."

Nigel smiles thinly as Guy strides back down the corridor. "Well done, Georgie," he finally manages as he sits down.

"Oh, it was definitely a team effort," I say, raising my eyebrow at Denise, who splutters into her coffee.

*   *   *

I leave work on time and get home in time to have a hot bath before "Buffy the Vampire Slayer" starts on BBC2. I know I'm probably not the target age group for this program, but I like it, and anyway, no one has to know. Not that I'm a Buffy nut, or anything. I mean, I haven't even watched its spin-off, "Angel." It's just something I do if I have the time. And I generally make sure that I do. Have the time, that is. Anyway, Buffy has just managed to pin down a particularly nasty-looking demon when the phone rings.

"Georgie Beauchamp." I am so engrossed in the fight action that I answer the phone as if I was at work. "Sorry, I mean, hello?"

"Hello Georgie Beauchamp. It's Mr. Bradley here," says David, mocking me.

"Oh sod off, I'm just have a bad day. How are you?"

"Busy. But missing you. Do you want to do dinner later?"

"When you say later, just how late do you mean?" I'm looking at my watch and it's already gone seven.

"Eight-ish."

"I have a better idea. How about you come round here at eight-ish with a take-away and we can watch the Paramount Comedy channel?"

I love television. I mean, I do other things, it's not like I just sit on my own and watch TV all day long, but there's really nothing better than curling up on the sofa with a good take-away and "Friends" or "Cheers" or something.

"Sounds perfect. See you then."

When I first started going out with David we went out constantly. I was so pleased to finally have a boyfriend who would actually do some of the things I wanted to do, instead of Mike, who always told me where he was going and asked if I wanted to come, too, which just isn't the same at all. It was so great to be asked what I wanted to do that I got a bit carried away. In one week we would go to the cinema twice, check out two exhibitions, go to the theater, and eat out at any new restaurant that opened. After a couple of months we were both exhausted, but neither of us wanted to admit it, so we carried on for another month. I think it was me who finally broke, and one night suggested staying in rather than going to an Albanian film night at our local arts club. David thought it was because I thought he didn't want to go, and spent twenty minutes trying to convince me of his enthusiasm for film as an artistic medium and the importance of emerging cinema from countries like Albania. I was all "no, really, we don't have to go," and David was like "I really want to." Finally I told him that I didn't know anything about Albanian cinema, didn't care about it, and wanted nothing more than to watch reruns of "Friends" eating takeout. As I said it I suddenly got really scared that he would realize that I wasn't his type after all and would dump me immediately, but instead he burst out laughing and gave me a huge hug.

We talked for hours that night—it was the first time we both admitted which bits of us were real and which were more for effect. You know, like I always say that my favorite band is some really obscure one with lyrics that are really deep, when, in actual fact, when no one's there I dance around to Madonna. And I always say I much prefer homemade food and hate artificial additives, but I've actually got a cupboard full of chocolate biscuits and cakes with bright pink icing that bears no resemblance to anything in the natural world. David admitted that he doesn't really understand poetry, that he likes Jack Higgins novels, and that he prefers Stallone films to anything with subtitles.

Since then, we probably stay in more than we go out,

which I actually love, but there's still a bit of me that wants to be the person who would prefer the Albanian film evening.

David arrives at eight-thirty with fish and chips. I carefully arrange the food on two large white plates. (I always try to re-create the look of food in expensive restaurants. So the fish goes on top of the chips, with the mushy peas kind of circled round them, interlaced with the ketchup. Actually, a lot of really smart restaurants serve fish and chips and it's not like it's that much better than the stuff you get from the chip shop; the only difference is presentation and ambience. So by re-creating the presentation I'm sort of making our night more of a postmodern ironic statement. At least that's what it said in some magazine article I picked up on how eating in is the new eating out, and really I think it's true.) We position ourselves on the sofa, food resting on cushions.

"Nice day at the office?" I'm not really expecting an answer, but I always ask the question.

David looks distracted for a moment. "Mmmm. No, not really."

It's not like David to say anything other than "Oh, not bad," so I look at him quizzically.

For a moment he looks like he's about to tell me all about it, but then the music for "Frasier" starts and my eyes flicker away for a second or two. By the time I've refocused on David, the moment has gone.

I tell him about my star turn today over the Pensions Bulletin research, and he laughs, but I don't mention my lunch with Mike. If things are tough at work, he's hardly going to be in the mood to hear about his girlfriend going out to lunch with her ex. And anyway, I'm not going to see Mike again, I think to myself as I nestle into David's shoulder.

I don't think about it again until later that night as we're falling asleep. "You haven't heard from Mike, have you?" David murmurs. Suddenly I'm wide awake.

"No," I lie, trying to work out why David would think that I had. "Why would I?"

"Oh, nothing," David says, rolling over. "It's just . . . I don't know. You will tell me if he tries to get in touch with you, won't you?"

Does he know about the lunch? Why would he ask that?

"You're not jealous are you?" I ask hesitantly.

"Jealous? Why on earth would I be jealous?" David says incredulously. I start to sulk slightly, but then figure that he's hardly going to admit that he's jealous. I know I should be feeling bad but instead I feel like a femme fatale.

But before I can sink into dreams of men fighting over me, David turns on the light and looks at me intently. "Look, I just don't trust Mike," he says seriously. "So tell me if he calls you, okay?"

I don't ask him if e-mails count.

4

I don't hear from Mike until Friday. All week I have been telling myself that I am relieved that he hasn't tried to get back in touch. But my stomach has been lurching every time I get an external e-mail, just in case it's him.

I'm on the phone to Candy, arranging a shopping and gossip session for the following afternoon when I hear the familiar *"ping."*

Candy and I are discussing the relative merits of Kensington High Street and Oxford Street. (I favor Ken High Street. Oxford Street is too busy, and anyway, my favorite shop on Oxford Street is Top Shop, and I'd never be able to go in there with Candy. She buys things featured in *Vogue* instead of searching the high street for rip-offs like the rest of us.) I absentmindedly go to my e-mail inbox, and there it is.

MIKE MARSHALL: So, I went away. Now it's Friday afternoon and you can't tell me you're still busy. I feel like getting drunk tonight, fancy joining me?

My heart starts beating. I'm meant to be going round to David's tonight. I *am* going round to David's tonight. At least I think I am. I mean, of course that's what I want to do, but it could be a good idea to meet Mike, just to, you know, reinforce the fact that he wants me and can't have me. If you think about it, that would actually be really good for David, too, because it would show Mike that David is way better than him. And if I don't go, he might think I'm too scared to go, that I don't trust myself around him, which is obviously ridiculous because I don't find him attractive anymore. Really. And David won't mind, I'm sure.

"George? Are you still there?" Candy has always called me George rather than Georgie. I think it started at school—though we lived near each other during my Kensington Church Street phase, we went to different schools, and Candy liked being able to tell her friends at school about her friend George, without mentioning that I was actually a girl. I've had a couple of odd meetings with people who went to school with Candy who looked really astonished to find out I was "George."

I realize I haven't been listening to Candy for five minutes. "Sorry, something's just come up," I say. "So, tomorrow at twelve?"

Candy is not happy. She was at the beginning of some story or other and is obviously annoyed to have lost my attention. "Fine," she says casually, as we agree on a meeting place (Oxford Street—arguing with Candy, I remember in time, is hopeless).

I stare at my computer screen and read Mike's message again and again, searching for the meaning behind it. Could it be that he is actually interested in me again? Why now? Having made no effort to contact me in years, why is Mike now so keen to see me? Of course, it's possible that he saw me with David and realized how much he missed me, but somehow that doesn't entirely ring true. I mean, he could have anyone, why would he come back for me? Perhaps he has some ulterior motive? In the past I'd have assumed he wanted to borrow money, but now he seems to have enough of his own, so it must be something else. But what?

Only one way to find out, I reason, and hit the Reply button.

GEORGIE BEAUCHAMP: I suppose I could meet you for a couple of drinks. The Atlantic Bar at 7?

As I hit the Send button I feel a pang of guilt. The Atlantic Bar is where Mike and I always used to go. It was too expensive for us to actually drink there, but we would hang out anyway, and he would steal drinks from the bar for us. I wish I had suggested somewhere more neutral, but reason that changing the venue now would be worse. I don't want to acknowledge to myself or anyone else that what I'm doing is of any consequence.

Not wanting to talk to David directly about it, I send him an e-mail, blushing at my lie as I send it.

GEORGIE BEAUCHAMP: Hi gorgeous, do you mind if I don't come round tonight? Going for drinks after work for someone's birthday. I'll see you tomorrow evening? Seeing Candy in the afternoon, so wish me luck! xx

About thirty seconds later, the phone rings.

"You're seeing Candy? I didn't know you two were still friends." It's David.

"Hello to you, too. Just because I haven't seen her for a while doesn't mean we're not friends anymore. Why should you care anyway?"

"Nothing. I don't care. I just thought it was a bit odd, that's all, suddenly seeing her again."

"David, is everything all right?"

"Of course it is. You have a great time tomorrow. I'll come round afterward, shall I?"

"Yes, come round about six. And give me loads of compliments because I'll be feeling dreadful after spending time in changing rooms with Candy."

"Gorgeous girl. You're much prettier than that skinny creature. See you then."

Gorgeous girl. When David says that, I know he actually means it. So why am I getting so excited about meeting Mike tonight?

At 7:05 P.M. I'm at the Atlantic Bar and Grill. I managed to get home early and had time to change and redo my makeup, and to tell the truth I'm feeling pretty hot to trot. Or is it just that I haven't been properly dressed up for a while? David and I do go out to nice restaurants, and I'm always going to the pub after work, but there never seems to be a reason to really dress up with full makeup and stuff. David always says I look better without it anyway, so there's not much point putting on more than a bit of mascara when we go out. Tonight, though, I've gone for the full works. I need to—you should see the girls in the Atlantic Bar; I'm sure they're all models or something.

I walk up to the bar and have a look around for Mike, trying to be as casual as I can. It doesn't look like he's here, so I order a gin and tonic. Turning my back on the bar, I survey the room. It isn't very busy but it'll be packed later on. There are lots of tall thin girls walking around with amazing tans and high-heeled shoes pointing out from the bottom of their jeans. And not wearing very much on top at all—one girl appears to have wrapped a ball of wool around her breasts and that's pretty much it. The men are either in suits with gold AmEx cards or arty types with odd haircuts.

I take a sip of my drink and remember why I used to

smoke—waiting in a bar is so much easier if you have a cigarette in your hand. It's something to focus on, something to do. You don't feel quite so vulnerable. For some reason, when I met David I stopped wanting to smoke. Plus, of course, he happened to mention over dinner that he hated the habit, so I just didn't mention the packet of Marlboro Lights in my bag and I haven't smoked since.

The bartender is trying to attract my attention, and I turn round, slightly irritated, to discover that I haven't actually paid for my drink yet. I get out my purse to find some cash and feel an arm slip round my waist.

"Put it on my tab, will you?" says a familiar voice, and a gold-colored credit card is passed to the barman.

"Mike!" I experience a frisson of excitement as I turn to kiss him hello. He's slightly unshaven and wearing a black suit and black shirt open at the neck. He has such an air of confidence about him, an insouciance that is so attractive. His hands move round my waist and my instinctive reaction is to turn and kiss him on the lips and move my body into his, but instead I manage a light kiss on the cheek. I am doing, I hope, a pretty good impression of someone who is totally unfazed and unimpressed.

"Georgie, this is Tracey, my PA. And this is Brian, a top DJ—at least he is when he plays our records, eh Brian?"

Brian grins and Tracey titters. Brian, I notice, is more interested in Tracey's expansive cleavage than anything Mike has to say.

"You known each other long?" Tracey inquires.

"Years and years," Mike replies before I can speak. He has turned to face Tracey and Brian, but his left arm is still wrapped round my waist. When we were together, Mike's arm would rarely be anywhere near me if we were out. I told myself then that public demonstrations of affection were really tacky and that I was pleased not to be in a couple that kissed and hugged in bars and clubs. But I had always suspected that Mike didn't touch me because he liked to give the impression that he was single.

"Have you got any cigarettes?"

Willpower be damned—this is an emergency; I need something to steady my nerves. Tracey offers me a Silk Cut, and I put it in my mouth gratefully. It is lit immediately by a platinum lighter that Mike has whisked out of his pocket. This really is the four-star treatment—I didn't know Mike had it in him.

"Georgie's the one who encouraged me to start my own business," Mike tells Tracey and Brian. This is news to me. I do remember shouting at Mike and telling him to "go and get a bloody job, or start making some money out of your stupid plans," but I'm not sure I would class that as encouragement. Then again, maybe that was the kick-start he had needed. Brian and Tracey both give me a sort of "well done" smile and I smile back.

Mike gives me a little squeeze and starts stroking my side. I feel myself stiffen. It isn't that I'm not enjoying this—to be honest, I have dreamed of this moment for ages. It's just that now I seem to have Mike all over me, I feel extremely self-conscious and awkward. It's all wrong, like I've missed a couple of steps, that things have been decided while I was out of the room, and no one thought to tell me. Plus, of course, I'm not here to get back together with Mike; just to make him realize what he's missing. If David knew that I was in the Atlantic Bar with Mike's arm round my waist, he would be devastated. I decide I need a bit of breathing space.

"Um, just nipping to the loo," I say hurriedly and prize myself out of Mike's arms. There is a long queue, which I join, and it's only after five minutes of not moving that I realize the queue is actually people putting on makeup and doing their hair—there are two empty cubicles. Trying to look nonchalant, like I knew all along there wasn't a queue, I go into one of them, lock the door, and sit down to gather my thoughts.

I have come for a drink, I tell myself. Mike cannot just waltz in like this and start treating me like his girlfriend. Even though I'm rather enjoying having the best-looking guy in the room all over me. When I go back to the bar I'm not going to let him put his arm round me. I'm going to be friendly but aloof. Absolutely no flirting.

Some girls come in, laughing loudly. I love listening to conversations in the loos at bars and clubs; you learn more than you could from any magazine or therapy session. Frankly, it beats "Oprah" hands down.

The girls are talking about a guy one of them fancies and is trying to establish whether he fancies her, too. From what they are saying, I'm tempted to conclude that he probably isn't interested.

I am about to flush the chain when I hear someone talking about a "Mike." It could be anyone, I know, but I hesitate anyway.

"So, d'you think she's the one?"

"What, the girl he's with tonight? Could be. Thought she'd be thinner, but he's certainly all over her. Don't know what he sees in her though. And did you see how much makeup she was wearing?"

"You don't think they're going to get married, do you?" asks one of the girls.

"Mike get married? Give me a break! Still, I bet he'd throw a great party if he did." At this the girls laugh raucously.

I'm fixed to the spot. They are definitely talking about Mike. But how do they know about me? What has Mike been saying? And more to the point, am I really wearing too much makeup? I'm desperate to get out of the cubicle to check my reflection in the mirror, but there's no way I can move until the girls leave the room.

They spend what seems like hours talking about other people in the bar—listening to some of the stinging comments, I feel like I've got away quite lightly with the makeup criticism. Finally they leave, and I unlock the cubicle door. My face is pale and with plenty of black eyeliner round my eye I resemble a Panda. Dabbing at my eyes with a tissue, I try to work out why those girls would think for a minute that Mike and I could be getting married. A week ago Mike and I hadn't seen each other for two years; now complete strangers are talking about us spending the rest of our lives together. He must have been talking about me to people. Washing my hands, I wonder if at long last my fantasies must have come true and Mike has realized he needs me in his life. And if he does, why don't I feel more excited? Why do I have this little thought buzzing around my head, asking whether I still need him?

I walk back to the bar, feeling slightly unsteady on my feet. Mike and Brian are talking about dance acts and clubs they have been to/played at around the world, and Tracey is giggling a lot. I am finding it hard to listen to a word they say.

"You've been a while, haven't you?" asks Mike, ruffling my hair. "Been sniffing drugs in there, have you?"

He laughs and Brian winks at me. I manage a smile.

"Oh, I'm sorry, you're far too good for that, aren't you," Mike continues. "Georgie is a good woman," he says to Brian and Tracey, as if to explain. "I need her to keep me on the straight and narrow."

"Fat chance!" Tracey replies and giggles again. She is really beginning to irritate me.

The conversation moves back to music. I try to join in,

but my knowledge of dance music is very limited, so mostly I just smile and nod at appropriate moments. It's such a cool life they lead, I think—all bars and clubs and interviews in style magazines. So why is it that I'm feeling tired and bored? What's wrong with me?

After a couple of hours I decide I've got to go home. The music's getting louder, Mike is getting more drunk, and I need some time to think.

"Mike, I've got to go now—I'm meeting some friends," I lie. Well, I'm hardly going to say I want to get back home in time for "Will and Grace," am I?

He puts on his puppy-dog expression. "What, already? But I've barely seen you."

"Call me during the week," I say and kiss him on the cheek. He turns his head so that his lips meet mine, then he grabs my hand and gives it a squeeze. "Try and stop me."

Out in the cold night air I go over the evening's events in my mind. The arm round the waist, the girls in the loo, the hand squeezing, the kiss. Especially the kiss. The truth is, I wanted it to last longer. Even though I was the one who pulled away, I wanted it to go on and on. My little plan to make Mike feel bad about dumping me might be backfiring slightly, and I need to be careful. I have a lovely boyfriend who adores me, and I really don't want to hurt him.

But as I walk down the street, I can't help my lips breaking into a little smile. Mike was doing a pretty good impression of someone who wants me back. I am maybe, just maybe, a bit of a femme fatale. After all this time of thinking I wasn't cool or pretty enough for Mike, I suddenly feel like I'm in control, and it feels really good. Seeing Candy tomorrow is suddenly looking far more appealing. I'm going to enjoy telling this particular story.

❧ 5

I'm just about to leave when the phone rings. I look at the caller ID and it's my mother. Should I pick it up and risk being late for Candy because of an hour-long diatribe from my mother on nutrition or the joys of gardening/macramé/ weekends in the Dordogne, or should I ignore it and risk her calling me on my mobile at an even worse moment? I decide to pick up.

"Darling," she begins before I've even said hello. "Tell me, are you taking iron supplements? I think you should go and get some. I've been listening to the radio and vegetarians are in real danger of becoming anemic. And you'll need to take vitamin C, because it helps you absorb the iron. Now, do you want me to send you some? Let me see how much I've got . . ."

I can hear her sorting through jars and containers. My mother and James, her latest husband, have an entire cupboard full of supplements. They eat supplements for breakfast with a plate full of the oddest assortment of foods—a brazil nut, a piece of avocado, some tofu, dried apricots, that sort of thing—which they eat with freshly juiced carrots and celery. My mother calls it their insurance plan: whatever foods the latest health magazines tell them to eat, they add to the plate; they then feel free to eat and drink whatever they want for the rest of the day because they've had all their essential nutrients already.

"Mum, I'm not a vegetarian."

"Here we are, maximum strength iron. Oh and this has added vitamin C, so you don't even need to buy it separately. Shall I pop some round to you later?"

"Mum, I am not a vegetarian."

"But you always eat so many vegetables, darling. You're always eating salads."

"Yes, but I also eat meat. I get plenty of iron."

My mother pauses. "You're absolutely sure you're not a vegetarian? I could have sworn—"

"Look, I'm sure, really. I don't need any vitamins."

"Fine, fine, well, if everything's okay, I'd better be getting on. I've got a reflexology appointment this afternoon, although I'm not sure this new woman they've got is any good. I mean, Paul really knew what he was doing and he also did cranial, which is very beneficial, but of course he's moved to L.A. now, and this new girl—can't remember her name—I'm not sure she's entirely up to scratch. I suppose she does have all the best qualifications—the Club would never employ someone who wasn't absolutely top notch . . . I suppose we'll just have to see, won't we. I'm thinking about trying some lymphatic drainage massage, though. Apparently it does wonders for the thighs. Are you still going to that nice masseuse in Kensington darling?"

After nutrition, my mother's favorite pastime is alternative health. Actually, I think it started with reflexology, and the supplements came next. She's a member of a very smart gym in Chelsea, but as far as I know has never actually gone to the gym. She does go there very regularly, though, to have her feet rubbed, neck yanked about, or skin covered in oil. She has been trying to get me to join for about five years now—I think she has visions of us sitting in the steam room talking about colonic irrigation or something.

"Mum, I don't go to a masseuse. I had a massage once at my hairdressers—there was a special offer." Actually, it was lovely, and I had been meaning to go back, but somehow I can't commit an hour and £50. And undressing in front of a complete stranger to have them rub your back, well, it's a bit weird, isn't it?

"You should go more, you know," continues my mother. "Why don't you come down to the Club one day and have a massage there? They only employ the best of the best, you know. And then we could have a spot of lunch? Why not today?"

"Sorry, Mum, I'm meeting Candida in about half an hour. Maybe next week?"

"As you wish," says my mother in a slightly cross tone. Honestly, it's as if I've said "No, I'm washing my hair."

"Shall I call you during the week?" I venture.

"Well, I'm going to be very busy next week, but you can always leave a message with James. Right, well, I've got to go now. Bye!" Before I can say anything further, she's put the phone down.

James and my mother have been together for about four years now, so I'm beginning to see him as a semi-permanent fixture. It's always difficult when you never know if your mother is about to up and leave the person you are starting to bond with. James is very solid though, physically and mentally. I like him a lot actually. He has learned how to tune my mother out when she's going off on some tangent and doesn't seem to mind that she picks up a new hobby/obsession/ailment each week, only to discard it the following week for another fad. And he's even quite good-looking, in an "older man" kind of way. Most important, my mother seems really happy.

I look at my watch. Bollocks. I've got ten minutes to get to Oxford Street. I'm going to have to get a cab even though I promised myself I would use my Tube pass more. Seventy pounds a month! No wonder people who live in London need so many massages to get over their stressful lives.

I grab my bag and run outside.

Of course I'm late. I'm always late for Candy. I haven't seen her for years and it's still the same old story. With Mike, it was always me who was on time and him who was late. With David, we pretty much get to places the same time. With my mother, well, she's either really early or really late, or one of us doesn't turn up at all.

I think you develop certain patterns with people that get so ingrained, you can't get out of them—like Candy never compensates and gets places a bit late. And even if I'm early when I leave to meet Candy, something always happens. Or maybe it's just that I'm always so worried about what I'm going to wear that I end up changing ten times.

Take today. A girly catch-up and shopping trip round Oxford Street. So that's jeans, maybe a nice top (wearing crap clothes when you're shopping is very dangerous—shop assistants sneer at you and anything you try on looks better than what you're wearing so you end up buying too much), and some cool flat-ish shoes. Flat because of all the walking. But not too flat because then my legs look stumpy and I won't be able to try on anything that requires heels, which is pretty much everything. Plus also, flat shoes make me look about forty, unless they're really pointed, in which case they're so uncomfortable that they defeat the object of wearing flats in the first place.

Getting dressed isn't usually this complicated for me. I manage to dress myself most days without a second thought. But Candy is one of those tall, thin, Gwyneth Pal-

trow types—blond hair, a constant light tan, and the ability
to make a pantomime cow outfit look sexy. In fact, it's
worse than that. I know plenty of beautiful people, and they
don't make me react this way. No, with Candy, it's the way
she looks at my clothes and says things like "That skirt's a
really nice idea. So I guess you need some cowboy boots
now to make it work. Shall we try . . ." and then lists a
whole load of shops that sell cowboy boots, when I had got
the skirt specifically to go with my trainers, or whatever I'm
wearing. She talks about "looks" instead of outfits, and as
yet I don't think I've ever got a "look" right, in her opinion.
But rather than accept defeat, I just keep on trying.

Today I think I've cracked it, though. Tod's loafers—
they're comfortable, but they're also Italian, and I once
saw Elle McPherson wearing a pair, which demonstrates
just how stylish they are. (If I'm really honest it was seeing
Elle wearing them that got me extending my overdraft to
buy a pair.) So with my black trousers and black turtleneck
I think I'm actually looking quite Audrey Hepburn in
Funny Face. A kind of beatnik Euro-chic look. Shit, I'm
even talking like Candy now.

Luckily I get a cab without too much difficulty and am
only ten minutes late. Candy is waiting for me outside
Browns on South Molton Street. She is in combats, trainers, and a little pink T-shirt that sits just above her belly
button, revealing an expanse of tanned skin. She looks me
up and down when we've kissed hello.

"You look very formal. Have you been working this
morning?" she asks.

This is not going to go well.

We decide to go for a coffee first. Last time I saw her,
Candy insisted on drinking cocktails—"makes shopping so
much more fun, don't you think?"—but today she is order-

ing a large latte with extra cream. I decide to order the same thing—it's sunny but windy outside and I need warming up.

We sit down in the Starbucks next to Office Shoes and I find that I am actually rather excited. I can't wait for Candy to say "So tell me, what's going on with you," so that I can give a little smile and say "Oh, you know, the usual. Although, you know I bumped into Mike recently? Well, you'll never believe it, but he's been pursuing me . . ." She'll probably squeal and fill me in on his side of the story ("He just called me up and asked how you were—said he'd seen you in the street and he just couldn't stop talking about you"), and we can laugh about it. I can talk at length about the relative merits of David and Mike, and the problems that come with being so darn desirable. And then we can go shopping and buy some fabulous new clothes to go with my fabulous new heartbreaker image.

Our seats are by the window and the sun is streaming through the glass, giving the impression that it's summer even though it's barely April. The coffee shop is full of glamorous-looking people with huge numbers of shopping bags. I notice that none of them are from shops that I frequent—I don't suppose Top Shop and Oasis bags really hold their own against Miu Miu and Fenwicks.

Maybe I should start buying designer clothes like Candy. I wonder if Mike would take me shopping with his platinum credit card and then I immediately feel guilty. David hates shopping, unless it's for gadgets—he can happily spend four hours finding out just how many functions a television has, but try and get him into French Connection and he suddenly remembers how much work he's got to do. But he is my boyfriend and I love him. There is no way I would ever go shopping with Mike. I'll just max-out my own credit card like normal people.

Candy has arranged herself delicately over her chair. She is looking amazing. Her cheeks are pink, her skin is glowing, and her blue eyes are gleaming. I resolve that I will only try clothes on in shops with separate changing facilities.

I wait for her to start talking, but strangely, she's silent.

"So," I begin. "How's things?"

She's about to start talking, when, before I can help it, I interrupt with "Seen much of Mike?"

It's no use. I just can't wait for her to tell me about her life. I've been bottling this Mike thing up for days, and I need to talk about it. I try to sound nonchalant, but unfortunately the question comes out a bit quickly, with a little bit too much emotion attached.

Candy looks up sharply.

Okay, so maybe that wasn't the best thing to say. I've got to impress upon Candy that I am over Mike, but that he is obviously not over me. Far from it. Maybe I should try a different tack.

"I mean, well, you're friends, aren't you?" I mutter, trying to make out that there was no significance to my question. I don't want to just tell her about Mike. I want her to ask. I want her to drag the facts out of me.

"So how are you?" I ask again.

"George, look, I'm sorry we haven't seen each other for such a long time. I've been really busy at work and . . . well, you know. The things is, I kind of brought you out under false pretenses today," she begins slowly.

Oh God, Mike's here, I think. He's asked her to get me out so that he can spend the afternoon with me. I look around, but can't see him.

Candy is staring into her coffee.

"The thing is, George, I'm pregnant."

Okay, I was not expecting that. "Pregnant? Candy, I didn't even know you were seeing anyone!"

It occurs to me that I wouldn't really know.

"How . . . how did it happen?"

Candy sort of snorts and stares at me. "George, I don't think I need to go into that level of detail do I?"

"No, sorry, of course not. I just . . . it . . . I'm just surprised, that's all. So, are you, I mean, do you think you'll . . ."

"Keep it?" she asks. "Oh yes, definitely. But I don't know. I haven't told my parents yet. I haven't dared."

I can see why she's scared. Candy's parents are completely terrifying. Even my mother is scared of them—she met them once at a party and couldn't get away quickly enough. They are like your worst nightmare headmistress and headmaster rolled into one. And they certainly aren't the sort to embrace single motherhood. Her mother went into a complete decline when Candy had her belly button pierced; the prospect of a baby would probably finish her off.

"So who's the father? Do you think you'll get married?"

Actually this is really cool. I could be godmother or something. A bad thought comes into my head and I try to push it out with little success. Candy will get stretch marks. Well, I told you it wasn't a nice thought. But it's true, isn't it. She might even get fat and not be able to lose the weight. Okay, Georgie, focus on the real issues here. This is *important*.

"I don't really want to say who the father is, actually, if that's okay," Candy is saying, still staring into her coffee cup. "He's . . . well, he needs time to get used to the idea, obviously. But we're really in love and stuff. I mean, he adores me."

Wow. Candy pregnant. I can hardly believe it. And even if she doesn't get married, all her friends are so loaded that at least she'll be okay financially. I'm sure she will get mar-

ried, though. Ooh, I could be a bridesmaid. I resolve to be
a really good friend and listen to everything Candy says—
if she gets married, she's bound to have really lovely bridesmaids dresses. And, obviously, I want to be there for her on
her special day. Bridesmaids generally get presents, too,
don't they?

"Are you going to give up work if you keep it?" The only
reason I can ever think of for having a baby is all the time
off work you get. Actually it's quite a compelling one. Although you'd also need a nanny, wouldn't you, otherwise
you'd spend all your free time having to look after a baby
instead of doing nice things. But if Candy doesn't get married, who's going to pay for the nanny?

"Work?" says Candy thoughtfully, as if it's something
she hasn't even considered. "Oh, I'm sure I won't have to
work."

I look at her uncertainly.

"I mean even if . . . well, even if we didn't get married,
which I'm sure we will, I'm sure Daddy would increase my
allowance if I needed it," she continues.

"Really?" I'd forgotten about Candy's allowance.

"God yes. He'd hate it, of course. But he'd definitely
make sure we had enough money. . . ."

I smile sweetly. It's so unfair. Why can't I have a nice trust
fund or something? I feel the beginnings of Candy-envy
creeping up through my body. I used to get this all the
time—being friends with Candy is not good for anyone's
health. But I realize that I now have a really good way of
dealing with it. I just picture Candy with stretch marks and
a large stomach and I start to feel much better. It's like the
old technique for giving presentations: imagine everyone
with just their underwear on. Except this image is actually
going to happen.

"What about the father? Is it one of your investment

banker admirers? Is it someone I've met? And are you going to have a huge big wedding? Oh, Candy, tell me," I beg,
but she shakes her head.

Instead, I slurp my coffee while Candy tells me about a
house she's seen in Kensington (a flat is just not suitable to
have a baby in) and about schools in the area, great clothes
shops for pregnant women and the possibility of having
a quick tummy tuck after the birth—naturally I advise
against it.

I keep looking for an opportune moment to tell Candy
about my stuff, but somehow the fact that after all this
time Mike seems to really fancy me doesn't really warrant
much airspace when Candy's about to become a mother.

I look at my watch. We've been sitting in the coffee shop
for nearly an hour now and I know more about pregnancy
than I ever thought possible. Certainly more than I want to
know. Surely it must be okay to talk about Mike for a bit
now. Actually, Candy would probably really appreciate me
changing the subject and talking about something other
than babies. But how can I gradually introduce Mike into
the conversation?

"So, anyway," I venture, "it looks like Mike is up to his
old tricks again!" Hmmm, not really what I was looking
for, but it'll have to do.

Candy looks at me strangely. "Meaning what, exactly?"

"Well, I think he might want me back," I say gleefully,
delighted to finally get an opportunity to tell my story. "I
mean, he's been calling and e-mailing, and then we went
out for a drink last night and he was all over me! Nothing
happened, of course—I'm, you know, with David now, but
it's a funny old world isn't it!"

It's all come out wrong. I wanted her to tease the facts
out of me, and only suggest that Mike has been flirting
with me. But at least I've opened up the subject for discus-

sion. I look up at Candy expectantly, waiting for her to tell me to stay away from Mike so I can explain that this time it's him doing all the chasing and that actually I'm not *really* interested, but instead she just says "You went out last night?"

I suddenly remember that Candy may be cross on behalf of David. She did introduce us, after all. And the last thing I want is for her to say anything to him. God, why didn't I think of that before?

"Well, it was more of a chance meeting really," I say uncertainly, backtracking furiously. "We just had a quick drink. You know, for old time's sake."

Candy looks at me accusingly. "There's nothing in it," I say quickly. "I think Mike's just made a real success of things and is realizing too late that it's no fun if you haven't got anyone to share it with."

It feels good to be saying this. I have wanted to be able to say this ever since Mike walked out on me. I'm not entirely sure it's true, but it's near enough.

Candy does not look pleased. "Georgie, I thought you were going out with David? Or have I missed something here? For God's sake, you go for one drink and now you think he wants you back? When are you going to grow up and realize that Mike is just not interested in you and never was?"

It's obviously bad timing. I shouldn't have brought up my men issues. Candy is pregnant, and that's far more important than my stupid ruminations on whether or not my flirting with Mike is completely wicked or just a bit of innocent fun.

But doesn't she realize that Mike *is* interested in me? That things have changed? I'm going to have to leave the subject, but I wish she'd been there. You know, to see that he was all over me. That I wasn't just imagining it.

"I'm sorry, Candy, I didn't mean it, really. Of course I'm going out with David, and I'm completely over Mike—you know that. It's not my fault if he calls, though, is it?"

I give her a smile, but am disconcerted to see that there are tears in her eyes. God, what have I done?

"Candy, honestly, forget it, it's nothing," I say hurriedly. "Look, I'm sorry I even brought it up. You haven't even told me when the baby's due or about names or anything! We could go to Mothercare or something!"

But it's too late. Candy is gathering up her things. "Candy?" I look at her in alarm. Is she really that upset? Can pregnancy hormones make you that temperamental?

"Look, I'm really sorry, George, I've got to go now," says Candy, sniffing. "I . . . I'm just a bit emotional, you know. It was nice seeing you, and I'll give you a call. Okay?" She gets up and starts walking out of the coffee shop very quickly.

"Look after yourself!" I manage to yell after her.

I look around the shop convinced that people are staring at me. This is awful. I haven't seen Candy for about two years, and within an hour or so I've managed to upset her so much that she's actually walked out on me.

Of course, if I'd really thought about it I'd have seen this coming. Candy always thought Mike was bad news where I was concerned. I mean, the two of them do get on very well—they've known each other for years—but she warned me from the start not to take things seriously with him, told me that I shouldn't get too involved because he was a heartbreaker. Not that I had listened to her then, or later, when she told me again and again to leave him while I still had my dignity intact. She probably thought that now, finally, I'd have stopped going on and on about what a shithead he was, only to find that the first thing I talk about is Mike again. I suppose she has a point. To be honest, I'm

not exactly proud of myself for thinking about Mike so
But the important point that she has completely missed is
that it is *him* chasing *me*. I am the one in control here, and
I don't even like him anymore. Well, not as much as I did.

I take a final gulp of coffee, but it's gone cold. I can't decide what to do. Now that I've come all the way into Oxford Street I don't want to go back home, but I'm not really
in the mood to go shopping either. I could try calling
Candy, attempt to persuade her that I can talk about the
weather or anything else she wants to discuss, but I'm not
sure it would work. And anyway, the only reason I really
wanted to see Candy was so I could brag about Mike. If I
can't do that, then what's the point?

I consider buying a chocolate brownie and another latte,
but my stomach is full of butterflies. The sad truth is that I
need to talk to someone properly about Mike. I need someone who will delve into every bit of conversation with me,
say that based on the evidence it is highly likely that Mike
does indeed fancy me like mad, and congratulate me on finally getting my own back. I know it's wrong, and I know
it's probably very boring to anyone other than me, but
surely that's what friends are for? The whole time I was going out with Mike everyone kept giving me little looks and
having "chats" with me that basically consisted of them
saying "It's never going to last, why don't you cut your
losses and go." And then when he dumped me I got sympathetic looks and lots of "I told you so" little chats. Now,
Mike is chasing after me. Now, girls in bars are talking
about us getting married. I can't contain this for another
minute.

There's only one thing for it: I'm going to have to see my
mother.

❧ 6

James is reading the *FT*'s "How to Spend It" supplement and is staring at an advert for a large four-by-four car.

"This is what you should be driving," he says to my mother, who is making tea in the kitchen. "Not that ridiculous little thing that could break down at any minute."

"We are not spending thousands of pounds on a new car," my mother says firmly, bringing a tray into the dining room. On it are two cups of normal tea and one cup of green . . . well, I'm assuming it's some sort of tea, though it looks utterly vile. She has poured the milk into the real cups of tea already, but has brought a separate bowl for the sugar. She always does this so that she can look at James and me reproachfully when we heap our teaspoonfuls and stir it into our tea. Sugar is enemy number one, according to my mother, worse than cocaine, even. Not that she knows the slightest thing about cocaine.

"Lovely." James takes a big gulp of tea and puts the car advert in front of my mother.

"Look how much more comfortable you'd be. And it can give you directions, too. It's got a TV screen in the front that has maps and information, and it's all voice-activated. Camilla, why don't we get you one?"

My mother looks at James sternly.

"We have discussed this a thousand times already, James. I do not need a new car, and that's that."

James is in property. At least he used to be. I'm not sure what, if anything, he does now apart from playing golf. I approve of James's outlook thoroughly. His philosophy on life is to lie back and enjoy it. He never lets the little things worry him, which is why, I suppose, he manages to live with my mother so contentedly.

"Okay, what if I buy another car for myself and I just let you drive it all the time?"

"I knew it!"

"What?"

"I knew you didn't want a new car because of the Mini being unsafe. It's because you just want the excitement of buying a new car!"

"I give up," says James and mooches off into the sitting room with his newspaper and cup of tea.

My mother sits down at the table.

"So, what happened to your exciting afternoon out with Candy? I thought you were too busy to see your boring mother?"

"Mum, don't be silly. I met Candy, we just didn't spend as long shopping as I thought we would."

"Darling, you look drained."

"Drained? No, I'm fine, really. Maybe a bit tired, but nothing serious."

My mother is peering at me for clues.

"Are you suffering from executive stress?"

"What?"

"Well, I was reading an article the other day on young women like you with stressful jobs, who can't keep their friendships going because they don't have anything of themselves to give. It all gets zapped at work. I think it might have something to do with sick building syndrome."

"Mum, what are you talking about?" My mother, when faced with a new syndrome or complaint that she cannot possibly say she has, will generally try and convince me or James that we have it. That way, next time she's discussing it with her friends at the Club, she has a real life example to bring up.

"I do not have executive stress. And I can keep my friendships going. I just . . ."

"Yes?"

Having waited so long to tell someone about Mike, I now can't quite find the words. Somehow telling Mum that my ex-boyfriend fancies me doesn't sound like a particularly compelling story.

"Do you remember Mike?" I ask tentatively. You never know, she might say something like "Oh, the one who left you so foolishly?" and I can tell her triumphantly that he's seen the error of his ways now.

"Of course I remember Mike. Very cheeky, I always thought. Perfect charmer. Why?"

Why? Good question.

"He's just been in touch, that's all."

"I see. And does David know?"

"Not really. I mean, you know, it's not really important."

"If this is the level of your conversational skill, darling, I'm not surprised you don't have any friends. Really, you are barely stringing sentences together."

Don't have any friends? I come and see my mother, taking time out of my busy day to spend time with her, and she starts jumping to conclusions about the number of friends I have. No wonder I don't come here more often.

"I do have a wide social circle, actually," I say, trying to convince myself as much as anything. I can't help wondering why I have resorted to spending Saturday afternoon with my mother.

"It's just that Candy's pregnant and she's all emotional so she went home early," I continue. "Anyway, the point is I bumped into him. Mike, I mean. And he's finally got himself together, you know, he's actually successful and running a proper business and stuff. And he's been e-mailing me, we had lunch, we . . ."

"Yes . . . ?" My mother is doing a crossword. Will no one listen to me?

"Mum, do you think David was a rebound? Do you think that I could still be in love with Mike? I never thought we could really be serious before, but he's really changed and I think he wants me back. Mum, I don't know what to do."

As I listen to myself I am surprised by my words. Am I really saying that I'm still in love with Mike after all this time? And that lovely, sweet David was just a rebound? Do I seriously think Mike is trying to get me back rather than just indulging in some innocent flirting? And more to the point, am I actually considering it as an option? These thoughts may have been vaguely circling around my mind for the past week, but I certainly haven't admitted as much even to myself. I thought I just wanted to brag a bit about having a gorgeous man chasing me around. But I now realize that the situation is far more serious. And I have no idea what to do.

I fold my arms on the table and rest my head on them.

"Six months ago you were telling me that you wanted to marry David."

"I know, I know. I do, I mean I would. He hasn't asked or anything. At least, I think I would. I just don't know anymore."

"Darling, has anything actually happened yet?" My mother puts her newspaper down. At last, a proper audience.

"No. Apart from, you know, a bit of flirting. But he's really been pursuing me. And he's actually got a proper business that's doing really well. And these girls were talking in the loo about him being serious about me when I hadn't seen him for ages. But obviously I'm with David so . . ."

"So, what? Why are you with David?"

Why am I with David? Why does my mother ask such silly questions?

"Because I am. Because I love him. Because he's, well, just because," I reply hotly.

"Eloquent as always, darling," says my mother, folding up her newspaper. "Look, it's really very simple. If you love David, then that's all there is to it. You wave good-bye to Michael and wish him well. If, on the other hand, David is just a stopgap, a poor man who happened to be there at the right time—or, rather, the wrong time, as far as he is concerned—then you need to tell him before you take things with Michael any further." My mother doesn't like shortening names. If Candy ever asked to speak to "George" on the phone when I was younger, my mother would reply that no one of that name lived in her house. And I'm sure she warmed to David more when he confirmed that he hated being called Dave.

"You can't have both," continues my mother. "And don't always think that the grass is greener."

"That's a bit rich," I mutter before I can stop myself.

Mum stares at me and her eyes narrow.

"We all make mistakes," she says quietly. "That doesn't mean we advise others to. And anyway, whatever I may or may not have done, I have never cheated on anyone. I make my choices and I stick by them."

I know she's right, but I don't like looking at the situation in such a black-and-white way. The idea of leaving

David is just awful—I couldn't bear it. But still, I can't quite push the fantasy of Mike from my mind. He's so exciting, and I long to flirt with him, to dance the evening away and have him seduce me. He's so sexy, and the idea of him being in love with me is very intoxicating. You know, if he actually is. And maybe David and I are just a bit too comfortable. I know everything about him, he knows everything about me, and there's no real potential for flirting anymore. I mean, when Audrey Hepburn met Gregory Peck in Rome, they didn't stay in and watch television, did they? She took a risk, she chose excitement.

James wanders back in. "Have you seen my reading glasses, Cammy?"

"On the mantelpiece, James."

"Of course, there they are."

The two of them live so happily together, I muse. Will I ever achieve that with someone, the ability to be contented without wondering what else is out there? Will I also have to go through four husbands and who knows how many relationships to get there?

"Anyway," continues my mother. "You don't want to end up like that Bellinger girl, do you?"

I look up in annoyance. The Bellingers are friends of my mother. Their daughter Sarah is a hugely successful lawyer and has a great big house in Chelsea or somewhere. She is also a lesbian. A well-adjusted lesbian with a long-term partner, two dogs, and lots of paintings by real artists, as opposed to framed prints. She's far more sorted and successful than I could ever hope to be, but evidently my mother thinks otherwise.

"Mum, how could my situation possibly lead to me ending up like Sarah?"

My mother looks at me as if I am mad.

"She could have had any number of young men, if she'd been more sensible."

"Mum, she's a lesbian. She doesn't fancy men!"

"If you say so." My mother turns back to her crossword.

So much for sensible advice. Draining my teacup, I decide to make my way home. I need to clear my head and decide what I want. David or Mike. Comfort and reliability or flirtation and uncertainty? I decide to write a list when I get home. A sort of pros and cons on both of them. Perhaps I could do a SWOT analysis. It's something I learned from Nigel last year: you look at the strengths, weaknesses, opportunities, and threats of a new product and assess whether it's viable or not. I could do one on both of them and then I'll have my answer!

My mobile rings. I look at the caller ID. Shit, it's Mike, and I haven't had time to do my analysis yet.

"Hello?"

"Georgie Porgie Pudding and Pie, Kissed the Boys and made them—"

"Mike! I thought I told you to call me next week?"

"Ah yes, but that was before I found out that I have to go to Rome next weekend, and I thought you could come with me."

Ohmygod. Breathe, Georgie, breathe.

"Rome, you say. Are you serious?" Immediately my mind starts racing. Rome, of all places. Already I'm seeing us kissing at the Coliseum, walking hand in hand down little cobbled streets. But then an image of David and me wandering round Rome hand in hand comes into my head. I couldn't possibly go to Rome with Mike. I mean, I've promised David so many times we'd go together. And actually I want to go with David, I really do. It's just that David never has the time. Two years of promises and we've never come close to actually going. Maybe, just maybe, fate is telling me that a trip to Rome with David isn't in the cards. That I should go with Mike instead.

"Totally. Got to check out a new band and meet with some people. Look, we'll be staying in a great hotel, we'll have a cool time. Tell me you'll come with me—it'll be so much better if you're there!"

Rome. I want to go there so much, but how could I go there with Mike when I've watched *Roman Holiday* so many times with David? Actually I've always had a little suspicion that when David proposes to me it's going to be in Rome. But to be honest I've sort of given up on the whole proposing thing, too. He hasn't mentioned Rome for a while—even when we watched *Roman Holiday* on Sunday he didn't do his usual "One day, my darling, I'm going to take you up those Spanish Steps, and show you how beautiful Rome is." But obviously that doesn't mean I should go with Mike. I mean, how dare he think that he can just ring up out of the blue and that I'll just drop everything?

I'm going to say no. I'm going to tell him that I have plans.

"I'd love to." Did I say that?

"You won't regret it. Look, I'll e-mail you the details, okay? We leave Friday evening. Bye!"

I'm grinning ear to ear. I know that I'm going to have a hard time explaining a weekend away to David. I know that I haven't written up any pros and cons, and I know that I am a very bad person. But Rome with Mike! Italy! This is so exciting!

By the time I turn onto my street I've planned every minute of the weekend. I've allowed two hours for Mike's meetings—very generous in my opinion—and decided where we're going to go and exactly what I'm going to wear. It's going to be the most amazing weekend ever.

As I approach my building I see someone standing outside the door. For a moment I think it's Mike and my heart lurches with alarm. I know I've agreed to go to Rome with him, but somehow I don't want to see him in the flesh just yet—it would make everything a bit too real. I have managed to justify the Rome trip to myself on the grounds that it is something completely unrelated to my normal life; I keep telling myself I can just go, have a lovely time, and then come back home as if it never happened. Just like Audrey Hepburn did. But I don't want to see Mike, especially not here at my flat. I don't want to really face the fact that I'm doing something very bad. I squint to see if it's definitely Mike—if it is, I can always turn round. But my eyes pick out a more familiar figure . . . it's not Mike. It's David. He's carrying groceries and reading the *FT*. Gorgeous, dependable David. My stomach is lurching again, but for very different reasons.

You've got to hand it to David. If we're talking pros and cons, David's got to be doing pretty well. He has brought food, and he is going to cook it himself, too.

I open the door and we go inside. David nearly knocks the curtain rail over.

"Must put that up," he mutters as he walks into the kitchen. As he turns round to give me a kiss I notice a cut and a bruise on his cheek. He smiles sheepishly. "Got hit by a squash ball this morning," he explains.

He opens a bottle of wine and pours me a large glass.

"Ooh, that's lovely."

"It isn't Bulgarian, I'm afraid," David grins, "but I believe that the French, too, produce a number of good wines."

He turns round and starts unloading the shopping bags. Spaghetti, minced beef, tinned tomatoes, garlic, onions, basil, and oregano. I love the fact that David knows that I never have any food in my flat. He used to ask me things like "Where do you keep the sun-dried tomatoes" or "You don't happen to have any capers, do you?" but now he always brings everything he needs when he's cooking and I just watch in admiration as he turns ingredients into proper food without even using a ready-made sauce.

"The trick to a really good spag Bol is to leave it bubbling for a while," David tells me as he starts to chop the onions. I sit down and slug wine as the kitchen warms up and David, wearing my floral Liberty apron, browns the beef. We are the picture of domestic bliss. I try to picture Mike doing the same thing, and can't. Mike would never spend an evening in like this. He used to prowl around like a caged animal waiting for the phone to ring whenever we didn't have plans. If it didn't ring by eight, he'd make a couple of calls and get us onto some guest list or other. Life indoors didn't count to Mike. Am I really contemplating going to the city of romance with him?

David hums as he cooks and every so often he turns round and winks at me. I get a huge pang of guilt about Rome. How could I do that to David? He's so much nicer than Mike. I'm going to cancel. Definitely. Although if he was really serious about me, wouldn't he have taken me to Rome himself? Suddenly my eyes, which have been staring into the middle distance, focus on David's shirt. There's a small rip on the shoulder, and it looks like he's been cut.

"David, is that blood on your shoulder?"

I get up to inspect it more closely.

"Oh, that. Hmmm. Yes, yes it is."

As I approach him he turns round to kiss me, deflecting my attempts to look more closely at the rip.

"David, let me see!"

"It's nothing, darling. Look, I've just had a run-in with a couple of idiots. Should have been more careful."

"What sort of idiots?" I persist. "Were you mugged?"

"Not exactly. Look, it's nothing—just a risk that comes with the job," David says, turning away.

"With the job? David, you're an accountant, not a bouncer."

"Of course I am. As I said, it's really nothing."

I'm cross now. I hate it when David avoids my questions.

"Tell me," I say firmly and pull him away from the stove. David leans down and kisses my forehead.

"Darling, when you're investigating fraud, you very occasionally encounter this sort of thing. People who get involved in fraud can often be involved in a whole host of unsavory activities alongside it. And they generally don't like the idea of being found out. So every once in a while I get some lunatic thinking that sending in the heavies, or sending me a bribe, is going to get me off their case. Which it doesn't."

He kisses me again and turns back to the spaghetti.

"So, what did you buy?"

I stare at David vacantly. Buy? What's he talking about? And who dared to send the heavies round to David? Why hasn't he mentioned it before?

"Today with Candy. Shopping," continues David. "Don't tell me you didn't get anything?"

"Oh, right. Um, no I didn't actually. We talked mostly. Didn't get round to going in any shops."

"Oh, that's right."

"What?"

"What?" David turns round.

"What you just said—'oh that's right'—as if you knew or something. Have you seen Candy?"

David slugs back some wine and turns back again.

"What? No, course not. I just remembered that you were going to have a catch-up. It's been a while, hasn't it?"

"A couple of years actually." If I didn't know David better, I'd think he was hiding something from me. Something other than the fact that he's regularly threatened by horrible criminals, that is. Shuddering at the thought of anyone trying to attack David I lean my forehead against his back.

"How about you?" I murmur. "What have you been up to today apart from getting into fights with gangsters?"

"Oh, just a bit of work," says David absentmindedly.

"Again? David, this is ridiculous. You're working all the time. Can't you put your foot down?" I put my arms around him protectively. I can't believe his firm. They expect him to work constantly and don't even give him a bodyguard.

David smiles. "Darling, it's me that's making all the work. There are people in my team whose wives and husbands will be cursing my name right now. But when you've got an assignment, there's nothing else for it."

David always talks about people's wives and husbands rather than girlfriends and boyfriends. And about a year ago he said something about wanting a family. So naturally I thought it was only a matter of time before he proposed. Every time we went out for a meal, I prepared myself for him getting down on one knee and saying he wanted to be with me forever. Each time I bought a new dress or pair of shoes I'd wonder if I'd be wearing them when we got engaged. But he never asked. For a while I was a bit upset. I started thinking that David didn't see me as wife material. Plus he never asked me to even move in with him. But I'm fine about it now. I mean, when you think about it, what's so great about being married? Why should I want some stupid piece of paper that legally binds us? Why should I care if David doesn't really want to commit to me? It's fine the way things are. We're very happy.

Although that should register on the SWOT analysis, shouldn't it? If Mike is in love with me enough to want to marry me, that should count toward him, shouldn't it? And if David isn't serious enough about me to want to spend the rest of his life with me, then I should maybe *contemplate* going to Rome with Mike, shouldn't I? I mean, a girl's got to keep her options open, hasn't she?

Feeling bad about thinking about going to Rome with Mike while David is cooking for me, I quickly try to focus on something else.

"So is it interesting, what you're doing?"

"Interesting?" David puts a lid on the saucepan and sits down at the kitchen table, looking serious. "Yes. Enjoyable? No. Actually, right now it's pretty bloody awful."

I stare at him. It's not like David to talk about his work like this.

"David, is everything all right?"

"Of course it is." He gives my hand a squeeze. "But I'm afraid I'm going to be away next weekend. I've got to go to Geneva on Thursday and I'm probably not going to be back till Monday."

"Next weekend?"

It's as if fate wants me to go to Rome. As if I'm *meant* to go.

"Yes. It's a bugger, but I need to go. Are you going to be okay?"

"Of course I am," I say brightly. "David, I am a grown-up, you know."

"I know. I just enjoy our weekends together, that's all. I like waking up with you on Sundays . . ." He's kissing my hand.

"Uh huh, and what else do you like?"

David stands up and starts kissing my neck.

"I like going to bed with you on Saturdays."

"I see. And what's the day today? I can't seem to remember . . ."

"Saturday."

"Of course it is."

David puts his arms around me and picks me up. Eliminating all thoughts of Rome from my head, I wrap my legs around him and he carries me to the bedroom.

"I also like taking your clothes off on Saturdays . . ."

"I see . . ."

"And I like . . ."

An hour later we manage to salvage some of the Bolognese sauce, but the spaghetti is completely burned and the pan is ruined. Evidently leaving the sauce to cook for an hour while you ravage your girlfriend is not the same as leaving it to simmer, stirring regularly. We opt for Bolognese on toast and eat it watching "Casualty."

I hate watching "Casualty." Whenever you see someone do anything, you know it's going to end in tears. Like, crossing a road? They're going to get hit by a car. Cooking something? There's going to be boiling oil everywhere and probably a lifelong handicap. It's too gruesome. I'm watching with my hands over my eyes as a small boy climbs onto a tall wall, and I know he's going to have a horrible fall, when the phone rings. Without thinking, I tell David to pick it up.

I assume it must be a crank caller, because I hear David say "Who is this?" in a really shitty tone. I often get calls from people thinking my number is a Chinese take-away.

"Yes, I thought it was you," he continues in a voice I hardly recognize. "Look, you know the situation. Don't press your luck or you won't enjoy the consequences." And he hangs up.

His cheeks are red. I look up, bewildered. "Who the hell was that?"

"Your friend Mike," says David in a very clipped voice.

"Mike?"

I need a second or two to gather my thoughts. My heart is racing. What if Mike said something about Rome? And how dare David tell Mike not to call me again, even if Mike is trying to seduce me. Unless he knows, that is? This is terrible. Guilt surges through my veins and I go on the offensive to make myself feel better.

"I'm sorry, did you just tell someone, a friend of mine, a friend of ours, actually, not to call me again? How dare you?"

My voice is quivering, but as expected my feelings of guilt are ebbing away as anger and indignation take their place. If we were on "Oprah," I'm sure I'd have a lot of the audience on my side. It just isn't on for David to talk to my friends like that.

"Georgie," David says firmly, "Mike is bad news. I don't want you to have anything to do with him." This is so unlike him; he never tells me what to do. Except when he's worried, like the time I walked into a busy road without looking. He was very cross with me then.

David isn't looking at me either, which is odd. I suddenly remember the strange comment he made earlier when I told him about catching up with Candy. He must have seen her. She's probably told him everything I said about Mike. Oh shit, shit, shit.

I reach for his hand in a conciliatory gesture. "David, me and Mike, you know, we go back a long way, but you know that there's nothing between us now. Come on, don't overreact. We're just friends."

"I'm perfectly aware how far you go back—I was there, remember," David says bitterly. "And I would hardly call someone you've barely seen for two years a friend. Georgie, there are things about Mike that you don't know and don't want to know. Just do as I say and have nothing further to do with him."

"Do as you say? Did you just say 'do as I say'? Who the bloody hell do you think I am?" I am livid now. Even if David does suspect something, he can't start ordering me around like a schoolgirl.

"I think you are a sensible, rational person. I think you should trust me." David is talking very slowly.

"Yeah, well, I think you should start treating me with a bit of respect."

"Respect? Is that what Mike showed you? Screwing around and spending your money? Would you prefer me to do that?"

"Oh just fuck off, will you." How dare he throw that at me? And anyway, he didn't screw around. I mean, I don't think he did, did he? Yes, he borrowed money and stuff, but if I want to lend people money, well, that's up to me, isn't it? I feel my eyes well up with tears and blink them back furiously. I don't want to cry. I want to be strong and in control.

"If that's what you want." David's eyes are thunderous. He turns and walks out of the room.

It's not what I want at all. But somehow as I watch him pick up his things and leave, I find myself unable to call after him. Not when he's being so horrible. I can't believe I was all set to cancel my trip to Rome, too. Well, I will go, and it'll just serve David right.

❧ 7

DAVID BRADLEY
STRENGTHS: cooks, kind, generous, good-looking, likes TV, nice car
WEAKNESSES: jealous, bossy, accountant, hasn't asked me to marry him
OPPORTUNITIES: could do something incredibly romantic, like take me away
   somewhere and propose; but very unlikely—especially after last night.
THREATS: Mike

MIKE MARSHALL
STRENGTHS: absolutely gorgeous, successful business, cool, sexy, is taking me to
   Rome
WEAKNESSES : doesn't keep promises; bad with money—at least he used to be;
   dumped me by leaving a note; flirts with other girls—although he hasn't done that
   recently either; could be changed character; calls me at inopportune moments
OPPORTUNITIES: well, Rome has to be a pretty big one. I mean, I suppose we're
   going to be sharing a room . . .
THREATS : David

I didn't know that so many people get to work a whole hour before they have to. What is that all about? I have an excuse: I haven't been able to sleep, and when you're up at six A.M., and there's nothing good on the telly, you may as well get some brownie points and come into work early, right? But all these other people—I'd say half the people who work on my floor at Leary are already at their desks, and it's only 8:15 A.M.

I place my freshly made cappuccino down on my desk and sit down. My weekend has been a complete disaster. All I've been thinking about is the argument with David and going to Rome with Mike. I want to go so much, but every time I shut my eyes I see David's face looking all cross and upset.

Nigel is looking at me suspiciously.

"Decided to make up for all the late mornings, have you?"

I can't even be bothered to answer, so I grunt and sit down.

"Well, it's a good thing you're in on time, because we've got a departmental meeting at nine-thirty sharp," Nigel continues. "Guy wants to talk to us about a new project."

"Can't wait," I mutter and swallow two white pills with my coffee. Coffee and painkillers. What a great start to the week.

At nine-thirty, we all troop dutifully into the third-floor meeting room. I thought it was going to be just our team, but there are about thirty of us, including Gary, the head of IT, who I snogged in my first month here. It was more than five years ago now, but I still feel mildly uncomfortable every time I see him. It was my first proper "drinks after work on payday," and I was so excited to have some money to spend that I went a bit over the top. I remember going back into the building with Gary quite late in the evening because I'd left my keys on my desk, and the next thing I knew, we were being woken up by a rather bemused cleaner. We were kind of tangled up under my desk. At least I had all my clothes on. From that day on, I have never called the IT help desk for anything, just in case.

Gary is grinning at me, and I manage a smile. He's married with two kids now. We are both mature, responsible adults, I tell myself, and take out my notepad. I start doodling. Georgie Marshall. Georgie Marshall. It has a nice ring to it. Georgie Bradley. Hmmm, that's not bad either.

Guy clears his throat.

"Ladies and gentlemen," he starts in faux-formal tones and then grins. "Guys and gals." Okay, now too jovial. Can't he just get on with it?

"Globalization has made the world a smaller place. As more and more process-driven functions are outsourced and taken over by enhanced technology, firms around the world are refocusing and joining forces to produce a real value add proposition for their customers. The business-to-business sector is no different, and so I am very excited to tell you today about a proposed partnership with a great business-to-business publisher in the States, Horowitz and Gold. HG are based in New York, and they are pioneers in the enhanced client interface and Web-based profiling, and through our partnership we will be able to strengthen and develop our portfolio of products, ensuring that we are at the forefront of business information in this new millennium." In other words, "blah blah blah blah blah blah blah."

I start writing a list of things to take to Rome on one side of my notepad. On the other, I'm writing a list of things I'll need to buy.

Guy has started showing us a whole bunch of slides with charts and diagrams. I approach this sort of thing on a need-to-know basis. If I need to know any of it, I reason, Nigel will tell me. So, black trousers because they go with everything, black polo neck, obviously; orange halter neck top in case I manage to get a tan . . .

"And this paradigm shift in cultural and emotional intelligence can only improve the working of our great team,"

Guy is saying. "I hope I can bank on your support. It's going to be hard work over the next few months, but I think we can all be sure it will be worth it."

He stops talking and I look up with what I hope is an attentive look on my face. There is a deathly silence in the room.

"Are there going to be any redundancies?" asks a man I haven't seen before. I think he might be in marketing.

"There may be some reshuffling of the pack, some essential maneuvering of personnel to ensure peak performance and integration throughout all our business units, yes," says Guy.

I'm getting the feeling I may have missed something big. Redundancies? What has Guy been talking about? He is always talking about strategic business propositions and win-win partnerships—he and Nigel use that language when they are discussing what they ate for dinner last night, for heaven's sake. So why is everyone looking so shell-shocked?

We all troop back and I immediately corner Nigel.

"Nigel, what was he talking about in there?"

Nigel looks at me mournfully. "Well, under the merger with Horowitz Gold there's going to be some inevitable structural realignment," he says.

"Structural what? And what merger? Nigel, tell me what's happening in proper English. Why were they talking about redundancies?"

"Weren't you listening?" Nigel looks as if he's about to give me a lecture and then a sort of "oh, what's the use" look appears on his face. "We need to be able to compete on a global scale, but we haven't got the capital or resources to enter the U.S. market, so we're merging with HG, a U.S.-based company. We do broadly similar things."

I still don't really get it. "But why redundancies?"

"Look, Georgie," Nigel says slowly. "You've got two companies, and they merge. In each company you've got marketing people, IT people, research people, salespeople, and you've got products. Now, what you want to do is combine the two companies' strengths and sell more products to all the customers, but without spending so much. Which means that you won't need as many salespeople or IT people or marketing and research people."

Shit. This sounds quite serious. What if they have really good research people in the States who know what they're talking about and don't spend their time surfing around on the Internet?

"And when will we find out? If we've still got a job, I mean."

"Not till the merger's gone through," says Nigel. "If it does."

"So it isn't certain then?"

"Nothing's certain till signatures are on a legal document. But it's unlikely they'll call it off."

I long to call David and ask his opinion—he knows a lot about this sort of stuff and will be able to tell me first who HG are, and second what I should do about it. But we're still not talking after Saturday night's argument—at least he hasn't called to apologize and there's no way I'm going to be the first to call him. So instead I do a search on the Internet for Horowitz and Gold. There's a lot of stuff.

"They're huge!" I exclaim. "They've got offices all over the world! I thought Guy said they were based in New York?"

"That's where their head offices are."

"So will we get to go over there? For research purposes, I mean?"

For a moment, the whole merger thing starts sounding a bit more interesting. Monthly meetings in Manhattan, tha sort of thing. I visualize myself stepping off a plane, being met by a group of serious-looking people in suits. Going to HG's amazingly cool offices and giving major presentations on the latest research techniques and developments. I wonder if I'll get any time to go sightseeing—I've never been to New York and I've always wanted to go up the Empire State Building.

"Georgie, by the time the merger has all gone through, we'll be lucky if there's still a research department in the U.K."

"You don't mean that. Tell me you didn't mean that."

"Sorry," Nigel says. "I didn't really mean that, you're right. I'm sure we'll be fine."

No one does any work for the rest of the day. We've all been sworn to secrecy, but word spreads pretty quickly. Denise spends the afternoon applying for jobs, and everyone else seems to spend their time lurking in corridors having hushed conversations. All anyone wants to talk about is: did anyone know about this; what is the management team planning to do; and who's in the firing line. Most people seem to think IT will be the first to go, but I think that's because IT aren't on our floor, so people can say that without risking offense.

Guy has asked us to do some in-depth research on HG's brand in the U.K.—how well they are known and whether their products are rated. According to Nigel, we need to skew the research to show that no one has heard of them; that way, they'll have to keep the U.K. brand and operations. If HG products are really well known, they'll just start replacing Leary products with the HG ones and that'll be that. I start digging out names of our customers to start calling them, but then Nigel comes over.

"I think Denise can probably do that," he says. Oh great, so he's trying to get rid of me already.

"I'm perfectly capable of making phone calls, you know," I say crossly and pick up the phone, just to prove my point.

"No." Nigel takes the receiver and puts it down. I look up, shocked. Nigel never does things like that. Are all the men in my life turning into tyrants?

"I want you to help me do some proper research," says Nigel quietly.

"I always do proper research," I say. "Usually, any-way . . ."

"Look," he hisses. "Shut up, will you. I want to find out some more about HG. Find out what this merger is really about. I want you to help me track recent mergers and the fallout."

"Fallout?" I think I know what he means, but you can never be sure with Nigel. Once he asked me to do some research on the relevance of ABC to today's accountant. I rung round a whole load of bemused accountants to find out whether the alphabet was really a useful tool for them in their current roles, only to discover (when the report was complete) that Nigel was actually talking about some business tool called Activity Based Costing. I never dared tell him my mistake, and we continued publishing the ABC CD-ROM because everyone in my research report said it was absolutely essential.

"I mean, what happens afterward. What happens to the companies."

Well, obviously, that's what I thought he meant.

Nigel and I sit at his desk going back through the last twenty years of publishing mergers. I had no idea there were so many publishing firms. Nor did I know how many publishers are owned by one company. Like, take the Fi *nancial Times*. Did you know that they are owned by Pearson, who used to own London Weekend Television? No? Well, neither did I. We put together a big list, focusing on cross-border mergers, then we highlight all the U.K.-U.S. ones.

I take my half of our final list back to my desk, and I'm about to do a search on the Internet, when I suddenly notice something. On the screen from my original search on HG, a name on one of the documents rings a bell.

"Nigel."

"What?"

"Come here."

Nigel reluctantly gets up and walks over to my desk. I am looking at a news report on a previous merger—HG and a French book publisher.

"Isn't this the same company that was involved in the Brightman-Glover merger?"

Nigel looks closely at my machine.

"Scroll down," he orders.

We search through old news reports looking for information on all the U.S.-Europe mergers in the past ten years. Sure enough, in nearly all of them the same name keeps appearing: Tryton.

"Not a company I've heard of," admits Nigel. I haven't either, but that doesn't mean much. I mean, I haven't heard of any of these companies.

Nigel doesn't say any more about it, so I assume it isn't really that interesting after all, and I carry on noting down share prices and collecting information.

By twelve, I'm starving from all this hard work so I go out to get some lunch. When I come back Nigel's in exactly the same position, hunched over his computer.

I guess it's because he thinks his job is on the line and he's trying to demonstrate how hard he works and how essen-

tial he is. Personally I prefer the *qué será será* approach. I
I'm going to lose my job, then there isn't much I can do
about it, so I may as well make the most of it while I'm
here. I sit down at my desk and take out my new copy of
Marie Claire to flick through while eating a tuna sandwich.

There's an article about people who have slept with their
boyfriend's/husband's/wife's/girlfriend's best friends. One
girl slept with her boyfriend's best friend and is now married to him with three kids; one girl slept with her best
friend's husband and is now miserable and on her own.
look at the pictures and can't understand why anyone
would want to sleep with any of them, but it does make me
wonder. If I go to Rome with Mike, could I get carried
away and end up sleeping with him? The thought has
crossed my mind. And as David hasn't even called or anything, I may not have a boyfriend anymore, so sleeping
with Mike wouldn't even be wrong. But if I did sleep
with Mike would I be the happy-ever-after one, or the
miserable-on-her-own one? There's a counselor giving advice in the article, and she suggests looking deep inside
yourself to discover whether you are happy, and to see if
there's something else that needs fixing before you sleep
with someone else. Well, my curtains still haven't been put
up, but I'm not sure that will have much of an impact on
my Mike/David dilemma.

"Got it!"

I look up startled. Nigel has just punched the air. You
know, like a footballer or something. Believe me, Nigel is
not the sort to punch the air.

"Nigel?"

He looks round quickly. Everyone except Angela, the
telesales team leader, is out at lunch, and she's taking a

call—she's got her headphones on so she won't have heard his celebratory cry.

He motions for me to come and look at his computer screen. Reluctantly I put down a rather interesting article on plastic surgery and wander over.

"Stand behind me," orders Nigel.

"What?"

"Just do it. I don't want anyone seeing what I'm going to show you."

"Nigel, you haven't just downloaded some porn, have you?"

"Look!"

Proudly, Nigel shows me what he's got. All I can see is lists and lists of names and details. He opens another screen and there are loads of figures.

"Wow, Nigel, that's amazing!" I'm bluffing, of course. I have no idea what any of it means.

"You don't know what it means, do you?" Nigel asks.

"Of course I do," I reply hotly. "It's, well, it's really important information on the merger!"

Nigel is breathless. I've never seen him this excited. "Not exactly, but close," he says. "In front of you are the personnel and financial records of every HG company around the world."

I'm still not sure why this is so exciting, but I'm pretty certain Nigel shouldn't have that sort of information. He could find out how much everyone is paid, and that's definitely not allowed.

"Find out how much their researchers are paid," I beg.

Nigel shakes his head.

"Not relevant," he says firmly. "What I want to know is what happened to employees from companies that HG has merged with in the past."

"Ooh, yes, find out about that, too," I gush. I never

knew work could be so exciting. "So how did you find this information anyway?"

"We have our ways." Nigel's eyes are glinting.

"We? Who's we? Nigel, isn't that like really illegal or something?"

"Only if you get caught."

"Nigel, you're scaring me now. Tell me how you did this!"

Nigel's hands are trembling. "It's something I learned from one of the people at the Security Convention," he tells me. "All networks have weaknesses. You just figure out what they are, and wham, you're in."

"And in this case?"

"A chink in their firewall. This information is on their network, and I got in through the Boston office. You just send an e-mail to the right person, they respond, and bingo, you're in."

"And will they find out?"

"Not if I'm quick enough. Go to the printer."

My heart is beating faster as I race over. Reams of names and figures are coming out of the printer. I'm just picking the first lot up when suddenly Guy appears out of nowhere and I jump.

"So, how did you think it went this morning?" He's standing right in front of me. I can't let him see what Nigel and I are doing.

"Oh, great, you know, um, really interesting." I turn round quickly, clutching the papers to my chest. I'm standing in front of the printer, but pages and pages are coming out, straight onto the floor.

I need to create a diversion. If Guy sees what we're printing out, or what Nigel is downloading, we won't be waiting for the merger before we lose our jobs.

"Your, um, hair looks nice today," I say.

Guy looks at me uncertainly. He has a receding hairline and has cut his hair to within an inch of its life to make it less obvious that he's going bald. Why couldn't I have complimented him on his suit?

"It's a bit like the Mitchell brothers in 'EastEnders,' " I say. Why? Why? Say something nice, I beg myself.

"Although, you know, a lot more professional. In that suit, I mean. That suit is more godfather than East End gangster, isn't it? I mean Italians always dress better than the English and—"

Nigel intervenes just in time. "The presentation this morning was most enlightening," he says, getting up and herding Guy toward the coffee machine. "The strategic alignment does seem to be exceptionally favorable, and . . ."

As soon as they have turned their backs on me, I grab all the printouts and take them back to my desk, hiding them under my *Marie Claire*.

Denise comes back from lunch. "Bloody Nigel," she mutters to me. "We could all be about to lose our jobs, and all he can do is smarm up to Guy and talk about business process reengineering or what have you. They're standing by the coffee machine now, talking about downsizing like it's not human beings who'll be affected. He's got no emotion, that man."

I nod sympathetically and put a few more files on top of my *Marie Claire*, just for good measure.

8

Nigel doesn't come back as expected five minutes later. I try to get on with some work, but keep wondering if Guy saw what I was printing out. Maybe he's issuing my termination notice right now. Maybe he's keeping Nigel busy while he calls the police and we're both going to prison and . . .

The phone rings. It'll be them! Oh God! The police are calling me and I haven't thought up any excuse!

I pick up the phone tentatively.

"Hello?"

"Hello?"

"Hello, who is this please?"

My voice is faltering and my palms are sweating.

"Georgie?"

Oh, thank God, I recognize the voice.

"Mike," I say with relief.

"I knew you'd be pleased to hear from me."

"No, it's not that . . . I thought you were someone else."

"My, your life is full of little intrigues, isn't it. So, who am I up against? What's his name? I'll have him."

"No, you idiot. It's a work thing."

"Right." Mike has never been interested in what I do at work. I wish I'd let him think it was another man now.

"So, anyway, about Rome."

I hold my breath. For a moment I think he's going to say it's all off, that it was a mistake, that he's taking someone else and no hard feelings. To my astonishment I'm almost relieved. I suppose it'll be one less thing to worry about.

"What about Rome?" I say, trying to sound cool.

"Well, how do you fancy meeting me there on Friday instead of us going together? I've got some business stuff to do first, so I thought rather than you having to hang around on your own, I could get it all done on Thursday and Friday, and then meet you in the evening."

Well, that's okay then. Actually I'm really pleased we're still going. Obviously I wasn't *really* relieved when I thought Mike might be calling it off. This trip is going to be the best.

"Sounds good to me," I say enthusiastically.

"So, I could meet you at the station at nine-thirty P.M. Italian time. There's a Eurostar at five and you change at Paris. Sound all right to you?"

"Okay, I'll just book the tickets shall I?"

"You're gorgeous. Oh, one other thing. Would you mind taking a bag for me? I have to go straight from the airport to a meeting and I don't want to be lugging loads of stuff with me. I thought you could maybe pop round to my offices later and pick it up."

"But . . ." I'm about to tell him that I've got enough luggage to bring myself and won't have room for any of his stupid papers, but then decide against it. I mean, one bag— it's not that much to ask, is it?

"Okay, that's fine."

"You're a star, thanks Georgie. I'll see you later then? I'll e-mail you the address of my office. Bye, honey."

And he's gone. I am sufficiently buoyed up by the prospect of a weekend in the city of romance to ignore the fact that now, apparently, I am buying my own ticket,

which isn't quite what I had in mind when Mike said he'd
"take me."

As I put the phone down, Nigel reappears. He walks over
to my desk and bends down so his face is at the same level
as mine. I meet his eyes, but, as always, my attention is
drawn by a large red protuberance just to the right of his
nose. What a nightmare to still get loads of spots at Nigel's
age. I mean, I get the odd one or two every so often, but
Nigel's skin is truly adolescent. I wonder if he'll have really
young-looking skin when he's older—you know, because
of all the natural oils. It occurs to me that I have no idea
how old Nigel is. Somewhere in thirty to forty territory I
would imagine, but who knows?

"Georgie," he says in a loud, jovial voice, "Guy was very
impressed with your report on Pensions Bulletin. Do you
have another copy you could give me?

"Pensions Bulletin?" I look blankly at him. I've already
e-mailed the report to Guy, and who knows where I saved
it to on my computer. Me and filing don't really go too well
together.

"Um, couldn't you just use Guy's copy?"

"No. Could you just give it to me now?"

Nigel is looking at me strangely. Why does he want it? I
thought we'd finished with all that mundane sort of work
now. And anyway, doesn't he know that I totally ripped off
his report?

"Nigel, could you, um, just give me a while to dig it out,
and then I could e-mail it to you?"

"I want the *hard* copy."

He wants me to give it to him now, and he wants the
hard copy. Is Nigel flirting with me? Is this his idea of office
banter?

"Nigel, really, I had no idea . . ." I grin at him. But he
doesn't grin back.

"The report that we were working on earlier," he hisses, and I suddenly twig.

"You mean the HG stuff?"

Nigel looks at me as if I am a complete idiot. Humbled, I pass over the printouts, sandwiched between my *Marie Claire* and a random pile of files.

"Thank you, Georgie, much obliged," says Nigel loudly in a "nothing untoward going on around here" kind of voice, then he gives me a thin little smile before going back to his desk. I'm not entirely sure I'm wild on this "getting to know Nigel better" lark. Still, at least he's going to be absorbed in those files for the rest of the afternoon, which means I can get on with more important things.

My trip to Rome is proving problematic. I can't get a seat on Eurostar—apparently there is some special offer on or something and all the tickets have gone—which means I'll have to fly instead. Flying's okay; actually it will be quicker than taking the train, but there aren't many cheap flights to Rome, and I also need to get from the airport to the train station in time to meet Mike.

Nigel looks over and I give him a big smile. The great thing about the Internet is that you can be buying flights for a fab weekend away, and as far as everyone else is concerned you're sitting at your desk working incredibly hard. David thinks a constructive day in the office is one where he's performed really well and got things done. I think a constructive day in the office is one where I've paid all my bills online, booked a holiday, and compared ten different horoscope readings.

I find a flight for £60 that gets in at 8 P.M., which will give me loads of time to get to the station in time to meet Mike. Relieved, I fill in my credit card details and press "Buy Now."

It's only when I've pressed the button that what I'm doing really hits me. I'm going to Rome with Mike. I'm going to Rome with the person David hates and has asked (okay, told) me never to see. If David's cross with me now, he will be livid if he ever finds out. He'll probably never talk to me again. The horrible guilt I felt on Sunday begins to wash over me again. I need to rationalize the trip to myself. The truth is, I decide, that I'm only going away with Mike because David hasn't ever managed to get a free weekend. If he took me away I wouldn't need to go with other men, would I? And anyway, he's going to Geneva, isn't he? And he won't take me with him. So in a way, it's pretty much his fault that I'm going to Rome.

I glance up and see Nigel sifting through all the printouts on HG, but he's trying to do it secretly so he's got some Leary report on top of it. Every time someone walks past he slams the Leary report down on top of the figures and looks around furtively. Honestly, he'd be rubbish as a double agent.

I try to stop thinking about David, but every time the phone rings I expect it to be him. It's so unlike him not to call me, even if we have an argument. I don't want to be the one to call him because frankly he was totally out of line over the weekend, telling me what to do and everything. But I usually talk to David at least once a day and I miss telling him stuff. And I don't want to go to Rome without seeing him first. I need to make sure we're okay, that everything's fine before I go. To be honest, I'm almost hoping that David will cancel his Geneva plans and suggest that we go somewhere instead. Then I can cancel Rome and we can just have a lovely time together.

Except David never cancels his work plans. I can't help wondering if this trip to Rome is a sign. David obviously doesn't want to marry me or anything, and this could be the wake-up call I need. Maybe David just doesn't love me enough.

I pick up the phone and hit "1." (David is on my speed dial. I love speed dial, like I'm far too important and busy to press more than one digit.)

"Hello?" I'm immediately unsettled—this isn't Jane on the line. Jane always says "Good afternoon, David Bradley's office" or "Good morning, David Bradley's office." She speaks a bit like the Queen actually. Or like a newsreader from the 1950s. Intimidating, but nice.

"Hi, can I speak to David?" I'm not looking for reassurance that David loves me. I just want to see how he is. You know, in a totally nonparanoid kind of way.

"May I ask who's calling?"

"Yes, it's Georgie."

"Georgie . . . from where, please?"

"Georgie, his girlfriend, actually." I sound a bit more agitated than I'd like to, but who is this woman making me feel like I need to justify myself? Why doesn't everyone in David's office know my name?

Okay, I'm overreacting a bit. Must be the guilt.

I go on hold briefly, and then I hear David's voice.

"Georgie. I'm so glad you called. I'm really sorry about the other night. I had no right to talk to you that way."

"I'm sorry, too," I say and I actually mean it. There's something incredibly reassuring about David's voice. Whenever I'm feeling even slightly unsure of myself, or don't know what to do about something, I just talk to David and feel like everything's okay again.

"I wish I wasn't going away this weekend. I'd invite you along but there's a new partner working on this case with me and I don't think I'm going to get a lot of free time."

"That's fine, don't worry," I say quickly. "I mean, I've

got loads to do this weekend anyway. We've got lots on at work."

"You've got a lot on?"

He sounds really surprised and I find myself getting defensive. Why should David have the monopoly on being really busy at work? I also have important things to do.

"Yes, you know, strategic stuff," I say airily.

He chuckles. "Right, well, you have fun with that. Is my girl becoming a fearsome business executive?"

"Sort of." Fearsome. I like that.

"Look, darling, I've got to go. I'll see you after the weekend, okay?"

"Okay, have fun."

"Bye."

For some reason I feel very flat as I put the receiver back.

It isn't too far to walk to Mike's offices, even though it isn't exactly on my way home. Although I use the word *offices* in its loosest sense. For one thing, they're in Soho, right in the middle of Frith Street, near all the cool pubs and bars. And for another thing, inside they don't have nasty flecked wallpaper like the Leary building; they have exposed brickwork with groovy circular desks and posters from gigs and clubs covering the walls. The radio is on and there are beanbags on the floor, a TV in the corner, and a bar. A bar, for God's sake!

Tracey, the girl I had met at the Atlantic Bar, is sitting at a desk at the front of the office with two phones on it. She's looking pretty bored. I smile at her.

"Hiya! Do you always have to work this late?"

"I wouldn't feel sorry for her if I were you. She doesn't get in till twelve," says Mike, who's just appeared. Tracey raises her eyebrows at me and then goes back to looking bored. Mike gives me a kiss on the cheek.

"Drink?"

I look around and take in my surroundings. "Mike, I an't believe you have a bar in your office. Do you ever actually work?"

"Bar's essential. Need it to keep DJs and bands happy," hrugs Mike. I sit down on one of the beanbags and immediately regret it. I've always liked the idea of beanbags—I nean they look really cool—but somehow the reality never ives up to expectations. They aren't very comfortable, and t's impossible to look good when you're on one.

Mike brings me over a beer and then tosses a holdall nto my lap. It's heavier than I expected and larger, too. till, I'm going to Rome, I keep reminding myself.

"Won't be a problem, will it?" I wonder what Mike vould say if I said "yes."

"It's quite heavy," I say instead, but Mike doesn't answer.

"So what's in it?" I ask. I mean, I have a right to know, lon't I?

Mike looks up sharply. "Georgie," he says with a sigh, if you don't want to help me out here, just say so, okay? f you want me to have to pay another £500 in excess baggage costs to take it with me, just say the word and I'll lo it."

I stare at him. I forgot he could be such a drama queen.

"Fine, I'll take it," I say crossly. "I was only asking a uestion."

"Thanks, Georgie. Look, sorry for snapping. I've just got o much shit to deal with right now, y'know?"

I wonder what sort of shit, but don't think it's really the ime to ask. Instead, I lean back on the beanbag and take a ulp of my beer. These are seriously cool offices. Maybe if get made redundant from Leary's I could get a job at a ecord label or something. I could sit around and listen to

records and sign up cool young things. I could end up go‐
ing out with a pop star.

"Do you have to do much research—into bands and
stuff, I mean?" I ask Mike.

He looks at me uncertainly. "Research? Nah. It's all i
here." He points to his head.

I lean back again, imagining myself in an interview a
Polygram or somewhere, pointing to my head and sayin
confidently "All my music knowledge doesn't come fror
research—it's all in here."

There's a loud buzzing noise and Tracey calls over t
Mike, "The boys are here. They say they've come for th
gear."

Mike stands up quickly. "Yeah, right. Um, let them ir
will you?"

He turns to me. "So don't you have to make a move?"

"I'm sorry?"

"We've got to clear out in a minute. Got a record launc
to go to. I'd love you to come but it's a stupid guest-lis
thing. You can get back all right, can't you?"

I struggle to my feet. I was rather enjoying my beer actu
ally.

"Oh, no problem—I'm going out tonight anyway." I'r
not really, but I can't help lying—something about Mike a
ways makes me want to make out like I've got a more ex
citing life than I actually do. As I pick up the holdall tw
men appear at the door. They don't look like record labe
types. For one thing, they're wearing really bad jeans, th
sort of thing people wore in the eighties. Although I sur
pose the eighties is meant to be back in again. It could b
me who's out of touch.

"Drink?" asks Mike.

The two men both stare at me.

"Georgie's just leaving, aren't you," he says, looking at me pointedly.

I walk toward the door. Honestly, I'm doing Mike a favor with this stupid bag, and he's desperate to get rid of me. I'm going to be revisiting my SWOT analysis just as soon as I get home.

"Sorry mate, can't stay," says one of the men. "Just give us the goods and we'll be on our way."

Tracey places a blue carrier bag with a large package in it on the reception desk.

"Got a sample, have you?" the other one asks. I pause at the door. I somehow don't think they're talking about music samples.

Sure enough I see Mike reach into his back pocket and pull out a small wrap.

"Drugs?" I say indignantly before I can stop myself. "Mike, I can't believe you."

Everyone stares at me.

"Georgie, weren't you on your way out?" Mike says angrily.

"Yes, yes I was," I fume, dumping the holdall and slamming the door behind me. As I stomp down the steps I wonder if this is what David meant when he said that Mike was involved in stuff I didn't want to know about. I knew that Mike sometimes did a few lines of coke—I mean, everyone in the music industry does it, he says. But this . . . well, this is different. Is this how he's been making his money? God, what a bloody idiot. As I reach the main front door, I hear someone coming down the stairs after me.

"Georgie, stop a minute, will you?" It's Mike.

"No, I won't stop," I say, walking more quickly. "I just can't believe you. You tell me you're running a successful record label, and all you're doing is selling drugs. No wonder David didn't want me associating with you."

"David? What did he say?" Mike is looking agitated.

"Just that I should give you a wide berth. And I think he's right."

"Georgie, it's not what you think," Mike says quickly. "Honestly, you've got to believe me. I'm not into that stuff anymore. It was just a favor for a client. A major client, actually, and we need to keep him onside otherwise we're screwed. I don't want to do it, but I just said we'd hold on to some gear for him for a bit—and now we're giving it back. End of story. Please don't be angry."

I give Mike my best withering stare.

"So why were they asking for a sample if it's their gear?"

"They're just the idiots who do the collections," Mike replies quickly. "They don't know me from Adam, so they want to check I'm not ripping their boss off. Come on, Georgie, you've got to believe me. Look, come and ask them if you like. I mean, we'll probably lose the client, but I'd rather that than have you think I'm a drug dealer."

He stands aside so I can go back to the office. If it's a bluff, it's a clever one. I mean, there's no way I'm going back in there.

"Georgie Porgie, look, you know me. I'm not a drug dealer," Mike pleads, looking me right in the eye. "Don't let this mess things up for us, please?"

He looks so sweet, I think, when his eyes do that gooey thing. I mean, it's so hard to stay angry. Resignedly, I take the holdall from him. "Okay, but don't do it again, okay? It's so stupid. You could end up in prison."

He nods sheepishly. "Thanks Georgie. And thanks for being fucked off. It means a lot to me that you care enough to be pissed."

"So I'll see you in Rome?"

"Rome," says Mike softly as he kisses me on the lips. Dropping the holdall again, I reach my arms around his neck. I can feel his light stubble grazing my cheeks and can taste beer on his tongue as my lips part.

"Better go," says Mike reluctantly as he gives me a final kiss.

I nod, wave good-bye, and, clutching the holdall as I walk down the street, assure myself everything is great. I'm going to Rome and I'm going to have a fantastic time. Aren't I?

9

I don't like flying. It's not that I get scared or anything, I just hate the tedium. I mean, you don't just jump on and jump off, do you? There's getting to the airport, all the waiting around, passport control, and getting your baggage at the other end. If I was rich enough I wouldn't have luggage. I'd just buy everything at the other end. I hate airports.

So far today I have been traveling for exactly five and a half hours, and I'm still in Rome airport waiting for my luggage. I wish I'd just taken my stuff in a small bag that I didn't have to check, but I wanted a fancy suitcase to bring with me, and the salesman convinced me that I should get a larger size because it would be so much more practical. On the plus side, it was big enough to fit Mike's bag in it along with all my clothes. Still, I wouldn't call having to wait forty minutes for my luggage practical.

I manage to get a trolley and wheel it over to the conveyor belt. Two little boys are seeing how far they can jump off the belt, and their harassed mother is trying to stop them. At least I don't have to worry about anyone else, I think to myself. Traveling on your own is quite hard enough; traveling with someone else brings a whole load more stress. Except traveling with David, that is. He's the sort of person who looks after everything so all you have to do is sit around and drink tea. I get a slight pang and wonder what he's doing now in Geneva.

According to the screen in front of me, my flight's luggage is next in line for this conveyor belt. Mind you, that doesn't mean much; it's been next in line for twenty minutes at least. The airport is heaving with people, and I let the Italian conversations wash over me. It's such a romantic language. I resolve to start learning it as soon as possible. I can already ask for a bottle of mineral water without gas in Italian, so I've probably got a flair for languages. Plus Italians are so well dressed—if I could learn to speak Italian I'm sure I would start dressing in tan, black, and beige like the women around me. And I wonder if I'd suit highlights? I gaze at a couple of women standing a few yards away from me, both wearing floppy linen trousers with really nice sandals and smart tops. One of them looks like Sophia Loren and the other one could easily be Penelope Cruz, just a few years older. They are talking animatedly about something and I wish I could understand what they are saying.

There's no doubt about it, when I get back to London, I'm going to start Italian classes. How great would it be to have another language under my belt! I'll be able to really impress people in restaurants—well, Italian restaurants anyway. And then I could even come and work in Italy. I could work for an Italian record label!

I imagine Nigel and Guy's shocked faces as I tell them that I'm leaving Leary to pursue a career at . . . well, I can't think of the name of any Italian record labels, but they must have them. I'll move to Rome and get a gorgeous little apartment, and I'll walk around in full skirts and chic little shoes. Actually, if I'm working for a record label, I'll probably be wearing low slung jeans and trainers most of the time. I wonder what David would say if I told him I was moving to Rome. Would he want to come with me?

As my thoughts turn to David, my eyes start to play tricks on me because I could swear I can see him on the other side of the airport walking toward the "nothing to declare" sign. I mean, it's obviously impossible because David's in Geneva, but it does look very like him. And he's with a woman.

Of course it can't actually be him. I mean, what on earth would David be doing with some other woman in Rome? But I could almost swear it's him. I'm about to call out when it occurs to me that if it is David, it wouldn't be very sensible to go charging across the airport to confront him. For one thing, there is the teeny-weeny problem that I'm not actually meant to be in Rome myself. If it is David, and if there is a perfectly reasonable explanation for all this, bounding up to him when he's with some gorgeous-looking woman and explaining that I'm actually here to meet my ex-boyfriend who David has explicitly asked me not to see or even speak to, is not the best idea in the world.

But it really does look like him, and he's even wearing a coat like David's. I whip out my mobile and dial David's number. You know, just to see how he is. In Geneva. The phone rings, and the man keeps walking toward the "nothing to declare" sign. He's walking. It's ringing. Ooh, he's stopped. Still ringing. Now, he's walking again, but he's reaching, he's . . . damn, he's out of sight.

"Georgie!"

I always forget about other people's caller ID.

"Hi darling!" I'm trying to sound all breezy. "Just wanted to see how things are going in Geneva!"

"Oh, you know, it's not exactly a laugh a minute, but I'd say we're making progress. I'd much rather be at home with you, though."

Now that I can't see whether the man I saw in the airport is on the phone or not I can't think of anything to say to David.

"So what's Geneva like?"

"To be honest, I haven't really seen much of Geneva, just the inside of offices."

"Okay, well, have a lovely time," I say, and hang up just in time to hear an announcement telling me my luggage has arrived on carousel number four.

Of course my suitcase is the last to appear on the carousel, and I'm half an hour late by the time I get to the station to meet Mike. I even take a taxi, which wipes out a whole load of cash. But naturally Mike hasn't arrived yet. Maybe he hasn't adjusted to Italian time. I sit on my suitcase and start reading a copy of Italian *Vogue* I bought at a kiosk. Not that I really understand any of it, but I like the pictures, and also I like the idea that people walking past me may think I'm Italian.

"Georgina," I mutter under my breath, practicing my accent. "*Buon giorno,* Georgina." A man sitting next to me looks at me oddly and I refocus on my magazine.

I can't stop thinking about the man in the airport. It couldn't have been David, could it? Before I've even asked myself the question, I know the answer. Of course it wasn't David. David is the most predictable man I've ever known. If he says he's in Geneva, well, that's exactly where he must be. I get another pang of guilt about being in Rome. But decide to ignore it. You are Audrey Hepburn, I tell myself. This is your weekend of indulgence. It's fine. David had loads of chances to bring you here, and he didn't. End of story.

But if I'm Audrey Hepburn and this is my Roman Holiday, who is my Gregory Peck going to be? I know David's not exactly rough around the edges, but I did always think that he would be my Gregory Peck. And now I'm going to be spending the weekend here with Mike instead. I try to imagine Mike wearing a baggy 1950s suit and driving me around on a Vespa and smile slightly at the thought. I mean, I can imagine Mike on a Vespa, I'm just not sure about the suit. Plus, if he did get a scooter, he'd almost certainly become a boy-racer, trying to beat everyone else on the street.

I put down my magazine and look around. To be honest, Rome station isn't particularly different from any other major station I've been in; there's a big sign for departures and arrivals, and lots of people waiting around. But the air is warmer, and people look more … well, not exactly glamorous but certainly more Italian. There are lots of curvaceous women wandering around wearing skin-tight jeans and high heels, and men in sharp suits talking into mobile phones. In Italian.

I look at my watch. Mike is nearly an hour late. I would get annoyed, but I figure I'm in Italy now; you can't get too hung up on people being a bit late, can you? And I quite like the people watching. I'm absorbed in a couple standing about twenty feet away who seem to be having a massive argument when Mike appears. Even when he's late, he doesn't run, I notice. He ambles slowly over and gives me a kiss on the lips.

"Been here long?"

"Oh, you know, a bit."

"Sorry I'm late, gorgeous, had a nightmare meeting this afternoon," he says, putting his fingers through his hair and looking around the station. "Still, made a wad of cash, so what the fuck. Have you got the bag?"

"It's in my suitcase."

"Cool. Come on then, let's go!"

I trot after Mike, dragging my suitcase. I can't believe I

didn't get one with wheels. I look ahead at Mike and am pleased to see he's looking utterly gorgeous. He's wearing a gray V-neck jumper and dark blue jeans, with a sixties-style beaten up leather jacket.

He looks like he's come straight out of a really cool black-and-white film. Only it isn't *Roman Holiday*, it's *The Thomas Crown Affair* or *Bullit*, and he's Steve McQueen. He looks a bit dangerous, like a lion that's prowling around looking for its next prey. His eyes are incredibly alert and watchful, and you get the feeling that he could pounce at any minute. I get a little flutter in my stomach, as if I'm nervous, but that's ridiculous. I have no reason to be nervous.

We jump in a cab and make our way to a small hotel near the Castel Sant'Angelo. A short man in uniform takes my luggage and says something to me in Italian. Not wanting to appear really English, I just smile sweetly as Mike presses the button for the lift. But the guy keeps standing there, looking like I should be saying something. I feel myself go red—I can hardly admit now that I didn't understand a word he said, can I? Hoping he'll go away, I stare ahead at the lift doors, but instead he starts talking to me again.

"Room Fifty-four," says Mike, and the man nods and walks away. I go redder and look up to see Mike laughing at me.

"Italian's a bit rusty," I mutter.

"Idiot," laughs Mike, "he was speaking English! The guy just has a thick accent!"

Mortified, I get into the lift, but Mike doesn't join me. Instead he winks and grins.

"Why don't you take your stuff to our room. Brian and I'll be in the bar," he suggests.

Our room. Okay, that's fine. We're sharing a room. I

mean, I expected that. But hang on, what was the other thing he said?

"Brian?"

"Yeah, you know, you met him at the Atlantic Bar."

"I know who he is; I just didn't know he was here." I try very hard to stop my voice going squeaky and indignant, and tell myself not to get upset. I want this weekend to be perfect, and getting upset because Brian is here is not going to get things off on the right note.

"Yeah, well, we had some business stuff to sort out, you know. He's only here till tomorrow. Come on, he's a laugh, Brian."

I smile. Of course it's fine. Why wouldn't it be fine? Actually, this is more than fine. Two men taking me out in Rome. What could be better than that?

As soon as I get to the room, I dump my things on the floor and run myself a bath. Then I have a quick look around the room (nice view, huge big wardrobe). By the time I get into the bath, the whole room is steamy and smells of the orange flower and lavender bath oils that I found by the basin. Quite frankly, I could stay here all evening. There is something very nurturing and comforting about hot water, and if the bath oil smells this nice, I want to check out the face wash and shower gel, too. David and I once stayed at a lovely hotel in Bath and they had Molton Brown stuff all over the bathroom. How cool is that? Hot water and fluffy white towels—frankly, that's a recipe for happiness in my book. I decide that when I get back I'm going to take a good look at my bathroom and fill it with nice things. I can't believe I haven't done it before. So much pleasure for such a small amount of effort.

After a good long soak I force myself to get out, wrap myself in a waffle robe, and shuffle back into the bedroom.

Getting dressed is not going to be easy. I'm looking for sexy but chic and none of my clothes really seem to fit the bill. I don't understand how that works. I mean, how many times do you buy something thinking of all the millions of occasions you'll wear it and look amazing? And how many times do you stare frustratedly at your wardrobe unable to find a thing to put on? It's even more weird when you've packed a suitcase full of clothes you consider to be sexy and gorgeous, only to arrive at your destination unable to find anything that makes you look halfway decent. Maybe Nigel is right about all that conspiracy stuff.

After getting everything out of my suitcase I finally decide that maybe with a dash of red lipstick my tight pencil skirt and sleeveless cashmere tank top will do the business. I actually wanted to bring more clothes but Mike's holdall took up quite a bit of room so I had to leave a few things behind. Like my gym kit, which I was going to bring, just in case the hotel had a spa or something.

I take the holdall out of my suitcase and gaze at it. I really want to know what could be so important that I had to sacrifice packing space, but obviously I couldn't look inside because that would be really wrong. And anyway, it's got a padlock on it. Mike said it was important papers and it certainly feels like paper, but why would Mike carry important papers around in a holdall rather than a briefcase? David's got a lovely old battered briefcase that used to be his grandfather's. But I don't want to think about David. If I even let the thought of him seep into my consciousness, I get huge pangs of guilt and I start wanting to call him, which would obviously be a very stupid thing to do. Instead, I pull out the wide selection of underwear I bought for Rome and try to decide between silk and lace.

On my way down to the bar I start feeling a bit light-headed and realize I haven't eaten anything since lunchtime. Unless you count the little chocolates the hotel left on my pillow. The hotel's quite a smart one—lots of leather seats and important-looking people striding around purposefully. Brian and Mike are sitting at a small table in the corner drinking champagne and look very pleased with themselves. As I approach them Mike pulls up a chair and Brian pours me a glass of champagne. "To success," grins Mike, and we all drink a toast.

I don't know why, but I'm feeling very jumpy. Or is it excited? It's probably because I haven't eaten. Although, thinking about it, I've been feeling a bit odd ever since I thought I saw David. Maybe it's guilt. I look at Mike and Brian looking all relaxed and tell myself not to worry. I mean, I am not doing anything wrong; I'm just enjoying a night out with friends. I mean, who knows what David's doing in Geneva? It's fine. Everything's going to be fine.

"So," I say to Mike, "do you drink nothing but champagne now? Is that a strategic decision?" I smile at both of them and down the contents of my glass very quickly. If I'm tipsy, these feelings of guilt are bound to go away.

"He tries not to," grins Brian. "Spends all the money he owes people like me on champagne and caviar, don't you Mike?"

Mike looks at Brian sharply.

"I told you, that's all being dealt with. Next week I'll sort you out, okay?"

Brian slaps Mike on the back good-naturedly, but his face suggests he's more stressed than he's letting on. So Mike owes him money, does he? I wonder how much? It must be just lack of ready cash, though. I mean he's obviously loaded. I raise my eyebrows at Mike, but he looks away and lights a cigarette.

It's good champagne, and we're soon on the third bottle. Brian tells us stories about groupies in clubland and I can't stop laughing. Although in all the stories, the girls come out terribly. I mean, they do sound pretty awful—sleeping with anyone who owns a pair of decks and doing all sorts of unmentionable things in limousines, but still, I hope no man has ever talked about me like that. I'm sure they wouldn't have though, mainly because I've never done anything like that.

But I hope Brian doesn't put me in the same category as them. You know, thinking I'm some sort of floozy. During the evening Mike's hand has kind of maneuvered itself onto my leg, and while I've sort of been enjoying having it there, I'm now all self-conscious and paranoid. But at the same time, I kind of like the idea of having his hand there. I'm in Rome, with one very sexy man and one who is all right I suppose, and they are buying me champagne and Mike can't keep his hands off me. When I'm with David, I feel loved, looked after, and safe. But right now I'm feeling desirable, strong, and slightly wicked.

Except that while I like the hand being there, I'm not entirely comfortable with the implication. It's like I'm playing a role, and loving it, but I sort of want someone to shout "Cut" so I can go back to my own room and go to sleep without worrying that Mike is going to expect a bit more than that.

To my alarm, Brian yawns and says he might call it a night. That means it's just going to be Mike and me left down here. Although being down here is probably going to be easier than going up to the bedroom. I'd kind of hoped the two of them would settle down for a night of drinking and that I'd have been able to make my excuses.

I look at Mike, who grins at me. "Yeah, I think we should probably make a move, too. Early start tomorrow, gorgeous," he says, squeezing my knee. I move my legs quickly and stand up, but regret it immediately. I am, I realize, very drunk indeed. According to my watch, it's two in the morning and I appear to have drunk an entire bottle of something called Perrier Jouet Belle Epoque. I'm definitely going to have a truckload of the stuff delivered to my house on a regular basis, because it is just the most amazing champagne I've ever drunk in my life. However, I would rather have more control over my coordination.

Mike calls the lift and Brian staggers off to the Men's leaving Mike and me alone. I am swaying, or the room is—I'm not sure. All I know is that I want to go to sleep. A cloud of sleepiness has descended on me and I feel too drowsy to even attempt conversation. We get into the lift and as we travel up we don't say a word to each other. If Mike was David, I think to myself, I would lean my head on his chest now. I might even insist he carry me into our hotel room. And he would, too. But he isn't David. It's Mike. And we're sharing a room, which means sharing a bed. This thought wakes me up with a jolt. Sharing a bed with Mike? Oh my God, do I really want to do this?

At the door to our room, Mike slips his arm round me as he turns the key in the lock. Then he cups my head in his hands and kisses me. Before I can engage my brain and decide what to do, he maneuvers me onto the bed and gets on top of me, tugging at my skirt and sticking his tongue down my throat. There's just no way I can do this. I pull away and roll over onto my front.

"Playing coy with me, are you, Georgie Porgie?" grins Mike, undoing the zip of my skirt. "Come on, you little tease, get your kit off."

So this isn't exactly an ideal situation. I'm in a foreign city, sharing a room with someone who has just spent huge amounts of money on champagne for me. I am half undressed, and I don't want to sleep with him. Oh, and there's only one bed. I manage a little smile, and then with a flash of inspiration, I put my hand to my mouth.

"I'm sorry, I think I drank a bit too much champagne," I smile apologetically.

Mike moves back in alarm. "You're not going to puke are you?"

Once, when we were going out, I got horrendously drunk (we were at a party where Mike was flirting with pretty much everyone except me, and drinking wine straight from the bottle seemed to be a pretty good idea), and on the way back I was sick on Mike's shoulder. He was absolutely furious and wouldn't talk to me for weeks.

I shrug. "I don't know. I'll probably be okay . . ." I say, getting up quickly and walking toward the bathroom. It does the trick. Mike's squeamishness is stronger than his sexual appetite, and he grabs a blanket and a pillow. "Look, I'm going to sleep here, just in case," he says quickly, pulling a camp bed out of the wardrobe.

"You, um, get some sleep, okay?"

I'd be offended if I wasn't so relieved.

❦ 10

I wake up slowly. The sun is shining on my face and is deliciously warm. As soon as I open my eyes I feel a tremor of excitement pass through me. I'm in Rome! I'm really here, and it's sunny, and I didn't sleep with Mike, and I'm going to have a lovely day walking around the city, having coffee in little roadside cafes, and visiting the Coliseum. Maybe Brian could come, too, then it really would be like *Roman Holiday*. Although actually I'm a lot more clued up than Audrey Hepburn was. I would have sussed Gregory Peck right away if it had been me.

I sit up quickly and discover two things. First, moving quickly is not a great idea when you've been drinking champagne all night. Second, Mike's camp bed is empty.

To be honest, I'm actually a bit relieved that Mike isn't there. It means I can get up slowly and enjoy the morning. He's probably out getting us some breakfast or something. I notice that there's a television opposite me on the desk and the remote control is on the bedside table. Within moments the comforting sounds of BBC Worldwide news are filling the room.

I lie back down, propping my throbbing head up with pillows. It's the business news, which is a shame, but still, at least it's television and I can understand it. There's another corporate scandal in the States, and there's someone talking about the investment community being betrayed, how it's another Enron. I yawn, and a little box appears saying that "Top Gear" is going to be on in five minutes.

I get up slowly and wander into the bathroom. To my amazement, the television is as loud in the bathroom as in the bedroom. I look around, and sure enough, there are speakers in all four corners of the room. How cool is that? I turn on the shower and wash my hair as the newsreader drones on about the AMT Group propping up its revenues through multiple acquisitions and the disgraced board of directors being investigated. One of them has been arrested, and there's another one who they can't pin any blame on.

"Taylor has been exonerated in this episode, but the SEC is still questioning the auditors . . ." the newsreader says as I rinse out my hair. Honestly, I don't know how people like David manage to listen to this stuff and make sense of it. As soon as I hear the words "and now it's time for our business news" I start yawning. Luckily, as I get out of the shower, my head feeling almost back to normal, the familiar "Top Gear" music kicks in.

But before I can sit back down on the bed to watch it, the phone rings. It's Mike.

"Good sleep?"

"Um, yeah, great. Where are you?"

They're test-driving four-by-fours on the television. I think of my mother and poor James's attempts to get her out of her antiquated Mini.

"Oh, I woke up early, so I thought I'd get on with a few things. Fancy going to the Vatican?"

The Vatican? What a surprise! Mike is so not the sort to go sightseeing. It suddenly occurs to me that he could be Catholic. To be honest, I have no idea whether Mike is even religious or not. I don't think it's ever come up in conversation. I've never really done the whole church thing except for a couple of years during the Kensington Church Street period (I divide my life up by addresses) when I went to a Catholic boarding school because my mother thought I might "get into trouble" in London. I hated it at first but then got totally seduced by the structure of the day and the soft-spoken teachers who were all nuns and called "sister." They looked after us amazingly well—although the teaching was pretty appalling. In the end I left because my mother realized I'd never get my O levels if I stayed, but by then I had decided that I wanted to take my vows and join a convent. I argued fiercely with my mother and she said that if I got my O levels in a more academic private school I could go to a convent if I really wanted to, and of course, by then I'd forgotten all about becoming a nun and wanted to be in a band instead.

Still, I've always wanted to go to the Vatican. It's even on my planned list of activities—it's got the Sistine Chapel and everything! More to the point, does this mean Mike really has changed and is interested in things and people other than himself?

"Give me half an hour or something," I croak.

It looks lovely and sunny outside, so I put on a skirt and a T-shirt and slap on some sun cream just in case. I notice that Mike's holdall has disappeared and make a mental note to quiz him about it later.

By the time I get downstairs, I am absolutely starving. We had a few bar snacks last night, but no proper meal. Maybe this is how celebrities stay so thin; they just drink champagne all the time and don't have time to eat. Mike is on his mobile by the reception desk. He waves hello, then turns his back on me, continuing his conversation.

He looks irritated when he comes off the phone.

"Shall we go?" he says abruptly. Not even a "how are you."

"Why don't we get some breakfast first?" I suggest. "I haven't eaten since yesterday lunchtime."

"Oh, I grabbed something to eat when I got up," says Mike. "Look, you can buy a croissant on the way, can't you?"

"I s'pose," I say doubtfully. I was hoping for a long leisurely breakfast with lots of coffee and orange juice. Still, I should be able to grab something near the Vatican. It's so nice to be going somewhere cultural with Mike. He used to be so scathing of my attempts to get him to go to art galleries. He'd go if it was "cool" and the right people were going to be there—a Damien Hirst private view, or something—but anything else was out of the question. And even if we did go to a gallery, we'd never actually look at the paintings; Mike would always head straight to the bar and end up flirting with everyone.

But now, well, we are in Rome and I am finally going to fulfill my fantasies of walking round arm in arm, looking at beautiful works of art, and eating delicious ice cream. Okay, so the ice cream bit hasn't featured in my fantasies before, but I'm really starving.

Actually we don't walk; we take a cab. It's not far, but Mike doesn't do walking. He doesn't believe in it, he always says. I've never established whether he doesn't believe that walking is actually possible, or whether it's just the benefits of walking that he doesn't believe in. Not that it matters, taxis are absolutely fine by me.

As we pull up outside St. Peter's Square, I come over all overawed and amazed. It's absolutely huge, a massive courtyard surrounded by statues and engravings and pillars. We stand outside St. Peter's Basilica for about ten minutes, marveling. Then we stand outside for another ten minutes, kind of looking around.

"Do we need to buy tickets?" I ask.

Mike has shown no inclination to move from our current spot, next to a large fountain. Tourists are milling around everywhere. As he was in such a hurry to get here, I can't really work out why he doesn't seem too keen to go into the basilica.

He looks up absentmindedly. "Tickets? What for?"

"To get in."

"In?"

"Inside. The basilica. The Sistine Chapel. You know." I gesture at the buildings behind us.

"You want to go in?"

"Of course! Don't you?"

"Can't, meeting someone in five. But go ahead. I'll see you back at the hotel later, okay?"

I can't quite believe what I'm hearing.

"Meeting who?"

"Just business stuff, it won't take long."

"Business stuff? Oh, bloody marvelous. I'll just be your personal assistant, shall I?"

How could I have been so stupid? We are not actually going into the Vatican. No, we're just meeting some stupid contact of Mike's. We're not spending the day together at all. I feel so stupid. And now I've got tears in my eyes. Dammit. Why am I so upset? It's not like the pope is actually here or anything.

I turn away from Mike so he can't see how upset I am, but I needn't have bothered; he's already whipped out his mobile and is making another call.

I can't believe I've come all the way to Rome and lied to David, and Mike just expects me to fit in with his bloody meetings. And he doesn't even care that I'm hungry. If I'm not careful, the prickling around my eyes is going to turn into full-fledged crying, which would be incredibly uncool, particularly since I'm not wearing waterproof mascara.

I turn around and blink furiously. Mike is not worth crying over. I tell myself it doesn't matter, that I don't really care if he is meeting someone or not. But actually it does matter. Not just that we're not going to go into the Vatican when we're right outside, but that I'm never going to have my Roman Holiday. And the worst thing is, I knew it would be like this. At least, I should have known. This was what it was like when I was Mike's girlfriend. I was always just kind of tagging along. I never felt I was the focal point for Mike; I was an appendage, and if I disappeared, well, I was never entirely sure Mike would even have noticed.

Not for the first time I begin to wish I was here with David. David would come into the basilica with me and let me read out all the information in my guidebook, even though he'd have the same guide in his hand. David would take me somewhere lovely for breakfast as soon as I even hinted I was hungry, and would hold my hand when we walked down the street.

I take a deep breath and remind myself that David isn't perfect either—I mean, he wouldn't even have made it to Rome in the first place because he'd never manage to leave his beloved work behind.

No, if I want a Roman Holiday, I'm better off on my own.

Mike wanders over and I feel his arms wrap round me. I stiffen slightly—a hug from him is the last thing I want.

"You're not pissed off, are you, gorgeous?" he says into my ear. "I'm sorry, I didn't know you were interested in religious stuff. But we can look round later if you want? I just have to see this guy, okay? It won't take long. You have a wander around and then we can grab some lunch. What do you say?"

He turns me around and kisses me on the nose, then smiles at me hopefully. I relax slightly. I mean, I'm here with Mike, so I may as well make the best of it, even if he is a selfish guy. It's only two days, after all. And if he's got a business meeting, well, that's not so bad. To be honest, it'll be nice to have a bit of time on my own.

"Well, I am pissed off," I say pointedly, "but you've got time to make it up to me. You have your meeting. I'll see you back at the hotel, shall I?"

"You're one in a million. Have fun?" Mike grins and ruffles my hair.

"You too."

I walk over to the entrance to St. Peter's Basilica. There are hordes of people outside, shouting and screaming in every language possible. Mike turns away and makes another call. I join the queue. Already I'm feeling better, and actually, looking at art and architecture and stuff is better when you're on your own anyway—you can really think about what you're looking at and interpret it without being influenced. Plus, you don't get people asking you what you think. I once went to the National Gallery in London with this art student bloke I quite fancied, and every time I said something like "Oh, I like that," he'd start asking me why, and what I thought the artist was trying to say and stuff, when all I meant was that the colors were nice or I liked the look of the house/person in the painting. Looking at art can be hard work when you have to actually talk about it.

An English couple in front of me are arguing. Evidently the woman is less than keen on going into the Vatican and wants to go shopping instead.

"We always go bloody shopping," her husband says in a

weary tone. "We're in Rome; let's do something we can't do at home. We've come all this way; let's at least go inside, shall we?"

"But you hate churches! I hate churches! For God's sake, Alan, you don't want to be here, I don't want to be here. Let's just go."

"I don't want to go shopping."

"We don't have to go shopping—that was just one idea. We could go and drink coffee in a cafe. Or we could go back to bed. For one weekend we don't have the kids, and I don't want to be walking round a sodding church."

Apparently Alan doesn't want to either. He immediately agrees to the "go back to bed" option and they leave arm in arm. I watch them as they pass Mike, who is still on his mobile waiting for his elusive business partner to show up. I notice that he's getting really deep lines on his forehead— maybe running his own business is really getting to him.

I realize I've been so taken in by Mike's good looks and charm that I've never really looked much deeper. I never really noticed how troubled he looks, how worried he seems. Maybe the problem is that I've never really stood up to him. I mean, if I didn't just accept the fact that he had a business meeting and got really mad instead, maybe he would cancel it for me. He looks so distant, even though he's only forty feet away. Could it be that he just needs someone to talk to?

I leave the queue and wander back over to Mike.

"No good?" he asks me. He looks stressed.

"If the person you're meeting isn't showing, why don't we just bugger off?" I say, and tentatively put my arm through his. "We could explore Rome and—"

Before I can finish my sentence the mobile is ringing again. I've lost my chance, and he's already shouting down the phone and walking away from me.

"Look, what is this? You think I'm lying? Is that it? I take you on, you start doing well, and now I have to put up with your shit just because you think you're too good now. Is that where we are? Because if it is, you can stick your fucking record deal. . . . Fine, well, that's okay. Look mate, you'll get the money, okay? These things can just take some time. Fine, now put Bill on the phone . . ."

I give up. If Mike's going to act like he's still in London, I'm certainly not going to. I wander off to buy myself a coffee and something to eat. There's a cafe by the side of Via Republica, the road leading back into the town center. If he needs me, Mike will be able to see me from here. I order a latte and a croissant, sit back and let the spring sun warm my face.

When I open my eyes again I see Mike talking to someone. The guy looks pretty smartly dressed, considering it's Saturday; he's wearing a suit and carrying a briefcase. Maybe it's an Italian thing—he probably thinks the English are a really scruffy lot, because Mike's wearing jeans and a pretty old T-shirt. They walk off quickly before I've got time to shout and let them know where I am. To be honest, I really couldn't care less. Right now, I just want to sit here and enjoy Rome.

I pull out my guidebook and marvel at the photographs of the frescoes in the Sistine Chapel. I read all about how Michelangelo painted the ceiling (he delegated a lot by the looks of it), and by the time I've finished I almost feel like I've actually seen them for myself.

Having paid for my coffee I wander off down the road. A group of Italian men look me up and down appraisingly and murmur *bellisima!* as I walk past. I smile and get a warm glow inside. Personally I've never understood people who don't like being whistled at in the street. I mean, you wouldn't get upset if someone stopped you and said politely that the dress you're wearing really flatters you, would you? And that's all a wolf whistle is, just punctuated.

I weave in and out of the cobbled streets looking in shop windows and enjoying the warmth on my skin. If only England were warmer, I'm sure we'd all be a lot happier. I mean, it's really hard to be depressed when the sun's shining, isn't it?

I'm just trying to decide whether to wander round the shops or do something more cultural like go to the Coliseum when I see something and freeze. Down an alleyway to my right I see David. This time I know I'm not mistaken. It's definitely him. I can't believe he's here! When he said he was going to Geneva!

I step back so he can't see me. I need to think this through. So he was at the airport yesterday! But what on earth is he doing here? My mind flits between feeling angry at David lying to me and worrying about how to explain my being here, too. At least Mike isn't with me. Maybe I could tell him I needed to get away and Rome seemed the perfect place. Oh God, this is too much of a coincidence . . . I mean, who expects to bump into their boyfriend nine hundred miles away in a foreign city when he's meant to be eight hundred miles away somewhere completely different?

Unless . . . he couldn't have found out I was coming here and decided to spy on me, could he? My mind is racing. Of course, it's impossible that David would know I was here— no one knows I'm here except Mike, and he's hardly going to tell David, is he?

I peek round the corner to see if David's still there. He is, and looking pretty good too, if you ask me. He's wearing a crumpled creamy linen suit and he's putting his hand through his hair a lot. There are two men with him, both very smartly dressed (it's definitely an Italian thing), and I can see that David is being incredibly serious and attentive. When I take a proper look at his companions I can see why—they don't look like the sort of men you'd want to get on the wrong side of. I wonder if he's being attacked or something—his face is strained, and he's nodding and giving them money. Quite a lot of money by the looks of it. Except they don't look like muggers. I mean, they aren't holding a knife or anything, and David seems to be listening really carefully to them. Maybe they are fraudsters and they're trying to buy him off? Except then he would be getting money, not giving it.

I consider running away, but I'm surprised at how incredibly relieved I am to see David's lovely face. I can't possibly waste the opportunity of spending some time with him. And my curiosity over why he's here is a lot stronger than my fear of being found out.

I decide that my best course of action is to walk casually down the street—okay, alleyway—and bump into David. That way I might overhear what those two men are talking about. And I will just look utterly surprised to see David there.

But as I start walking nonchalantly toward David, I trip over a cobblestone. David looks up, startled. I wave and carry on walking toward him, but before I can get to him the two men disappear down a side alley.

"David! Are you all right? I saw those guys taking money from you. What the hell are you doing here?"

David looks slightly stunned.

"Who were those men, and what are you doing here?" I repeat. I've never seen David look so flummoxed.

"What? Oh, um, they were clients, of sorts . . ." David looks around him as if to get his bearings.

"Georgie," he continues slowly, "I . . . I didn't really expect to see you here." He looks utterly confused.

"But why would you be here?" I persist. "You're meant to be in Geneva. For a minute I thought you might be following me, but that's impossible . . ."

"Following you," says David slowly. "Yes, I suppose you may as well know. I . . . I was going to go to Geneva, but . . . then I found out you were going to Rome, and I just had to come and find you. Have a proper Roman Holiday."

I stare at him accusingly. "David, do not bloody lie to me, okay? You really expect me to believe that you were prepared to cancel a business trip just so you could follow me here? And anyway, how did you find out? And who were those men?"

But instead of answering, David leans down and kisses me.

"It's so good to see you here," he says softly, then straightens up and narrows his eyes at me. "But tell me something," David continues. "Why exactly are you in Rome?"

He's got me there. If he knew I was coming here, he might know that I'm supposedly here with Mike. Of course, then again, he might not.

"Because I wanted some romance in my life," I say defensively. "Because I thought, obviously mistakenly, that you'd never take me."

"Oh my darling." David gives me a hug. "I'm so sorry. I can't believe you came here all by yourself. But I'm here now, aren't I?"

"But why? How did you find out I was here? And why didn't you just suggest we go out together?"

"I thought it would be more romantic this way. And I wanted to find out what you were up to . . ." David grins at me and raises one eyebrow.

So you don't know about Mike, I think with relief. And now I've got someone to have lunch with!

"That's all very well," I say, pretending to still be cross, "but I still want to know who those men were."

"I just thought, while I was here, I would look up a couple of old business acquaintances," says David. He seems a lot calmer now. I suppose he wasn't expecting me to stumble across him like that.

"You said they were clients."

"One day a business acquaintance, the next a client," grins David.

"And you were giving them money."

"Their money. Money my firm had been looking after for them."

I stare at him. I'm not convinced, but I can't think of a good enough reason why David would be making it up. The thing is, David just doesn't lie. I mean, whenever he tries, he always fails miserably, like the time he tried to convince me that he'd forgotten all about Valentine's Day when actually he had organized a surprise late-night picnic in Hyde Park. Unlike Mike who actually did forget Valentine's Day.

At the thought of Mike, I feel the blood rushing from my face. What if we bump into him? I mean, Mike could be around the next corner, couldn't he, and then David would know why I came here and it would just be too awful.

And Mike, well, he would be furious, too. He brings me to Rome for a romantic weekend and I go off with David instead. I mean, it's not exactly good form, is it? I can just imagine what my mother would have to say about this. She would think it incredibly unethical, unreasonable, and downright rude. And she'd have a very good point.

"Are you okay, darling?"

"Yes, yes of course," I manage to say. "Just . . . well, I'm a bit hungry actually." I smile wanly at him.

David looks at his watch and scratches the back of his

neck like he does when he's worried about something. But then he grins again and puts his arm round me protectively.

"In that case, I think we should get you some food, don't you?"

Right answer. Very good response. Putting Mike firmly out of my mind, I follow David back up the alleyway and into a cafe.

Once I'm sitting down, I begin to relax. To be honest, it's probably the most relaxed I've been since I got to Rome. I mean, I was looking forward to walking around with Mike and going to cool record label parties and stuff, but with David here I feel much less on edge. Like I don't have to prove anything to anyone and don't have to worry about saying the right thing. And he's even buying me breakfast. How nice is that?

Every so often a few little questions start to creep into my mind about how David knew I'd be here, and what would have happened if I hadn't bumped into him like that. Would he have come to the hotel? Would he have seen me and Mike together? But I do my best to suppress them and after a while they seem to disappear altogether.

When the waiter comes over I order a cappuccino.

"Are you sure that's what you want?"

I look up at David curiously.

"I just thought a bottle of wine might be nice. Maybe an early lunch . . ."

I meet David's eyes and see that they are glinting slightly.

"Could we have a few minutes?" I ask the waiter and as soon as he's turned his back I reach over and give David a kiss. Somehow I think today is going to turn out much better than I thought.

This is the life. This is what fantasies of Rome are made of. David and me, sitting at a small, wobbly table, basking in the sun, drinking rosé and eating slices of pizza, and it's perfect. Well, nearly perfect. If David would just stop looking at his watch all the time I'd be a lot happier.

I look at him sternly. "Do you have somewhere you need to be?" I ask pointedly, and David reddens slightly.

"Um, well," he starts, then sees my eyes narrow and closes his mouth again. "I'll tell you what," he says, "let me make one phone call. Okay?"

I agree reluctantly—I've had enough of men and their phones for one day. He gets up from the table and I hear him talk in a low voice but I can't make out the words. After about five minutes, he sits back down and turns his phone off.

"Okay," he says with a smile, "I'm all yours."

And I really think he means it. I gaze at him, studying every little crease on his face. It's funny, today, when I was looking at Mike, I sort of got the feeling that I'd always been too bowled over by his amazing good looks to notice the hard lines on his face, whereas now, looking at David, it's as if I've never really appreciated his strong bone structure and beautiful eyes. Like Mike is a beautiful bracelet that you find out is only gold-plated, and David is solid gold but in a more simple design.

"Okay, so what do you have planned for this afternoon?" David asks as he takes a large mouthful of baked dough and mozzarella cheese.

What do I have planned? Is this a trick question? Does he know I'm meant to be meeting Mike back at the hotel?

"I don't know really," I say hesitantly. "Do you have plans?"

"Well, I was hoping that maybe you might agree to explore Rome with me, if you're not doing anything else, that is." David grins slightly and I relax.

"Definitely!" I exclaim and pull out my guidebook. In it

is a list I wrote on the plane of all the things I want to do. Frankly, you don't watch *Roman Holiday* fifty million times and not know how you want to spend a free afternoon in the great city itself.

"Right, well, I definitely want to see some culture. Art galleries, that sort of thing. And to see the ancient ruins—I mean, you can't come here and not see them, can you?"

I look at David for reassurance and he nods his approval.

"And I want to have my hair cut," I continue, now in my stride. "I want to sit in sidewalk cafes and look in shop windows. I want go get arrested and have a fight and . . ."

The best bit in *Roman Holiday* is when Audrey Hepburn runs around Rome flirting with people and dancing with dodgy hairdressers. And I know it's slightly silly to want to re-create a scene from a film but it would just be so much fun—and I'm sure other people have done it. I mean, how many people have walked down Rodeo Drive pretending to be Julia Roberts in *Pretty Woman*? Quite a few, I'm sure. So what if I want to have a gamine haircut and go a bit wild? There's nothing wrong with that, is there?

I look up to see David laughing.

"I'll tell you what," he says. "We can do all of those things. But let's maybe forget the being arrested part, shall we?"

Relieved that he's laughing with me and not at me, I nod reluctantly as David pays the bill.

"Now wait here," he says, and walks off.

"Where are you going?" I call after him. But he doesn't reply.

There's a bit of wine left in the bottle so I pour it into my glass and take a sip. Drinking at lunchtime always feels so utterly decadent. Particularly when the sun is shining like this. I sit back and sigh contentedly. I am so glad David came here. So glad I didn't sleep with Mike. I shudder at the thought. And then I shudder at the realization that I'm going to have to let Mike know I'm not going to be meeting him for lunch. I can't just leave him wondering, can I? Noticing that David has left his mobile on the table, I turn it on and take out the hotel postcard I took this morning to send to my mother. Luckily the telephone number is on it, and I manage to get through to a receptionist who speaks a bit of English. "Room Fifty-four," I say loudly. "Mike Marshall. Leave message. From Georgie, yes?" The man repeats what I said, which is hopefully a good sign. "I meet friend. Don't wait for me. Okay?"

"*Si, si,* no wait. Meet a friend. *Si,*" says the receptionist, and I hang up just as David appears, coming toward me on a Vespa.

I can hardly believe my eyes. It is just the coolest thing I've ever seen. It's duck-egg blue with a leather seat and even though David looks a little bit unsteady on it, he's grinning ear to ear.

"Fancy a ride?"

"David . . . where did you get this?"

I can't believe it. This is the most romantic thing I've ever heard of, and it's actually happening to me.

"Just round the corner—I saw they were renting out scooters on the way to the restaurant. So what do you think, are you game?"

"Are you joking? Of course I am!"

David hands me a helmet, and I jump on the back. We drive off, speeding down the little cobbled streets and weaving through the tourists. To start off with we drive pretty slowly, but within a few minutes David seems to get the hang of it. Actually, he gets more than the hang of it; he's really enjoying it. I can tell by the way he keeps speeding up and throwing back his head.

"Lean to your left!" David shouts at me as we approach

a corner, and instead of slowing down, we whiz round the bend. It's scary, but so exciting. I never thought I'd be doing this with David. I always thought he'd say that scooters are actually a bit dangerous really and maybe we should get a nice car instead. I hold on tightly and he takes his left hand off its handle to give my hand a squeeze.

Riding a Vespa is the coolest. Now I know how Audrey Hepburn felt. We weave through the streets, looking, I think, like a pretty cool couple. The wind is kind of blowing my skirt up round my legs, and I start to enjoy the appreciative looks I'm getting from people on the streets. I wish Nigel could see me now! I am the girl on the Vespa. Actually, I think I'm going to get a scooter when I get back to London. I mean, how cool would that be? I could drive it to work, to parties . . .

We go over a bump in the road and I yelp, clinging on tighter to David. How come he's so good at this, I wonder. It's like he's ridden one for years. It's strange. I thought if I went to Rome I'd find a whole new me waiting to get out, but actually I seem to have found a whole new David instead. The faster we go, the tighter I find myself holding on to him. And not just because it's safer.

Finally we stop in front of the Spanish Steps and David pulls off his helmet. I suppose he is still the David I know and love; none of the Italians are bothering with helmets.

"Recognize this?"

I look up at the tearoom David is pointing at. Caffé Greco. It couldn't be, could it? Sure enough, we are at the very cafe where Audrey and Gregory began to fall in love in *Roman Holiday*. David offers me his hand and we go inside. It's exactly the same as it was in the film—like something out of the 1920s. The seats are all in plush red velvet, and beautiful paintings adorn the walls.

"You want to sit outside, right?"

I nod gratefully. We order Earl Grey and our waiter, a man in his fifties, brings us a plate full of scones, pastries, and croissants.

I'm feeling a bit windswept after our Vespa outing—even the safety helmet hasn't stopped my hair getting all tangled at the back. I comb it with my fingers. This is Rome, after all, home of style. Matted hair is really not on at all.

"You know," murmurs David, leaning in and kissing me on the ear, "I know you really want to do the whole *Roman Holiday* thing, but you don't really have to have your hair cut, do you? I mean, Audrey's hair was all long and straggly before she cut it all off, wasn't it. Whereas your hair is quite beautiful the way it is."

He pulls a few loose strands of my hair and tucks them behind my ear.

"I never knew you liked my hair," I say, suddenly feeling shy.

"Darling, there is so much I like about you, I hardly know where to start."

I look at David intently. Does he really mean it? Is he really serious about me? I mean, I'm pretty sure he loves me, but I never know if he sees me as a proper long-term girlfriend or not. Or, you know, wife material. And the thing is, I know that I've been flirting with Mike and everything, but looking at David now I don't think Mike is really a patch on him. Okay, Mike may be very good-looking, but be doesn't have a strong face like David. He doesn't ooze confidence like David does. Plus, he's incredibly selfish, while David is really generous. And I don't trust Mike, whereas David is so utterly dependable.

"I'm so glad . . . so glad you are here," I breathe. I want to say more. I want to ask him where he sees us in five years. I also want to come clean about the Mike thing—

you know, to be honest and open. But I don't; I'm not stupid enough to ruin this perfect moment.

Instead I put my fingers through David's hair, and we plan out what we're doing next. I pretend that I've already been to the Vatican. (My guidebook is extremely good. David is very impressed by my in-depth knowledge of all the frescoes.) And when we finally finish all the delicious cakes and sweet things at the Caffé Greco, David takes me for a wander through the streets of Rome. I press my nose up against the window of shoe shops, marvel at statues and frescoes, and tie a scarf that David buys for me round my neck. I don't think I've ever been so happy.

By seven, we're exhausted, and find a restaurant. Over swordfish and roasted vegetables I tell David about the fiascos at work, and he laughs when he hears about Nigel's conference. I don't understand it, I think, looking at David's generous features and strong jaw. I've been going out with this man for ages, and yet today I've seen a side to him I've never seen before. Following me here, hiring a Vespa, sweeping me off my feet. I always thought David was so predictable. And yet I feel like I'm almost getting to know him all over again.

"It's nice, being out, isn't it?" I say.

"Lovely," David agrees.

"I mean . . . I think we should go out more," I say with conviction. "You know, properly going out."

David looks at me for a moment before speaking. "I really have been a pain, haven't I?" he says softly. "Always working, too tired to take you out."

I smile. To be honest, I think it could actually be my fault that we stay in most of the time. Don't get me wrong; I love going out. It's just that since I've been going out with David I've got lazy. I've got into the habit of scanning the television pages every week and refusing to go out when any of my favorite programs are on, which means pretty much every evening except Monday. I thought that David just wasn't as exciting as Mike, but maybe it's me who's holding him back.

"You're not a pain," I smile. "But you do have to work a lot. It must be great being here and not being worried that some client is going to call you any minute. Couldn't you do this more often?"

David half smiles and takes a slug of wine.

"Oh, you'd hate having me around all the time," he says jokingly. "I'm sure I'd cramp your style."

"I mean it," I persist. "For once, you're doing something just for me—I mean, you're meant to be in Geneva and you came here instead. You don't know how much that means to me."

I look at David with what I hope is a devoted expression, but he just looks slightly embarrassed.

"I'll tell you what," he says, after a short pause. "How about I make up for everything by taking you dancing?"

It's not quite the response I was looking for, but it'll do.

"What, now?"

"No time like the present. Come on, drink up."

This definitely isn't the David I know. But if he wants to take me dancing in Rome, who am I to say no? And anyway, even if I haven't really managed to have a heart-to-heart with David yet, there's always tomorrow, isn't there? We finish our wine and leave the restaurant arm in arm.

"The nightclubs won't be open yet, but there's a wonderful place near here where we can get some wine and dance the night away," David says, turning down a small side road. I follow him dubiously—it looks pretty deserted to me—but sure enough, five minutes later we alight upon a small establishment called Carlo's.

As we walk in, a short man greets David with open arms.

David introduces us—his name is Carlo, so I can only assume he's the owner. The place is fantastic. It's your perfect cheesy seventies venue, with flocked wallpaper and a guy with dark, slicked back hair is singing Bee Gees songs with a thick Italian accent. And the really weird thing is that it's completely packed—there's barely a free table. How did David know about this place, and how does he know Carlo, I wonder.

Carlo kisses me hello and leads us to a table. Several other people grin and wave at David as we walk past.

"Darling, how do you know these people so well?" I whisper, intrigued.

"Oh, it's work-related," David shrugs.

Carlo, who has overheard, puts his arm round me.

"Mr. Davido, he ees hero," he says loudly in my ear. "He stop the mafioso from closing me down, from taking all this away from me and my family." He looks around the restaurant proudly, reaching over to give David a hug.

"It really wasn't that dramatic," David says, grinning as he sits down at a table right next to the dance floor. "We just caught a guy running a prostitution ring in the U.K.—and he was also rather busy in these parts."

"Ees savior," says Carlo again, and signals for one of the waiters to bring us a menu.

"Since when do accountants get involved in prostitution rings?" I ask incredulously. I am completely blown away. I'm also very impressed, but am beginning to wonder what other surprises David is going to have for me.

"Well, it all comes down to money in the end. If you can trace where the money is and what's being done with it, you can track down the people. Now, some wine for the lady?" David attempts an Italian accent, and hands me the plastic rose that is adorning our table. "Ees, nice, yes?" he grins.

We order more wine and giggle as the singer wiggles his hips to "Staying Alive."

"David, you never really talk about your work."

"Yes, and for very good reason. It's dull as ditchwater. Why on earth would you want to hear about my days in an accountancy firm?"

"But all this stuff. Carlo's nightclub. Prostitution rings. Why didn't I know about any of this before?"

"Look, it's mostly pretty boring stuff," shrugs David. "And the bits that are more interesting are usually either very sensitive or slightly dangerous. A lot of the work I do involves some pretty horrible people. And I don't want you exposed to that again."

"Again?" I ask indignantly. What does he mean "again"? I don't remember being exposed to any horrible people.

David looks annoyed with himself. "At all. I meant at all."

I look at him accusingly. "David, don't lie to me. What do you mean, you don't want me exposed to that again? Tell me!"

"Oh, I suppose it won't hurt," he sighs. "About a year ago I was working on a case involving dodgy mini-cab drivers. I got a note saying that they knew who you were and that I should stop my investigations or you were going to be in real trouble. And then you were really late coming round to see me . . . and I panicked."

"You mean the time you freaked out and went and bought me a mobile phone?"

David smiles sheepishly. "Yes, I suppose I did freak out a bit. It's a bit of a special phone actually. It means that if anything happens to you, we can track you. I'm sorry, I didn't want you to have to deal with any of this rubbish."

I can't decide whether to be flattered, excited, scared, or concerned. "You mean you know where I am all the time?"

"God no," David laughs. "But if you did go missing, or if anything happened, we would be able to find you."

No wonder Nigel was so excited by the phone. I better not tell him why David gave it to me; he'd probably think David was one of "them" and was using me to spy on Nigel.

"When you say 'we,' do you mean your accountancy firm?" I'm confused. None of this really makes much sense.

"Not the firm, no. A lot of the work I'm doing now relates to government agencies. Organized crime, that sort of thing."

"So you're kind of like a spy?" I ask hopefully. I saw *True Lies* with Arnie and Jamie Lee Curtis the other day and rather like the idea of going out with my very own action man.

David laughs. "I'm afraid I'm not James Bond," he says slowly. "In reality, the vast majority of my work involves digging around and going through people's financial affairs. It isn't at all glamorous and usually isn't dangerous at all; it just gets difficult if people know you're on to them. No one likes getting caught out. But I thought we came here to dance?" He grabs my hand and leads me to the dance floor.

David has never been that great at dancing. We went to Starsky and Hutch, the seventies nightclub, once a couple of years ago and he was dreadful—funny, but dreadful. But our Italian singer has finished with the Bee Gees and is now crooning Frank Sinatra numbers.

I don't know how he does it, but with his hands holding me tightly round the waist David soon has me moving all over the floor, spinning around and everything. It's intoxicating. I feel like I'm in a Sophia Loren movie, with the man of my dreams smoldering at me as I glide around the dance floor.

I say glide, in reality I'm not actually the best dancer, but I'm definitely getting the hang of it. And to be honest, I think if I practiced I could be really good. Maybe David and I could go to classes when we get back home. And when we get married we can impress everyone with our amazing dancing—all our guests will just stand round the dance floor watching and clapping, and we'll smile modestly and say "Well, we do like going out dancing. . . ."

I let go of David's hands to twirl round, and when I spin round again I feel some unfamiliar hands round my waist. It's Carlo.

"You come to Carlo's, you 'ava to dance with Carlo," he grins. As we dance, I look at David watching us. He's smiling broadly and winks at me when I catch his eye. What is he thinking, I wonder. What do I really mean to him?

When the singer starts on "That's Amore," I break off from Carlo and walk back to David.

"You looked beautiful dancing," he tells me as I wrap my arms around his neck.

"Why don't you take me home," I say simply.

"Home?" David says, surprised.

"Home as in your hotel. I don't want to dance with my clothes on anymore."

"Just what I was thinking," murmurs David and places his hand firmly on my bottom, leading me to the door. Carlo meets us with our coats and puts us in a cab. "You'll sort out the Vespa for us?" David asks him.

"Of course!" He grins, then winks at me. "Too dangerous for a beautiful young lady like you to be on a scooter, no? I think a car is better."

I smile politely. To be honest, I'm a teensy bit disappointed. I was looking forward to jumping on the Vespa and putting my arms around David again. Still, I suppose a luxurious cab isn't too bad either.

"Hotel Inghilterra," David says to the driver and turns to look at me. He stares into my eyes as if looking for something.

"So, did today meet with your expectations?" he asks me.

I kiss him. "It did much more than that."

"And you're happy?" He is still looking at me intently. As if he wants to ask me something important. He couldn't be about to pop the question, could he?

"David, I'm always happy when you're around." I take his hand and look up expectantly.

"I don't want to lose you," David says softly.

Lose me? What's he talking about.

"David, you're not going to lose me," I whisper in his ear, then kiss him, nibbling his earlobe. He kisses me back urgently, wrapping his arms around me. Then he pulls back slightly.

"Darling, there's something I need to tell you."

"Mmmm?"

Before he can answer, the cab draws up in front of an impressive-looking hotel. David pulls away and gets some money out of his pocket for the driver.

As we walk into the hotel, I nestle my head in his shoulder.

"What was it you wanted to tell me?"

"Oh, nothing. It can wait," David says, stroking my head.

As we walk into the hotel, I stifle a yawn.

"Oh no you don't," David says firmly, and picks me up over his shoulder.

"David! Put me down!" I yelp. There are a few people in the reception area looking rather taken aback.

"Room number Thirty-four," David says calmly to the

concierge as if it was completely normal to have a girl hanging over his back.

"Put me down!" I squeak as we move toward the lift, but David just pats me on the bottom and presses the button.

"I am not having you yawn, Miss Beauchamp," he says sternly. "I have a number of activities planned for this evening and I think you need to conserve your energy."

As the lift doors open, David concedes defeat and puts me down again.

"No yawning?" he asks.

"No yawning," I agree. David picks me up again, but this time he has his arms securely under my bottom and my legs wrap round him. I can feel his slight stubble graze my cheeks as we kiss, our tongues exploring each other's mouth.

For a moment I wonder if we're going to make it to the bedroom, but the lift doors open and David carries me down the corridor.

I slither down his front as he puts the key in the door, and as David closes the door behind us he looks at me intensely.

"Beauchamp, get your clothes off."

In any event, there's no need; David has that under control, too. He kisses me urgently, deftly undoing my shirt and bra at the same time. Before I know it we're naked and making love, and I don't know if it's the wine, the dancing, being in Rome, or something else, but I can't help myself shouting out as waves of pleasure course through my body.

"That wasn't very princesslike," David smiles afterward as he kisses my breasts, kisses my shoulders.

"I think I did one better than Audrey Hepburn," I smile. "She didn't get a good seeing-to."

"Yes, well, she didn't wiggle her bottom when she was dancing, did she? You are a sexy little minx, aren't you?"

With David's arm wrapped round me and glistening in sweat, I feel myself begin to fall asleep.

"The best thing," I say sleepily to David just before I drop off, "is that unlike Audrey and Greg, we can stay with each other forever."

❧ 11

The alarm clock is ringing, but however hard I try to turn it off, it won't stop. God, it's the most annoying sound. As I gradually drift into consciousness I realize that it's the phone ringing. It's nine o'clock in the morning, and the phone's ringing.

Reluctantly I reach over and pick it up.

"Hello?" I croak, wondering too late if I should have said *"Buon giorno"* instead.

"Oh, hello." The clipped female voice on the other end sounds surprised. "I think I may have dialed the wrong number. I was looking for David. David Bradley."

"No, you've got the right number, but he's asleep. Can I take a message?"

There is a pause at the other end of the line.

"I'd like to speak to him if it wouldn't be too much trouble."

The frosty tone suggests that it better not be too much trouble, so I reluctantly prod David to wake him up. He looks gorgeous asleep, and I'm looking forward to spending the morning in bed with him. We can order room service and stay in bed till lunchtime . . .

David wakes with a start and I hand him the phone.

"Hi. Yes, of course I remembered. No, it's nothing. She's a . . . look, doesn't matter. Fine, see you then."

He jumps out of bed.

"Gorgeous, I've got to go I'm afraid. Shit, is that the time?" David wanders into the bathroom and turns on the shower.

I follow him in, trying to work out what's happening. How can David be rushing off when no one even knows he's here? Unless his colleagues in Geneva have tracked him down? That would be so typical.

"Darling, you don't have to go anywhere," I say, sitting down on the loo as David gets into the shower. I'm quite tempted to get in there with him. "You deserve a weekend to yourself. They can't make you work on Sunday."

"I'm afraid they can," he says, washing his hair. "I wish I didn't have to leave you, but I've wasted enough time already. I should have been working yesterday . . ."

"You've wasted enough time?" I can't believe what I'm hearing. Yesterday was the best day of my life, and David is describing it as wasting time. "I'm really very sorry, David, but I thought yesterday was a little bit more than that."

"Not *wasted* . . . oh, look Georgie, I'm sorry but there are some things I have to do here. I shouldn't really have had yesterday off, but I wanted to spend it with you. I'll call you later, shall I?"

He's looking at me like he's done me some huge favor. My heart is beating loudly and I can't quite believe what's happening.

"But . . . I thought you followed me here. How could you be working when you came to Rome to follow me? How could you?"

My voice breaks and I retreat into the bedroom. I am not going to cry. There is a perfectly rational reason for all of this. David is going to come out of the shower, and go back to being the David of yesterday.

I lie down on the bed in what I hope is a seductive pose. There is no way David will want to leave this hotel room when he realizes he'll be giving up a day in bed with me.

But when David reemerges from the bathroom, he gives me a quick look over and then grins.

"Gorgeous girl. Look, I won't be too long. You order room service and watch some television, and I'll see you soon, okay?"

I sit up with a start. Last night I was a sex goddess and David couldn't get enough of me; now it's back to "gorgeous girl" and "why don't you watch some television"?

Patronizing bastard. How dare he talk to me like that? How dare he say he followed me here to be with me and then announce that actually he's here to do some work, and did me the huge favor of spending time with me yesterday? He didn't follow me here at all, did he? He was here for work, and happened to bump into me. Well, he and his work can go screw themselves. If David thinks I'm going to wait around for him he's got another think coming. A little voice inside my head points out that I'm hardly one to talk, and that perhaps being here for work is not quite as bad as me being here to have an illicit affair with my ex-boyfriend. But that's not the point. Or rather, we're not arguing about that now. God, I hope we never argue about that. If David found out . . . no, that's too horrible to even contemplate.

I struggle into my clothes, and the silence in the room is deafening. I know that David is not a bad person. I know that he would never intentionally be mean to me. And I know that I do not have much of a moral leg to stand on. But the fact remains that he is ditching me just like Mike did, and he doesn't even think there's a problem. There is no such thing as the perfect man. Jesus, Georgie, I chastise myself, when are you going to wake up and smell the roses?

As I put on my shoes, David comes over and sits down next to me on the bed. He's still unshaven and I can see some nail marks in his back that I remember giving him the night before. I kind of wish I'd dug harder.

"Darling, don't be cross," he pleads, taking my hand. "Look, okay, I'm here for work. But you don't know how pleased I was to see you. We had the best time yesterday, didn't we? Don't ruin it now, please."

"Me ruin it? Me?" I'm really cross now. "For your information, I am ruining nothing. You, on the other hand, have ruined everything."

I pick up the scarf David bought me and throw it at him. Too late I remember that scarves don't tend to throw very well. It glides softly down to the floor right in front of my feet. I kick it impatiently. This is our Roman Holiday, and David is leaving me here to meet some horrible work colleague. It's just not fair.

I pick up my things and head for the door without even kissing David good-bye. Why can't anything just go well? Why can't I just have one weekend in Rome with the man I love? Is it really too much to ask?

Arriving in the smart lobby, my anger subsides a little as I try to figure out what to do next. I don't want to go back to Mike's hotel now—to be honest, since bumping into David yesterday I've sort of tried to forget I ever came to Rome with Mike, as if it will cease to be true if I can convince myself otherwise. But what else am I going to do? Plus, my ticket home is in Mike's room, along with my things.

The other thing is, I don't want to leave on such bad terms with David. He's probably up in his room now realizing what a shit he's been. He might even be canceling his stupid meeting right now. Maybe I should wait for him down here. He'll come down to the reception, see me, and be relieved that he's got a chance to apologize. He'll pick me up again and tell me how sorry he is, and I can accept his apology graciously, tell him to go and get his meeting out of the way quickly, then I can sneak back to Mike's hotel, get my things, and be back here in time to have a relaxed lunch with David. Perfect.

I sit down on a sofa and discover that someone's conveniently left a copy of *InStyle* on a table in front of me, so I pick it up and flick through it idly. A young, glamorous-looking woman brushes past me as I turn to a feature called "How to Look Like a Million Bucks on a Budget." I'm so interested in the idea of making £40 shoes look like £400 shoes that I almost miss David coming out of the lift. But out of the corner of my eye I register the strong face and assured walk, and my heart flips slightly. I stand up and smooth down my clothes (according to *InStyle*, grooming is an easy way to make an inexpensive outfit ooze sophistication). But before I can get David's attention I see that the glamorous woman who brushed past me earlier is now hanging on his arm. How dare she! I'm about to shout out when I realize that this is not the first time I've seen her. She was also at the airport with David on Friday.

My heart feels like it's stopped beating. It's obviously the woman who called earlier. "My colleague," David had called her. But she doesn't look like a boring accountant. She's wearing red lipstick for a start. And why would a colleague hold on to his arm like that? I hesitate. I don't want to accost David with this woman yet, not until I'm sure what she's doing here. But as they swish through reception and walk up to the concierge's desk, I lose all sense of proportion. She is openly flirting with him, and he is hardly shrinking back. There is no apologetic moving away or look of embarrassment—David looks like he's enjoying it. Where is the sad look on his face because I've gone? Why isn't he wondering where I am? And to think that a minute ago I was all ready to forgive and forget. Well, we'll see about that.

I stand up and can feel my hands shaking. This is what people must mean by "shaking with rage."

"David," I call out. I was hoping for an accusatory tone, but instead my voice sounds shrill and stressed.

David turns round quickly.

"Georgie, you're still here." I wouldn't say his eyes are lighting up at the sight of me. And now he looks embarrassed. God, this is much worse than I thought. This is really serious—if it wasn't, he'd have run over and said how sorry he was. But he's just looking at me as if he wished I wasn't here.

"Yes, I'm still here. I just wanted to say how glad I am that you've got work to do. I hope you enjoy it," I say pointedly, looking at the brunette.

"Um, this is Georgie," David says to the bitch. "She's . . ." He seems to be having difficulties explaining who I am.

"I'm his ex-girlfriend," I announce loudly. "So you're welcome to him. Fucking welcome to him." My voice breaks as I fight back the tears, and I run from the hotel.

I walk around the block for about half an hour. I don't know where to go, what to do. The only place I can think to go is back to Mike's hotel, but somehow I can't face seeing him yet. I want to cry, but I'm too angry, too desperate. I can't believe that everything was a sham. I can't believe that David would lie to me like that. No sooner do I realize how much I love him than David turns out to have a whole life I know nothing about, complete with a total bitch of a mistress. Sorry, *colleague*.

I need to sit down. No I don't, I need to keep walking. To be honest I don't know what I need to do, but there must be something I can do to dull the pain. To stop my mind racing with horrible thoughts of David with that bitch on his arm, of them laughing behind my back. God, what a fool I've been.

I look around and see that I'm in the shopping district. Not just the shopping district, but the designer shopping district. David's hotel is right next door to Valentino. I turn the corner, and have to blink several times. I don't think I've ever seen so many designer shops in one place. All the names you usually see in magazines are here: Dior, Chanel, Louis Vuitton, Prada, Missoni. I always thought designer labels were only worn by pop stars and models in magazines, but here everyone seems to be walking around with Prada and Moschino shopping bags.

I am suddenly gripped with the desire to go shopping. I mean, I deserve some nice clothes, don't I? Maybe I'll find something that makes me look so gorgeous that David will ache with desire when he sees me. He'll take one look at me and forget all about the bitch. Yesterday was for Mike and David, for window shopping. Today is for me, and I want to buy.

I gear myself up to walk into one of the designer shops. I mean, how hard can it be? I'll just amble in, have a look around, and maybe buy a bag or something. My eyes alight on Prada. I take a deep breath and get ready to open the door. But just as I'm about to push it, it opens before me and I find myself almost falling over. This isn't a good start—of course, they have doormen. I should have known that. I start to look around. The walls are painted a duck-egg green and there is a hushed silence. I approach a row of shirts self-consciously and try to study them. I have no idea what I'm looking for. Within a second an assistant is at my side. Do I need any help? I shake my head. How did she know I was English, I wonder. But instead of walking away, she persists.

"Ees there something in particular you are looking for?"

I smile and say no.

"But Madam does know that this is the menswear shop?"

I can't believe it. I assumed that the men's and women's clothes would all be together. Actually that's a lie. I had no idea Prada even did menswear. I feel my cheeks flush and walk out as quickly as I can. I can hear the assistant calling after me explaining that the womenswear shop is right next door, but I don't want to listen. This is a mistake. I'm not a Prada person. I should just go and find the cheap shops I know so well. Unless . . . right in front of me is Gucci. Gucci! I can't simply walk past it, can I?

I loiter outside for a moment or two. It's incredibly busy and people (mainly Japanese, by the looks of it) are going in and out continuously. I should easily be able to wander around unnoticed. I see a group of people walk in and take my chance, following in behind. As the heavy scent and cool air hit me I almost gasp. It is amazing in here. The carpet is thick, the assistants are stunning, and everything looks better than in real life. Even the bags are presented like works of art in holes in the wall. People are quietly milling around and all I can hear is the busy hum of the cash desk. I make my way up to women's clothing on the first floor. Lots of black trousers. A couple of nice-looking tops. But to be honest I'm a bit at a loss. This isn't like Miss Selfridge where there are loads of different things to try on. Just as I'm about to give up and leave a nice-looking young man appears at my side.

"Would Madam like to try something on?" He smiles at me.

Would I like to try something on? In Gucci? Is he mad? Of course I would.

I nod gratefully and he looks at the trousers I've been eyeing up.

"These are nice," he says, "but we have a better style for you, I think." He walks over to the other side of the room and picks out a gorgeous pair of black trousers with a little leather buckle at the front. I swear I've seen Madonna in the same pair.

I grin at him and he picks out a few tops, which he takes over to a changing room. At first I'm almost too nervous to try anything on, but once I've got the trousers on I get into my stride. The tops are amazing—there's one with a kind of drawstring waist that makes me look like I'm really thin, and there's another that is really sheer but incredibly flattering. I suddenly understand why people happily spend so much money on clothes. These pieces work miracles. You don't need to go on a diet if you can afford to wear Gucci.

Each time I come out of the changing room my new friend, who I discover is called Roberto and speaks such good English because he studied in Berkshire for a year, gasps and tells me how gorgeous I look. He brings me drinks, tells me how to drape a chiffon shirt for maximum effect, and convinces me that I need to wear four-inch heels ("So what if they're difficult to walk in? Take a cab!"). But when he asks me whether I am going to buy them, I shake my head reluctantly. I'm just not sure I'm ready for four-inch heels yet, and without them, the trousers just don't look the same.

But just as I'm about to put my own clothes back on, Roberto appears with a dress. Not just any dress, you understand. It's a pale pink, silk dress. Thin straps and a slightly billowy skirt with a nipped-in waist. It's more beautiful than anything I've ever seen. It's the sort of dress you dream of finding when you're rummaging around in Top Shop and of course you never find because it's in Gucci. I take it uncertainly and go into the changing rooms.

Even before I've done up the zip I know it's perfect. I have never looked so amazing. I didn't know my waist could look this small, my legs this long (okay, so the shoes help, but still). I marvel at myself in the mirror. This isn't the Georgie that usually looks back at me every morning when I brush my teeth. I look like something precious. I am short of breath. This is exactly what Audrey Hepburn would wear in a twenty-first-century remake of *Roman Holiday*. I just have to have it.

When I come out of the changing room, Roberto gasps again, and so does a girl serving someone else. A woman trying on a black trouser suit looks at me in the mirror and tells me I look amazing. I do. I look incredible.

I give Roberto a little nod and go back into the changing room. I am on autopilot as I change back into my normal clothes. I haven't looked at the price tag and to be honest I don't dare. This is about more than money. This is about indulging myself. I mean, I deserve it. And this is about getting back at David. When he sees me looking this amazing, he will never forgive himself for daring to ruin what had been the best weekend of my life.

I come out and hand the dress and the shoes to Roberto. He asks for my credit card and disappears, leaving me with a cappuccino and Gucci's fall brochure. In Gucci, it seems, you don't have to do anything as mundane as going to a till. I sit down on a leather chair, flicking through the brochure, pretending to put together next season's wardrobe in my head. Roberto returns with a credit card slip inside a leather folder, like in smart restaurants. My eyes dart up to look at the amount. 1,500 Euros.

Wait a minute. Fifteen hundred Euros? That's over

£1,000. Oh my God! What am I doing? The blood drains from my face. There's no way I can pull out now. I mean, my card's gone through the machine and there are people in the shop. But £1,000! I sign the slip and manage to smile at Roberto before walking out of the shop feeling absolutely sick. A thousand pounds is my rent for nearly two months. It's three last-minute holidays. I take a peek in the bag. Maybe if I wear the dress and shoes every day for five years, it might be worth it?

By the time I get back to Mike's hotel tears are appearing in my eyes and there's nothing I can do about it. This isn't the Roman Holiday I have been dreaming about for two years, and I don't want to be here anymore. I don't want to have spent so much money on stupid clothes. I don't want David to be in Rome with the bitch. I don't want to go back and face Mike. I just want it all to go away.

I get to the hotel and to my huge relief Mike isn't there. Without thinking, I get into bed. Maybe I'm just overtired. If I can get some sleep, I'll wake up and everything will be okay again.

When I wake up, the room is dark and I feel like I've been asleep for hours. For a moment I forget where I am, but then I feel the unfamiliar blankets and everything starts flooding back. I'm in Rome. David is in Rome. Mike is in Rome. Neither of them is with me. And I have spent £1,000 on two items of clothing. Last night I thought that my life couldn't get any better. Now it couldn't be worse.

I look at the clock by the bed and discover that it's two-thirty in the afternoon. I try to tell myself that things aren't that bad, but it doesn't do much good.

I decide to run a bath. I can wash away the whole weekend, then I'll get my stuff together and go home. There is a new batch of thick white towels just waiting for me and some delicious-smelling bubble bath. On autopilot, I start to run the bath, and almost don't hear the phone ringing. I pick it up just in time, expecting it to be Mike. So what if he's cross that I didn't come back last night? I've had it with doing the right thing anyway. But instead of Mike's voice I hear an Italian voice on the line.

"Hello, could I speak to Meester Marshall, please?"

"Um, he's not here I'm afraid," I say. "Could I take a message?"

"You're sure he's not there?" The voice is charming but persistent.

"Absolutely!" I say. I mean, I would know if Mike was in the room, wouldn't I?

"And when do you expect him back?"

"Well, I don't know really," I say crossly. I'm actually a bit sick and tired of acting as a messenger service today. First the bitch woman for David, and now this guy. "I'm sure he'll be back eventually. I suggest you call again later."

"I see." Through the nice veneer, I get the impression that this man is not a very nice person.

"In that case I will call him this evening."

"Great. Can I say who called?"

"Oh, it's family," comes the reply and the phone goes dead.

Family? I didn't know Mike had family in Italy. I sit down on the bed, lost in thought. There's something about all this that doesn't add up. Threatening phone calls, all those barbed comments from Brian, and Mike holding drugs for people, maybe even selling them. What is Mike really doing in Rome? I notice the holdall that I carried for him sticking out from under the bed and pull it out quickly. Just what is inside? But it's empty. Whatever the papers were, they aren't there any longer.

Standing up, I kick the bag back under the bed. What do

I care what was in it anyway? Mike can do whatever he likes. I just don't want to be involved anymore.

I pad to the bathroom and immerse myself in the hot soapy water, washing the morning's events away. What's needed is a nice clean slate.

I am in the middle of a daydream (me in my pink dress, walking into a restaurant where David is eating with the bitch woman; David looking up at me with a look that says "I didn't realize how beautiful you are"; him leaving the bitch woman at their table and walking off into the sunset with me) when I hear a key in the door. I quickly cover myself up with bubbles.

Mike walks in and tries the bathroom door. Why didn't I lock it? He sticks his head round the door and then looks away again.

"When I said that I'd see you back at the hotel I meant the same fucking day," he says, turning on the television.

I get out of the bath quickly and wrap myself up in a robe. I consider making up a story, but don't have the energy.

"I left you a message. The thing is, I sort of bumped into David. I'm sorry, Mike."

He looks up at me and then looks back at the television. "So your accountant boyfriend thought he'd come along for the ride, did he? Well, that's about right. I see he took you shopping. Popped out of his fancy hotel to get you some new clothes, did he?" He has obviously noticed my Gucci bag. I can't be bothered to tell him the full story so I just nod. I wonder for a moment how Mike would know David was staying in a fancy hotel, but assume he must be guessing.

"Yeah, well, you missed a fucking great night. But I suppose these days you prefer nights in with a cup of cocoa with David."

Mike lies down on the bed and doubles a pillow up to act as a neck rest. He isn't looking at me so I choose to ignore his comments. I just want to go home, but my flight doesn't leave until 6 P.M. I want to defend David, to tell Mike that we had a fantastic night dancing and that David is far more exciting than Mike could possibly imagine, but I can't think about David without seeing an image of him with that woman in my head. David does have a more interesting side to him. I'm just not sure I like it all that much.

Mike is studying the back of a CD intently. Incredibly he doesn't seem particularly bothered that I left him in the lurch; he's mildly pissed off but that's all. I decide I am really bad at reading people. I mean, I thought Mike would be furious. And I never thought I'd see David with a glamorous cow on his arm.

"Someone called you, by the way."

Mike looks round, startled. "Here? At the hotel?"

"Yes. Some Italian bloke. Said he was family. Do you have Italian family?"

He gets up quickly and walks to the window, looking out furtively. "Family? Oh Christ."

"What? Mike, what's the matter?"

Mike looks dreadful for a minute, then he seems to pull himself together.

"Oh, nothing really. I've . . . I've got some family out here. Uncle . . . Uncle Pedro. It's family feud stuff. I . . . I borrowed some money off him a while back and I haven't paid it back, that's all."

"I thought Pedro was a Spanish name?"

"Yeah, well, maybe he's half Spanish. How do I fucking know?"

Mike glares at me and I smile sweetly at him. I can see that he's really unsettled and I'm quite enjoying it.

"You don't look particularly Italian. Or Spanish," I say

thoughtfully. "So why don't you pay back the money now that you're rolling in it?"

Mike looks at me strangely, then turns away. "Yeah. Yeah, I will. But look, if he calls again can you say I'm not here?"

I agree, dubiously. To be honest, I don't want to be here long enough to answer another call. I don't want to know what kind of trouble Mike is in, what kind of stupid things he's been doing. I'm tired of hanging around with people who have secrets. I want to go home. My Roman Holiday is well and truly over.

"So, does David know you're here with me?" Mike shoots me a wicked grin. Evidently his uncle Pedro isn't causing him too much concern.

I shake my head. "No. And he doesn't need to, does he?"

"Oh no, of course not," says Mike, winking. "I see no need to tell good old David that his lovely Georgie came out here for a dirty weekend with yours truly but couldn't take the pace." He lies back down on the bed and looks very pleased with himself.

"As it happens, I need a little favor from you. And, you know, one good deed deserves another . . ."

"Favor? Mike, I have done you a million favors. I think you probably owe me this one."

"Oh, sure, yes. But I'd just hate to accidentally tell David. I bet he thinks butter wouldn't melt in your mouth, doesn't he, Georgie girl?"

Angry as I am with David, I don't want him knowing about Mike. I can't let him find out—there's no way he'd ever forgive me.

"Fine. One favor. But you tell David anything and I'm telling someone about the drugs."

"Ooh, feisty," grins Mike as he lights a cigarette.

*   *   *

We order coffee from room service and spend the next couple of hours reading music magazines that Mike's brought with him and smoking cigarettes. Just like the old days, I think. No resentment, no big arguments. But no real emotion either. It's like Mike has very low standards in terms of how he treats other people, and he doesn't expect much from them either. I look at him laughing at an interview with some club diva and can't understand what I saw in him for so long. He's got nothing on David. He isn't as good-looking, as intelligent, as brave, kind, or exciting. He's actually very boring.

"So this favor," I say eventually, wanting to get whatever it is out of the way as soon as possible. "What is it?"

"All in good time, my pretty," says Mike, flicking ash onto the surface of the bedside table. "All in good time."

12

David hasn't called. It's Monday lunchtime, and he hasn't called once. Which is obviously fine. I mean, he's got lots of work to do, and he knows that I'm upset with him, so maybe he's just giving me some time to calm down and then he's going to call and explain everything. He's going to beg me to take him back, tell me that the bitch from Rome means nothing to him, and everything will be fine. Of course it will.

I check my mobile again to make sure I haven't missed any calls. I haven't.

"Do you think work is more important to some people than their family and friends?" God knows why I'm asking Nigel this. Well, actually I do know; it's because we're having lunch together and I can't think of anything else to say.

He looks at me sympathetically. "Georgie, don't let this HG thing get to you too much, will you?"

"No! No, of course not." God, if Nigel only knew—with Rome and David not calling, I haven't actually thought about the merger at all.

I dig into my sausage, bacon, and egg combo with extra baked beans. We are sitting in a greasy spoon round the corner from our office. Nigel doesn't like cafes; he thinks they're full of yuppies, even though yuppies don't exist anymore. But I think another reason why our "business lunch" is taking place in such a nonbusiness place is that he wants to go somewhere they don't serve alcohol. The research team went out for lunch together once, about a year ago—me, Nigel, and Denise. And Denise and I drank a bottle of wine between us, and Nigel was really twitchy all afternoon. It's not like a bottle is that much really, but there's a paragraph in our staff handbook that says we can't drink at lunchtime unless we're entertaining clients, and I think he was worried he'd get the sack for allowing it.

Nigel has ordered pasta, which is really stupid when you're in a greasy spoon. I mean, you wouldn't order a vegetarian meal in a restaurant that's famous for its steak, would you? Unless you were vegetarian, of course. In which case, I'm sure the vegetarian meal would be really nice, maybe even better than the steak. But the point is, Nigel's pasta is all glupey and the "tomato and basil" sauce looks like ketchup to me.

"Nice weekend?"

Nigel gives up trying to wind the spaghetti round his fork and starts shoveling it into his mouth instead. He shrugs. It takes me a while to realize that this is his answer to my question.

I'm not doing well engaging Nigel in conversation. I've tried talking about the weather, the food, even his dodgy-looking parka, all to no avail. And he hasn't asked me a single question, I notice, except to check that I've got cash on me (the greasy spoon doesn't take credit cards).

Reluctantly, I give up trying to talk about anything other than work. In offices all around the country, colleagues are bonding, I think; learning more about each other and cementing firm friendships. Offices all around the country, but not ours. At least not in the research department, at any rate.

"So did you go through those papers from HG?"

Nigel's eyes light up.

"It's funny you should ask," he begins, as if I have just asked a completely "out there" question. Still, at least he's looking up from his food.

Nigel looks around, to check if anyone is listening. There is an old lady at the next door table muttering to herself. I kick Nigel under the table and look at her meaningfully. "D'you think she's one of them?"

He looks round with a start, then turns back to me crossly. "You may not take this seriously, Georgie, but I think you will when you've heard what was in those files."

I seriously doubt it, but Nigel is looking so excited I stop teasing him and listen attentively.

"HG, or, if we go back to the original company, Horowitz and Sons, has grown steadily for a number of years," Nigel tells me. He is talking quietly, but the pace of his words suggests that he may have rehearsed this particular speech. "One hundred ten years to be precise," he adds.

"However, in the past ten years, the company has taken over and/or merged with more than fifty smaller publishing companies, both in the U.S. and around the world."

"So we're being swallowed up by a giant?" I ask.

Nigel nods. "The thing is, in each of those mergers, within a year of the deal being done, every single employee of the original firm has been fired or made redundant."

"What? Every single one? That's ridiculous—I mean, it must cost loads to get in a whole new team." In spite of myself, I am actually interested.

"Precisely. The point is, they don't get in a new team. They take over the companies, and they close them down. All they keep is the customer base and the local brand. They just exchange the existing products for their own."

"Yikes. So why would Leary want to go ahead?"

"Why indeed."

"You think they know?"

"Someone must know. But I don't think everyone does."

"What about Guy? Does he know?"

"I'm, well, I'm currently in the planning stages on how to best communicate this piece of information to him. If he doesn't know already, I think he should be informed."

"He can't know. If he did, he'd never be so excited about the merger! Nigel, you've got to just tell him. He won't want this any more than the rest of us."

Nigel concentrates hard on his plate. He looks apprehensive. Poor old Nigel is actually scared about getting into trouble.

"Let's think of a way in which you could have got those papers without breaking the law," I suggest.

This obviously doesn't help. Nigel looks more scared than before. "Breaking the law" may not have been the best choice of words.

"Or you could give them to him anonymously?"

"Anonymously?

"Yes, you know, put them in a blank envelope and leave it on his desk. Or even send it to him."

"I could send it to him," agrees Nigel. "I could photocopy the pages wearing gloves so there aren't any fingerprints on them, put them in an envelope and send it to him from the other side of London," he continues, but his voice is definitely faltering.

"Definitely. Nigel, you'll be doing the right thing. All you're doing is making sure Guy has all the information before he makes a huge mistake."

"Yes, yes, you're right. It's my duty," says Nigel. "And don't worry," he adds, "if I do get caught, I will tell them that I worked alone."

I look at Nigel with what I hope looks like a smile of relief.

* * *

When I get back to my desk there's an e-mail waiting for me from Mike. I'm about to open it when the phone rings.

"Hello, Georgie Beauchamp."

"Georgie, it's me."

There's a long pause. It's David.

"Are you still there?"

"Yes," I say quietly.

"Georgie, I'm so sorry about yesterday. Look, I need to explain properly. I would have called last night—I mean, I wanted to, but I couldn't. We just didn't stop until really late. Look, I've got to drop in on the Paris office today, but I'm back tomorrow. Are you around in the evening? I need to see you. I need to explain . . ."

His voice sounds so confident and trustworthy I can't believe he's the same person who was so dismissive in the hotel reception yesterday. I can feel myself melting. I want to forget all about the horrible brunette and have David come over and sweep me off my feet.

"You just didn't stop?" Well, I want to forget her, but I can't actually do it. I beg myself to play it cool, but my voice is tinged with bitterness.

"Georgie, don't. We were working. Just working. Please don't overreact."

"Overreact?" I hiss. "Oh, I'm so sorry. You're right, I really should be more understanding. I mean, it's absolutely fine for you to tell me you came to Rome to see me when actually it was for work. It's perfectly acceptable for you to say you love me and then to leave me on my own while you bugger off with some sneering bitch."

Okay, so I'm not going to play it cool. I'm going to play it extremely bloody hot under the collar.

Too late I realize I'm talking rather loudly. Nigel is looking up at me with wide eyes. As soon as he sees me look at him, he hunches back over his computer.

"So Vanessa is a sneering bitch?"

I realize David is chuckling. How dare he not take this seriously.

"It's not Vanessa I'm cross with," I lie. "I'm sure she's perfectly nice. But you . . . you wouldn't even introduce me as your girlfriend. How do you think that made me feel?"

"Georgie, my darling, I'm really sorry. Vanessa is working with me on a particular case. She had to work on her own on Saturday because I was with you—we actually owe her one, okay? I was hoping she wouldn't find out I was with you all day; I had made some excuse about being ill and told her that the maid had answered the phone. Then you turned up and started shouting at us!"

"Really?" I start to feel a bit silly.

"Yes, gorgeous." David's laughing now. "I am now the butt of a million jokes in the office. But that's okay—you, and our night together, are absolutely worth it. But don't read anything sinister into the fact that I had to work on Sunday, okay?"

"Okay," I agree. "But you could have said you were in Rome to work. And not told me you were going to Geneva," I say pointedly.

"I know. Georgie, I was a fool. I didn't want to tell you I was going to Rome because I knew you'd want me to take you. In the event, it turns out that I could have done—and I'm so glad you were there—but I didn't want our first trip to Rome together to be a business trip so I told you I was going to Switzerland instead. And then I was just so shocked to bump into you that I wasn't thinking straight. Look, don't be cross with me. I'll make it up to you. How about we go out tomorrow night? I'll take you out dancing again and if I even look at another woman you can get into a jealous rage and wallop me on the behind and—"

"Okay," I giggle, "enough! I forgive you. But less of the touchy-feely stuff in future."

"You don't like me touching and feeling you?"

"Not me, *her*."

"Okay, no touching. And certainly no feeling. I promise. So what do you say, shall we go out tomorrow for a night on the town?"

"We could . . ." To be honest I'm not really in the mood for going out.

"I hear hesitation. What's the matter?"

"No, I'd love to, it's just . . . I mean, I love dancing and everything, but it might be nice to, you know, stay in, just this once . . ."

Now David is laughing. "My darling, whatever you want. Why don't you come round and I'll cook?"

I agree gratefully and put the phone down. I know I thought I wanted a glamorous boyfriend who goes out all the time, but when it comes to it, I don't actually. I want David, who I like being at home with.

Nigel looks up and gives me an odd look. I realize that I'm talking to myself out loud. I go red and turn back to my computer. Mike's e-mail is waiting for me.

MIKE MARSHALL: Georgie Porgie. Can you come over this evening? I'm in St. John's Wood. 22 Arcacia Road—flat 14. I need to talk to you about this favor.

Oh God. I'd managed to push Mike out of my head, but it doesn't look like he's going to go away. If I don't go round, he might tell David I was in Rome with him, and I don't think David would forgive me for that. But I can't bear to see Mike again and find out what sordid little favor he wants me to do for him. Haven't I done enough? I keep wondering what was in the bag I took to Rome for him. What if there were drugs in there? I could have gone to prison. I shudder at the thought. Still, one more favor and then that's it. I will never see Mike again and everything will be fine again. I mean, how hard can one little favor be?

❦ 13

It's five o'clock, the time that I would usually be packing up my things in order to make a swift exit. But today I don't have my usual enthusiasm for leaving the building. I feel a mixture of frustration, nausea, and excitement. Excitement about seeing David tomorrow, frustration because I'm not seeing him tonight, and nausea because I don't want to go round to Mike's, don't want to spend any more time with him. If we're absolutely honest here, what Mike is doing is no better than blackmail: me doing him a favor in return for his silence. And I didn't even do anything! Well, nothing really bad anyway. But I can't risk it. I can't risk hurting David.

I feel like going for a run or something, which is odd because I never exercise. I mean, I go to a Pilates class about once a month (usually the week after I buy a copy of *Vogue* or *Cosmopolitan* and read an article on some glamorous super-model who swears by it) and got really into tennis for a week last year, but I never go to the gym and I absolutely hate jogging.

I decide to go for a walk before making my way up to Mike's flat. But as I walk past Nigel, he calls me over.

"Georgie, before you go, there's something I want to . . ."

Much as I don't want to get to Mike's any time soon, the last thing I need is more boring work.

"Nigel," I interrupt. "Is it really important? There's something urgent that I need to do, and I'm going to be late if I don't go now."

"Oh. Okay. I just thought you might be interested in seeing something."

Seeing something? Unlikely. But before I can say no Nigel is opening up his briefcase. Inside is a large, bright pink envelope with orange flowers all over it. It's so hideous it's quite wonderful.

"Nigel, I'm, well, I'm lost for words actually. Is it a present or something?"

Nigel looks at me as if I am completely stupid.

"The printouts," he hisses. "I thought this envelope would throw Guy off the track. He wouldn't expect me to send the information in an envelope like this, would he?"

He's got a point. Suddenly I get a huge urge to give Nigel a hug. He's probably been sitting here all afternoon waiting to show me the envelope. He must have gone out especially after lunch to get it.

"When he gets it, he'll assume that it's come from a drag queen or seven-year-old girl! Nigel, you're a genius."

He grins sheepishly. "Always pays to be thorough."

On my way out I wonder what Guy is going to think when all that HG information arrives on his doorstep in a bright pink envelope. I bet Nigel will be logging on to his chat rooms tonight, showing off and telling everyone about his cleverness. I wonder what his chat room pseudonym is.

As I approach Mike's road, I wish that I had a cozy group of chat room friends I could talk to. People who could sympathize with me and make me feel better about going round to Mike's flat. I want to forget I ever thought I might fancy him more than David.

Mike lives in a really smart apartment block with off-street parking. All the cars are BMWs and Mercedes, and there are bits of grass here and there with immaculate borders. He must be doing really well to afford a flat here. There is a For Sale sign outside, along with three Sold signs. I make a mental note to ring the estate agent to find out how much the flats are going for. Just out of interest.

"I've called out for take-out," Mike tells me as he kisses me hello. "You like Indian, don't you?"

I don't like Indian, actually, but I'm not going to remind Mike of that. I wonder if he remembers and has ordered it to spite me.

While we're waiting for the food, he shows me round the flat. There are spare bedrooms—in the plural. I mean who has spare bedrooms? And an office. The bathroom is even nicer than the one in the Rome hotel, complete with fluffy towels. And the kitchen, well, David would adore it. It's all chrome and full of gadgets. Mike doesn't cook, so I'm not sure why he's got so many cooking instruments, but it's incredibly pristine.

I'm impressed, in spite of myself. "Mike, this place is amazing! Is it all yours?"

"Course it is. Cool, isn't it."

It is cool. I mean, it's amazing. Although I can't help but think that he needs some more things in it. You know, pictures, books, old magazines. Maybe it's just me. Maybe other people don't need to clutter their flats with piles of junk that they keep because it has sentimental value (or because they never get round to throwing things out).

The flat does have amazing furniture, though. Sumptuous leather sofas and a glass coffee table that looks bigger than my sitting room. And he's got a huge television that swivels round when you turn it on. It's like a five-star hotel or something.

The doorbell goes and it's the curry. Mike cracks open a couple of beers and we perch at his huge dining room table.

"So," I say expectantly.

"So?"

"So what is it that you want from me?"

"My, you're impatient!"

"Yes, of course I am," I say crossly. Honestly, does he think I've got nothing better to do than to trek up to St. John's Wood for food I don't even like?

Mike pauses and then brings his hands together on the table. He looks a bit like Tony Blair when he's doing one of his "I'm a caring sort of bloke" speeches.

"Look," he starts, uncertainly. "There's some stuff you need to know about David. I didn't want to be the one to tell you, but I need your help, and this is the only way."

Something I should know about David? What's David got to do with anything?

"I see. Go on." I try to sound as businesslike as possible. I suddenly get a sickening feeling in my stomach. What if there is something going on between David and the brunette? What if Mike knows all about it and it's been going on for ages?

"Okay. Not sure where to start, really. David and me . . . you know we've never really got on, right?"

"Right." Please don't let it be about her, I pray. Please let it be something completely different.

"Well, I never really thought anything of it. I mean, I rarely see the guy, you know? But I think he's more obsessed than I thought."

"What?" I smile with relief. It has nothing to do with that woman. Thank God. "Mike, you're not talking about the time he hung up on you, are you? Look, I wouldn't take that too seriously."

Mike gives me a slightly patronizing smile.

"Georgie, I don't give a fuck if David hangs up on me. Quite honestly I'd rather that than have to actually talk to him. It's actually a bit more serious than that. The reason David hung up on me is that he was scared I was going to tell you what I'm telling you now."

Mike takes a cigarette out of the packet in front of him and lights it. He doesn't offer me one, but I take one anyway. I can feel that my palms are sweaty.

"So tell me!" I wish Mike would get to the point.

Mike lowers his eyes. "Georgie, your darling accountant is doing everything he can to destroy me and my business."

Okay, I didn't expect that.

"What?" What does he mean "destroy" him? Is Mike going mad? For a moment I wonder if he's become a paranoid freak like Nigel.

"David is not as gentlemanly as he likes to make out," continues Mike bitterly. "He is a ruthless bastard who loves making people squirm." He pauses and stares into the distance.

"Mike, what do you mean?"

"Georgie?" Mike looks back at me with a sorrowful look.

"Yes?"

"Would you mind not dripping curry on the table? It's brand new and I need to keep it in pristine condition."

"What? Oh, right." I can't believe Mike is worried about the table at a time like this. He certainly never cared about any of my furniture when we were together. I decide I don't want to be thinking about when we were together. "So, about David?"

"Right, of course. The thing is, Georgie, I don't think he can bear the fact that I'm doing rather well for myself. He's always been jealous of me, but recently he's just flipped. He hates knowing that I'm successful. And so he's doing what any other spoiled brat would try to do, and trying to ruin me. And because he's a fucking accountant he can spread a few lies about me without anyone noticing. He's doing everything he can to jeopardize my professional reputation."

"What do you mean?" My mind boggles at the idea of Mike having a professional reputation to ruin.

"I mean that my investors have been getting anonymous letters telling them not to trust me. That he's been contacting my bank trying to get my account information. That he's been following me around, talking to my employees, making everyone think I'm stealing money or something. He works for some huge firm so everyone believes him, and I'm having a fucking tough time convincing people to stick with it."

All Mike's arguments with DJs and tense mobile phone calls in Rome start to make sense. But surely David can't have anything to do with it? I mean, it's ridiculous.

"Mike, that's absurd. David wouldn't go to all that trouble. It must be someone else." My mind is racing. David did slam the phone down on Mike, and was determined that I shouldn't see him. But he would hardly try and ruin Mike's business, would he? I mean, he's so measured and sensible. Except when he's driving a Vespa . . . but no, the whole idea is stupid.

"Of course he would. Look, he's a jealous man. What do you think he was doing in Rome? Did he just *happen* to have some business out there the very weekend I go out to meet some potential bands? Or do you think it is a little bit coincidental that one band, who were about to sign on the dotted line, suddenly had second thoughts on Sunday evening? Oh, he would go to all that trouble all right." Mike stubs out his cigarette viciously in a beautiful large glass ashtray.

"But what's he got to be jealous of?" Obviously I'm hoping that it's me, but I'm hardly going to admit that.

"You."

I smile bashfully. But it still doesn't add up.

"Mike, David has nothing to be jealous of. We split up years ago, end of story. And so long as he never finds out that I went to Rome to meet you, there will be no problem."

Mike looks away quickly and then meets my eye again.

"Right. And David's just going to swallow the fact that you also just *happened* to be in Rome. Wake up, Georgie, for fuck's sake."

I feel myself go pale. So David knew? He knew all the time we were eating and talking and dancing and making love? He knew, and he didn't say anything?

"That's impossible," I say hotly. "If David knew, and if he's so jealous he wants to ruin your business, he would have said something to me. None of this makes any sense. David had no reason to be jealous of you before now, but you're making out he's been doing all this damage for ages."

"He's been jealous since the first night we met," says Mike flatly. "Jealous because I got you first. Jealous because he thinks you still love me just a bit."

I stare at him.

"Obviously it's not true," Mike continues quickly, "but David doesn't know that, does he? He found out from Candy that I was doing really well. And he knew that I'd come and find you."

"Why? Why would he know that?" Why didn't I know that either? I feel like Alice in Wonderland, like all the things I've been taking for granted have suddenly shifted into something strange and new.

Mike lights another cigarette. "When we were together,

Georgie, I knew I could never have stayed with you. You had your own flat, a proper job, you had everything. And I was totally skint and couldn't offer you anything. I felt like shit. I knew you deserved better. I had to go. I just didn't have any self-respect left. I wanted to be the sort of guy who could take you places you wanted to go. Buy you presents, y'know?"

My head is spinning. So let me get this straight: David is the exciting, dangerous guy who will do anything to prevent Mike winning me back, and Mike is the downtrodden ex-boyfriend who wanted nothing more than to prove himself worthy of me?

Something about this doesn't add up.

"So you left me because you didn't think you were good enough for me? Explain the girl, then."

Mike looks up, surprised. "What girl?"

"You left me for another girl, remember? My neighbor saw you leave with her."

"Oh, right. You knew about that?"

I nod.

Mike looks a bit nonplussed. "Look, she was nothing," he says eventually. "Is nothing. Just a fling, you know. Georgie, it was only ever you, but I wanted to sort myself out. I confided in David, even asked him if he could help me get a job. But instead he asked you out and convinced you I was the lowest of the low. And now he thinks I'm going to get you back and he's trying to ruin everything."

Mike looks up briefly and I almost think I can see a tear.

"You really left me because you didn't think you were good enough?" I still can't quite believe this is Mike talking.

"I wanted you to be happy."

"I was happy! Most of the time. Well, you know . . . some of the time anyway. I thought you left me because I wasn't cool enough." I'm almost laughing at the irony of all this. Except that I feel sick to my stomach.

"Georgie, you're the coolest."

"Yeah, well. Look, I'm sorry, Mike. I really am." I'm trying hard to sound sympathetic and reassuring, and I lower my voice. Two years ago I would have been over the moon to hear this—two weeks ago, even. But now I just don't care why Mike left me. Don't care if he has any feelings toward me. I just want to know what David knows about Rome.

"The thing is," I say slowly, trying not to sound as stressed out as I feel, "I love David now. So look, why don't you tell me what it is that you want me to do and that'll be the end of it?"

Mike looks up. "Okay, here's the deal. David has managed to get hold of something that could get me and him into a lot of trouble." This doesn't sound good.

"What kind of trouble? What thing?"

He pauses. "David sent one of his people to my offices posing as a DJ, and he managed to lift a disk with some information on it that I'm not particularly proud of."

"What sort of information? Does he know about the drugs?"

"Fuck no. And he doesn't need to know, okay? Look, what he found isn't *that* bad, but it could cause problems. It's just that I . . . well, I borrowed some money from my company to buy this place. I'm paying it back and everything, but I wanted to avoid some taxes and stuff, so it isn't strictly done by the book. And if my investors found out they could close me down. I worked so hard to get this company off the ground, and if David shows anyone the disk I'm completely screwed."

"You borrowed money from your company?" I ask skeptically. "Borrowed or took?"

Mike looks shocked. "Borrowed! God, Georgie, you're as bad as David. Look, I haven't been paying myself anywhere near what I should because I want the company to grow, so it's my money that I borrowed anyway, it just makes it easier this way."

"And you're going to pay it back?"

"Of course! I've already started."

"And David has evidence?"

"Yeah. And he'll use it, too. But it's not just me in trouble. David's also trying to fabricate stuff. If it comes out, he could lose his own job over this, but I don't think he cares."

David could lose his job? Now Mike's got my full attention. I mean obviously Mike's wrong—David would never fabricate anything. But he does really hate Mike. Maybe I underestimated how much.

"Mike, can't you just talk to him? Why don't I talk to him?"

"It won't do any good," Mike says mournfully. "It's gone too far. He's got too many people involved. The only way is for the disk to go missing. Then he'll just have to close the investigation."

"Can't you just tell them what you told me? No one would close your business down if you explained, would they?"

"I dunno. They're all just suits. They don't care if it's not my fault. And they're never going to believe me over David. Seriously, if I don't get that disk back, I'm going to be in trouble. I need you to get hold of it, Georgie. I need you to get it back for me. Then David will just walk away from this. I'll get my company back in order, and you and David can live happily ever after. Otherwise . . ."

So now I know what the favor is. I have got to steal a disk from David. Mind you, it doesn't look like I've got much of an option—I can't have David throwing his career away over some stupid rivalry with Mike. Mike just isn't worth it.

"Okay," I say crisply. "Tell me what it looks like."

"Like this." Mike pulls out a fat-looking disk with red markings on it. It doesn't look like a disk I've ever used before.

"It's a Zip disk," Mike says as if that explains the odd appearance.

"And you have no idea where it is?" It occurs to me that if the disk is at David's office I've got no chance of getting hold of it. I've never been to his office and I don't know if they'd even let me up.

"I don't know for sure, but I know it's in his flat, or in his briefcase, because I've got a friend at his firm and she says it definitely isn't in his office."

"You've got a friend at David's firm? Mike, since when do you have accountants for friends?"

"She isn't an accountant, at least she wasn't when I knew her. She used to be quite high up in the police but she had to leave and now she works with David. Anyway, it's no worse than he's doing to me. I just know someone, that's all, and she did me a favor. Okay?"

I take a deep breath. I need to think this through so I excuse myself and go to the bathroom. I don't trust Mike, not really, but this is not the sort of story he would make up. And David was in Rome, which he never really explained properly. Could he really be risking so much just for me? I want to enjoy the thought, but can't. If Mike is right, David must have known exactly why I was in Rome. I just hope he can forgive me.

I hear Mike go out onto the terrace and decide to have a quick nose around his flat. I don't know what I'm looking for, but before I start trying to find the disk that David has supposedly got, I want to know a bit more about Mike's business affairs. I poke my head round the door to Mike's bedroom. Like the other rooms in his apartment, it's full of expensive furniture. There's a huge big leather chair, for instance. And a cool-looking stereo. I can see why he had to borrow money from his company—this lot must have set him back thousands of pounds. Hundreds of thousands. There doesn't seem to be much of interest in here though. Just a wardrobe full of expensive-looking clothes and two full-length mirrors. I take a look at myself, and wonder where the Georgie from Gucci has gone. My hair looks flat and my face is pale. Maybe I should take my mother's advice and go to her Club for a few treatments.

Next, I duck quickly into Mike's study. It's got a huge desk in it with loads of bits sticking out for computers and keyboards and stuff. I sit down on the fake fur chair next to it and spin round. There's a neatly ordered pile of paper on one side of the desk. A pile of paper that I wouldn't dream of going through. Unless . . . unless I accidentally knock them onto the floor and have to pick them up. I mean, that could happen, right? I quickly pick up the papers and crouch down on the floor.

It's all pretty boring stuff really. Some bank statements, a plane ticket to Malaga . . . I didn't know Mike was going there! That must be his fallback plan if things do go pearshaped. And then I see a letter from David's office. My heart starts beating loudly.

Dear Mr. Marshall,

Further to our recent communications, we have not received the information we requested on 2 Feb 2003. In order for us to complete our investigations and close our file on Big Base Records Ltd, we require the

*following information to be sent to our offices within
28 working days:*

- *Financial Accounts for the year ending 31 Dec 2002*
- *Profit and loss account for the year ending 31 Dec
  2002*
- *Bank statements for BBR Ltd and any holding
  companies for the year ending 31 December 2002.*

*I look forward to hearing from you shortly. Please
do not hesitate to contact me with any queries.*

*Yours sincerely,
David Bradley
Partner*

Oh my God. What is David getting himself into? I'm
breathing quickly. It feels really weird looking at a letter
that David has sent to Mike. This makes it all so real. There
is no doubt in my mind: I've simply got to sort this out.

I finally get to the bathroom, and splash some water on
my face. There's too much information to take in. Dodgy
business deals; Mike leaving me because he wasn't good
enough; David being in trouble. As I wash my hands my
eyes alight on some Crème de la Mer by the basin. Evidently Mike's feelings for me haven't stopped him from entertaining girls with £100 plus to spend on face cream, I
think, smiling to myself. Then, checking that the door is
locked, I help myself to a scoop. Mike's hardly going to
miss it.

Mike is sifting through his records when I get back to the
sitting room.

"When shall I do it?"

"It's got to be tomorrow," Mike says without turning
round. "I've got a meeting with my investors on Wednes-
day and I know this thing will blow up if you don't get it
by then."

🍇 14

I oversleep on Tuesday and don't get to work till nine-thirty. Nigel is at his desk and I sidle past hoping he won't notice the time. Denise is at her desk, back from a short break in Tenerife and she looks amazing, all tanned skin and highlighted hair. Not that this necessarily has anything to do with Tenerife; Denise sometimes comes into the office in the middle of winter looking like she's just come back from the Caribbean, when all she's done is gone to the hairdressers and applied some fake tan. Still, she looks pretty good.

I can't do fake tan. I mean, it's not like I haven't tried; it's just that it always goes streaky and ends up looking worse than my painfully white skin. I don't go brown. I get freckles instead, and they never join up like my mother used to say they would when I was little. Once a boy told me that I looked like I'd been sunbathing with a sieve over my face and I never forgot it.

"You look fab!" I exclaim, walking over to Denise, and she smiles. That's another thing. If you compliment Denise she graciously accepts it, like she knows the compliment is true. Whereas if someone says something nice about something I'm wearing, I'll immediately say something like "This old thing? Oh, it's not that great really. It might look like silk, but it's a polyester mix really. And it's a nightmare to wash. It was very cheap. . . ."

I sit down at my desk and discover that in my rush to leave last night, I didn't actually turn off my computer and I already have some new e-mails.

The first one is from Guy, and it's been sent to both me and Nigel.

GUY JACKSON: Nigel/Georgie, some new information has come to light on the merger and I'd like you and your team to do some work for me. Can you both come to my office at 10am to discuss? Keep this confidential. Guy.

Ohmygod. He knows. He knows everything. He's getting us in on the pretext of helping us out when really he's going to make us admit that we, sorry, Nigel, has been illegally hacking into our future parent company's personnel files.

I quickly look up at Nigel and he meets my eye. By the look on his face I can tell that he's been sitting terrified at his desk waiting for me to get in since he got the e-mail. I try to give him a reassuring smile, but I don't feel very reassuring. Nigel grimaces and looks back at his computer. He looks really scared.

My next e-mail is from my mother. James has been trying to get her to use the Internet for ages, and it seems he has finally triumphed.

CAMILLA EDWARDS: Hello. This is an e-mail. James tells me you will get this. Personally I prefer the telephone.

There's another one from James.

JAMES EDWARDS: For God's sake, send your mother a message. Otherwise she'll never use e-mail again. Hope everything's going well? Love James.

E-mail is actually ideally suited to my mother, I realize.
She doesn't generally require someone to talk to; rather, she
likes people she can talk at. And with e-mail she can write
as much as she likes without anyone telling her that actually they have to go out now, or go to bed, or whatever.

I press Reply.

GEORGIE BEAUCHAMP: Hi Mum! Congratulations—welcome to the
information superhighway! Sorry can't write a long message
because very busy here. See you soon—maybe over the weekend?
Lots of Love Georgie x (P.S., James, are you sure you know what
you're doing?!)

I've also got an e-mail from David. I tentatively open it.

DAVID BRADLEY: Darling, I called you last night but you didn't
answer. Are you still okay for this evening? I've bought a Harry
Connick Junior CD for us to dance to . . . x

I want to smile but I feel sick to my stomach. David thinks
I'm coming over for a lovely supper and dancing and actually I'm going to be searching for some stupid Zip disk to
give to Mike. And if he does know why I went to Rome, he
must really hate me. It's all horrible. I've never been any
good at lying—I was always the one who went red in assem-
bly when the headmistress said something had been stolen
or something, even though it was never me. I have a highly
developed guilt complex and it's making me feel ill.

I hit Reply.

GEORGIE BEAUCHAMP: Can't wait! G x

More like "Can't think of anything else to say because
I'm going to be there under totally false pretenses!" I think

as I hit Send. I suppose everything will be okay eventually. That this is for the best. But I don't like it.

"Georgie?" Nigel's face is about two centimeters away from mine and I jump.

"Nigel, will you not do that, please? Can't you just stand back a bit like other people?"

Of course I don't really say that. I just move my head back and give him a look.

"I think we need to talk before going in to see Guy," he continues. "Get our story straight. There's a meeting room free if you've got a minute?"

Get our story straight? I'm not sure about this "our" business. All I did was stand in front of the printer and talk to Guy about his hair, or lack of it. I suppose in a court of law that could be considered aiding and abetting, but I didn't know what Nigel was doing. And even if I did, what was I meant to do? Tell someone? Well, yes, I suppose that's what I should have done instead of suggesting sending the material anonymously. But still. This is very much Nigel's problem.

"Okay," I shrug. "Nigel, do you think we're in trouble?"

"I don't know, Georgie. I really don't know."

We go to the second-floor meeting room. The second floor is where all our magazines and newsletters are actually produced. Everyone looks very po-faced. I don't recognize many faces; frankly, after my encounter with Gary from IT, I rather went off company socializing. And Nigel never ever goes to the pub after work, so I've kind of followed suit.

I sit down and Nigel shuts the door.

"The question is whether Guy will be able to establish any linkages between the envelope and my computer," says Nigel.

"Linkages? You mean links?"

Nigel shoots me a dark look. Nigel learned the word *linkages* at a management training course. He has never been able to give me one good reason why the word *linkages* is any different from the word *links*, but he always tries to drop it into conversation, particularly if any of the directors are around.

"If he has established any *linkages* . . ." Nigel emphasizes the word for good measure and continues to pace up and down. ". . . I will simply explain that I was actioning the research, and that I stumbled on the records through error." I nod seriously. I've never seen Nigel like this. He's pacing around and his face is all pink. I've seen the pink before, just not the pacing.

"How are you going to explain the envelope?"

"I've thought about that. I'm going to say that I was going to give him the pages, and I left them on my desk and they disappeared."

"So someone else found them on your desk and sent them to Guy, you mean?"

"Exactly."

"And that helps us how?"

"It means that we didn't enter into an agreement to deceive. We printed out information pertinent to a business-linked criticality and this information was circulated by someone else." Nigel is gripping the top of a chair and staring at the table. I'm not sure that even Guy would have understood a word of that, but the last thing I want is for him to repeat it for me. I look at my watch.

"Nigel, it's nearly ten now. Shouldn't we go up to Guy's office?"

Nigel looks a state. Dark patches have appeared under his arms and beads of sweat are evident on his forehead. If

Guy suspects Nigel of anything now, when he sees him his suspicions will be confirmed immediately.

I realize that this could be the last time I stand in this room as a Leary employee. If Guy knows, we could be escorted from the building never to return. I suddenly feel really attached to this dismal office block. I've worked here for five years, and it's sort of a home away from home. I take in the pink floor tiles, the white board on which someone once wrote "Technological advances" in black pen and underlined it three times only to find out that they'd used the wrong pen and it wouldn't come off. They can't make me leave, I think to myself. I belong here. I've even snogged Gary in IT, for God's sake. Nigel is combing his hair to one side. He looks truly dreadful. I realize that if I do get the sack, I will even miss him in a funny sort of way. I'll have no more stories to tell my friends.

We take the lift up to the fourth floor in complete silence. I feel like we're on our way to a really important exam or something. The fourth floor is nothing like the rest of the building. For one thing, the carpet is really thick so it's a lot quieter. And for another, there are no open plan areas, just offices with secretaries outside. The secretaries never smile at you. Guy's is particularly fearsome—I've been to see him a few times now and she always gives me this piercing look as if to say "I know you're a time waster" and I automatically feel like I have no right to be there at all. Like when I go to the doctor, I'm always convinced the doctor thinks I'm wasting her time. The moment I sit down I forget what my symptoms are, and end up apologizing and leaving, only to remember that I'm almost dying of food poisoning.

Luckily Guy's secretary isn't here today. His door is open and we enter in silence. So silently, in fact, that Guy doesn't seem to have noticed that we've come in.

I clear my throat and he looks up from some papers on

his desk. I scan the room quickly for any sign of the printouts or a pink flowery envelope, but can't see either.

"Nigel, Georgie, thanks for coming up. We've got a
slightly tricky situation on our hands."

Nigel and I exchange glances as Guy gets up to shut the
door of his office. He looks at us long and hard and says
nothing for a minute or two. I can almost hear Nigel sweating.

"Okay. I need to know if I can trust the two of you to do
some work for me."

Nigel and I look at each other and both turn earnestly to
Guy with "you can trust us" looks on our faces. Guy grimaces.

"Some information has come to me," he continues. "Information about HG that could only have come from
within HG. I need to find out if it's genuine."

"What information?" I ask, trying to sound as innocent
as I can.

"Personnel records, stuff that we shouldn't have."

"Gosh!"

Nigel shoots daggers at me. I know what he's thinking.
Use the word *gosh* and Guy will know we're guilty. I mean,
who says "gosh" these days? Mind you, Guy should be
used to me saying stupid things by now, surely. But he
doesn't seem to have noticed, which is a relief.

"The thing is, it appears that HG has a track record of
decimating all the companies they take over. They are telling us a very different story, according to the board, and I
need to find out what the truth is."

He pauses again, then looks up at us earnestly.

"Look, would you mind just digging around a bit? Find
out anything you can about HG and previous mergers. I've
got a board meeting on Friday, and if there's anything I

should know, I need to know it by then. Otherwise it could be too late. Okay?"

We both nod furiously and I mutter "Absolutely," but it doesn't come out loud enough because my throat is kind of caught, so I say it again and this time it comes out really loudly. Guy looks at me strangely.

"If this gets out now, it could jeopardize the future of the company, as well as our jobs," he says slowly. "I need to know I can rely on your discretion."

"Guy, you can depend on us. This won't get out." Nigel sounds amazingly calm, like an actor in a spy film or something. An actor with a really nasal London accent who sweats a lot.

Guy forces himself to smile as he stands up, but his forehead is creased in concentration. Personally, I'm grinning ear to ear. We're not fired! Not only does Guy not suspect us of giving him the information, but he's putting his trust in us to find out what's going on! We are truly employees of the month!

Nigel is also looking visibly relieved. "It worked!" he whispers as we wait for the lift. "He didn't suspect a thing! And now we've got the go-ahead to do some *real* research."

"Real?" I say uncertainly. "You do mean legal, don't you?"

"Sometimes you need to bend the law to get the information you need," says Nigel and his eyes are glinting. I wonder if Guy quite realizes what he is getting us all into.

Back at my desk I try to work out if there's any way I can talk David round without having to steal the disk from him. But each time I think I've found the right words, I realize that by admitting that I know all about it, I'll be revealing that I've been seeing Mike, and I just can't risk it. If

David doesn't know I went to Rome to meet Mike, imagine how he'll react if he finds out what I've been up to! It's no good—I'm going to have to go through with it.

My phone rings and I answer it to find Nigel on the other line. Even though his desk is about five feet away from mine.

"Um, Nigel, why are you calling me?"

"It's quieter. Honestly, Georgie, you're going to have to learn how to do this sort of work. Right, I'm going to dig around HG some more and see what I can find."

As he talks I can see him shoving everything on his desk to one side. That is so unlike Nigel—he isn't even labeling anything! I miss most of what he's saying because I'm so preoccupied with his new approach to paperwork, but I tune back in to the conversation to hear him say "What I want you to do is to find out more about Tryton. If they are involved in all the mergers, we need to know who they are—the people who run it, the investors, that kind of thing. Okay?"

I think it's okay. I mean, it's not the sort of research I usually do—it's not just a case of ringing up some accountants or lawyers and asking their opinion on something—but it beats having to think about the Zip disk and Mike.

"Leave it with me," I say in businesslike terms, and put the phone down purposefully. It feels good to have something proper to do. Something that is going to make a difference. I am Georgie Beauchamp, Private Investigator. It's just me and Nigel against the world. Well, against a rather large accountancy publishing company anyway.

15

Frankly, research isn't all it's cracked up to be. I mean, it's exciting to start with, but then it turns into work and that's pretty boring really. Tryton seem to be involved in everything from financing companies and buying them, to managing mergers and advising on acquisitions. They've been involved in hundreds of companies in the past few years, including every publishing company HG has been associated with, and it's making my brain ache tracking everything they've done.

I've written a list of the personnel on the new pad that I've just taken out of the stationery cupboard. I know I could easily type them onto a Word document, but having a notepad feels more gritty and exciting. Like I'm a reporter or something taking important notes. And to make it a bit more interesting, I've written each name in a different color, and assigned them each a Clue character—it's a lot more fun that way. There's a Duncan Taylor at the helm—he's the chairman (Colonel Mustard, written in yellow). Then there's a Graham Brightman, who's chief executive (Professor Plum, written in purple), and Jane Larcombe, who's the finance director (Miss Scarlet, written in red). I underline each name for good measure. For some reason, the name Duncan Taylor rings some sort of bell with me, but I can't think why. I had a teacher at school called Duncan Mailor, so maybe that's it.

To be honest, I'm pretty bored with all this. And even if the company is sold, or merged or whatever, it's not exactly the end of the world. I'm sure I can get another job. Probably a better one. I halfheartedly dig around a bit more and find a whole load of boring information aimed at investors, which I print out. I don't really understand it, but I'm sure Nigel will be impressed when I present it to him. Actually, this investigative work is pretty easy really. You just go to a Web site and copy stuff off it. I don't know how much people are paid for this kind of work, but I'm sure it's too much. Except for me, obviously.

I log on to Reuters and do a search under "Tryton." To my surprise there's loads of stuff, so I print all that, too. Then I do a search for HG and print a whole load more pages. I start feeling a lot better. I'm going to have a brilliantly huge pile of paper for Nigel to go through, I think as I happily watch pages spew onto the floor.

Nigel gets up and walks over to the printer. He picks up the pages for me and brings them over. Now that's what you call teamwork.

"What do you think you're doing?" he hisses.

"Research! I'm getting loads of stuff for you to go through!"

"Georgie." Nigel's fists are clenched. "Did you understand when Guy talked about discretion?"

"Yes, of course I did," I whisper confidently. "We've got to keep our mouths shut. I understand perfectly!"

"So then you may not want to have these pages coming out all over the floor. You may like to wait at the printer rather than leave them for someone else to find."

Nigel stomps back to his desk. Honestly, I think he might be taking this a bit far, but he is a paranoia junkie.

I read through all the pages of names and numbers, hoping that something will come out and grab me like in Agatha Christie novels and I can say "Of course, they did it with mirrors" or something and I'll have solved the mystery. But instead my eyes glaze over as I turn to story after story about finance and shares and profits and really boring stuff like that, and apart from some of the names being the same again and again, there's nothing else that stands out at all.

When I've got a sufficiently impressive pile of papers, I decide I need a break, and I go out to buy a sandwich for lunch, which I eat at my desk. I am enjoying the feeling of doing something important. I feel all charged up and serious. I finally understand what David meant when he said that he really enjoys his work and how once he gets started on a case he can't stop till it's finished. Maybe I could get a job as a top research analyst for the government or something. I think I'd be really good at it. Maybe I should get David to introduce me to someone at the fraud office.

By the end of the day I have a pile of papers that is about four inches high. I did actually take a rather extended lunch break (Denise bought *Heat* magazine at lunchtime and I spent most of the afternoon reading it), but still, it's not how long you work, but what you achieve that matters, and I even had to go to the stationery cupboard to get more paper for the printer. How dedicated is that? I call up Nigel—I think he'll prefer that to me walking over to his desk.

"Nigel, I've got some interesting information," I say, imagining I'm Scully from "The X-Files." "Maybe you should come over and take a look at it."

Nigel doesn't say anything; he just puts the phone down and comes over. This is so much better than what we used to do. He arrives at my desk looking quite exhilarated. "So what have you got?"

I show him my pile of printouts with a confident smile.

"Right," he begins uncertainly. "But what's the interesting information?"

"All of it!" I whisper excitedly. "I've got piles of stuff on Tryton, on HG, on Leary . . . look how many pages there are!"

Nigel looks at me strangely. "Georgie, interesting information means something that doesn't add up, or a link that we didn't know about. You need to go through the pages to find it."

"I have!" I say hotly. At least I read through some of it. The problem is, I didn't understand a word, but I'm not going to tell Nigel that.

"Right, well then, you'll be able to tell me what this interesting information is."

Nigel looks like he's smirking. How dare he; I do all this work and now he's making fun of me.

"Yes I can, actually," I say angrily. "It's that . . . that . . ."

I grab the top sheet from my pile and scan it for something to tell Nigel. It's a page of information on the Leary Group, its board of directors, and its major shareholders. I spot a name that I recognize. "That Duncan Taylor is a major shareholder in Leary, and . . ." I pause for dramatic effect, "and is the chairman of Tryton." I look at Nigel triumphantly. Actually, I'm not sure if it's interesting or not, but at least it's a link. Or should that be linkage?

Nigel looks really impressed in spite of himself. "I'm sorry, that's really good work," he says, the smirk disappearing from his face. "What else do we know about Duncan Taylor?"

I flick through the pages in front of me, but can't find his name anywhere. Frankly, one incredible insight is, I think, quite enough for one day.

"Nigel, it's been a long day. Maybe we should wait until tomorrow to find out about Duncan Taylor."

"You can wait?" says Nigel incredulously. "You don't need to know now?"

"Um, well, of course I *want* to, but, you know, sometimes you've got to be patient," I say knowledgeably. "If we rush it, we could screw up."

Nigel nods slowly. "You could be right. But can I take these anyway? Maybe a fresh set of eyes will be able to find out something else." A fresh set of eyes. Yes, that would be good.

"Why don't you brief me tomorrow morning?" I say crisply. I'm getting into this whole business lark. The good thing about going out with David is that you learn all sorts of phrases that make you sound incredibly businesslike. He's always asking people to brief him or to debrief him. I'm not entirely sure what the difference is, so I use them interchangeably. Actually I don't really use them at all, but I'm going to from now on. I might even buy a proper suit and a briefcase and start striding around purposefully. Who knows, when Guy sees all the work I've done, I may get promoted. I could be a high-flying business executive with loads of air miles and a mobile phone that never stops ringing.

I look at my watch and to my amazement it's nearly five-thirty. We finish at five, and I'm never late going home unless Nigel forces me. Everyone else has left already. I realize I'm going to be late for David if I'm not careful. I quickly turn off my computer and put on my coat. Nigel has gone back to his hunched-over-computer position, so I don't bother to say good-bye to him; I just give him a quick wave and go.

I decide against taking the lift. (It's superstition. I never take the lift on my way out of work in case it breaks down and I'm stuck in it overnight. Whereas I always take it in the morning; if it breaks down then, it means sitting in the lift instead of working and that's fine by me. So long as I've got a magazine or something, obviously.)

The stairs at Leary are at the back of the building so I make my way across the office quickly. I open the door to the stairwell and I've just started walking down when I hear two people having a fraught discussion. Any fraught discussions at Leary generally mean fantastic gossip; I once heard one of the directors telling a girl from communications that her backside was as whippable as a horse's. Denise loved that; she told everyone and no one ever found out that it came from me. I didn't mean for it to end up in the company newsletter and for the director to leave, but that was hardly my fault.

"What did he say exactly?" I hear one man say.

"He asked about HG's future plans. But in detail. He wanted to know the three-year plan and stuff. Wouldn't be a problem, but he said it in front of a couple of board members and got them all interested, too."

"Okay. We'll just have to fudge it. Why don't you send Guy to New York for a few weeks to do some reconnaissance work? If he's out of the picture, I can easily smooth things over with the board. Once they see the financial implications they won't give a fuck about three-year plans."

"Even the Learys? They always get so emotionally involved," says the other man sarcastically.

"The Learys? The guys are idiots. Come on, all three of them are about to pop their clogs anyway. Look, it'll be fine, so long as we get round Guy."

"If you say so. Are you still on for a spot of golf tomorrow?"

"Absolutely . . ."

The voices are getting closer so I nip back to the door and quickly close it behind me. This is like being in a film. So Guy could be sent to New York because of the information Nigel sent him. And by the time he gets back it'll be too late! I've got to warn him somehow. I peek through the glass panel of the stairway door and see our chief exec, Robin Friend, and some other guy I don't know walk past.

Breathlessly I slip back to my department and find Nigel.

"You won't believe what I've just heard!"

Nigel looks up with a start. "I thought you'd gone."

He isn't looking up at me, but staring at something on his computer screen.

"Stop it! This is important!" I tug his arm. "Nigel, I've just seen Robin and some other guy on the stairs. And they were talking about Guy and sending him to New York because he's asking questions about the merger, and then they were talking about the Learys and how they are so old that they don't know what they're doing anyway, and . . ." I tell him everything I can remember about the conversation.

"So Nigel, who are the Learys? Are they the owners of the company?"

"The Learys? They're the founders," he says. "At least their family founded it. Couple of generations ago. There are three Learys on the board now—they own about forty percent of the company between them."

"How come only forty percent? Don't they own it all if they founded it?"

Nigel looks distracted. "About twenty years ago the company needed more money so the family sold sixty percent of the shares to private investors. About ten percent is held by people owning just a few shares, and the rest is split between five people. They're all on the board, too.

"But you must know all this," Nigel continues, "because

it's all here." He looks pointedly at the pile of paper I'd given him earlier.

"Oh, yes, yes of course," I say dismissively, trying to ignore the hint of a smile on Nigel's lips.

"The Learys wouldn't be too happy if they knew that HG was going to shut down the company," Nigel continues. "We've got to warn them. We've got to stop this!"

He's looking all excited. I look at my watch. I've really got to go.

"Why don't you send them a pink envelope, too?" I venture. "Then they can sort it all out." I'm not too sure about all this "we" business. I mean, I don't mind printing out Web pages and stuff, but to be honest I've got more important things on my mind than the possibility that Leary's accounting products could be shut down. I mean, I'd hate for us to lose our jobs and everything, but right now I've got a Zip disk to get hold of.

"We could do . . ." says Nigel. "But they aren't majority shareholders anymore. If the rest of the board votes for the merger, they'll be outnumbered. And anyway, HG will no doubt be offering a superb deal to the board. They'll be making some serious money out of this."

"Maybe we should sleep on it," I suggest. I've really got to go now.

"Maybe we should."

Nigel is looking at his computer screen again. I'm about to go, but something makes me look at Nigel more closely. He looks really down and stressed out. I realize that he's worked at Leary for, well, forever pretty much. And if he loses his job, I don't know what he'll do. I certainly can't see anyone else employing him.

Squinting at some figures on the screen, Nigel takes his glasses off to clean them and for the first time ever I see his eyes properly. Actually, Nigel looks quite vulnerable without his glasses on—kind of like a mole or something. If he went out like that, he might have more luck with women; some girls have a real mothering instinct, and he could definitely take advantage. I consider suggesting this to him but before I can he puts his glasses back on and says, "I believe you were on your way home?"

"Yes, yes I am. Look, Nigel, you'll be okay, you know."

"Course I will," says Nigel with absolutely no feeling. "Look, it's fine. I'm just going to look into this Taylor guy before I go home. I want something good to show Guy, not just overheard conversations."

I look at my watch and it's five to six. I'm going to be seriously late for David. Promising myself that I'm going to do everything I can to help Nigel keep his job, I grab my bag and turn to go.

But for a second time that evening I don't make it past the door to the stairwell. I knew the name Taylor was familiar to me, and I think I've just remembered why.

"Nigel," I breathe as I race back to his desk, "do a search under the AMG Group. I'm sure Duncan Taylor is involved in a scandal in the U.S." It was on the news before "Top Gear" when I was in Italy. I'm sure it's the same name.

Nigel quickly brings up pages and pages on the story. Sure enough, the picture of Duncan Taylor on the AMG site is the same as the one on the Tryton site.

"Georgie, I think you might have just done it," Nigel grins as he begins to type a memo to Guy. "I think this might just get Guy's attention."

I try to feel as excited as Nigel, but I can't help thinking that sorting things out with David is going to be a lot more difficult.

❦ 16

David's wearing jeans. I only mention this because it's very rare for David to wear jeans at the weekend, let alone on a Tuesday evening.

He sees me staring and grins sheepishly. "Just something I'm trying," he says by way of explanation.

There are delicious smells emanating from the kitchen. When he leans down to kiss me I put my arms around him and give him a bear hug. I want to feel all wrapped up and safe, instead of wondering where the disk is.

"Sorry I'm late." I look at David's face. He has such a strong, open, honest face. I wonder if he's been working on Mike's "case" today.

"No problem. The food's going to take a while anyway—I wanted to cook something nice. I thought trout might be just the ticket?"

"Sounds lovely." I feel nervous. My eyes are flicking around the hallway as if looking for clues. Usually I just walk straight into the sitting room and watch TV while David cooks, and he brings me wine and olives. Now I'm standing here awkwardly and haven't even taken off my coat.

"Actually, now that you're here, would you mind keeping an eye on the fish while I nip out quickly? I forgot to buy some wine on my way home."

"Of course not." Grateful for something to do, I take off my coat and go through to the kitchen. A sauce is bubbling on the stove. I can't exactly do much with the fish because they're in the oven. The front door bangs as David leaves.

This is my chance. If I can find the disk now, I can forget about it for the rest of the evening, otherwise I'm not going to be able to enjoy a minute. Estimating that I've got around five minutes, possibly ten, I run round the flat looking everywhere for the disk—I check his bedroom, the spare bedroom, the study, and the sitting room. Nothing. I open his briefcase and go through every pocket, but it's nowhere to be found. I can't believe it. It's got to be somewhere. I rummage through his desk again, opening up all the drawers, but they just have boring stuff on tax returns and contracts from builders and stuff. I notice an invoice and stare at it. Oh my God, did David really spend £40K on his kitchen?

Suddenly I remember his laptop. Of course! The disk is probably inside it! I remember seeing it on his bed, so I run to David's bedroom. I look to see if there's a disk inside it but it's one of those computers that won't do anything, even allow you to open the disk drive, until it's on. I boot it up and sit swearing at it to hurry up as icon after icon appears on the screen. There's no way I'm going to have time to get the disk. I hear the door bang downstairs and I jump. If it's David I've got next to no time. Finally it springs into action. With a huge sigh of relief I press the button to the disk drive just as I hear David's key in the door. The drive opens and . . . nothing. Nothing! I haven't got time to shut the laptop down properly so I just slam it shut and run to the kitchen to find the sauce boiling over. David comes in and kisses me on the neck.

"Smells lovely," he says, giving me a hug. I manage a smile. Two things keep going through my mind: where is the disk, and does David know about me and Mike? He's acting so relaxed that I start to believe Mike was wrong, that David did think it was coincidence that I was in Rome. Or is he just putting on a brave face?

All I want to do is stir the food, but David puts his hands around my face and lifts it up so I'm looking right into his eyes. "Georgie, thank you for coming tonight. Look, I'm sorry about Rome, I really am. But we had a fantastic time, didn't we? I'd have loved to have spent Sunday with you as well, but maybe another time."

"Of course," I smile, turning back to the sauce.

"So what did you get up to when I was working?" David puts his arms around me and starts kissing the back of my neck. His words make me freeze, but I force myself to carry on talking as if everything is fine.

"Oh, just a bit of shopping. Actually, I went to Gucci."

"Gucci! Blimey. Sounds like you're turning into an expensive woman!"

"What do you mean 'turning into'? I've always been expensive," I say as David goes off to open the wine. Actually that's a lie, but dammit, if David can spend £40K on a kitchen, he's going to start spending more on me.

The food is really good. And the wine is lovely, too. I gradually find myself feeling less and less awkward and relax into the evening. "It Had to Be You" is playing on the stereo and David is singing along, particularly when it gets to the bit "with all your faults, I love you still." He keeps adding the word *many* before the word *faults* and then laughs to himself and winks at me.

I look at him closely. Could this lovely, open man really be doing everything he can to ensure that Mike's company doesn't succeed? I can't quite believe it, but then I remember the letter I found at Mike's.

We're eating at the table in the kitchen and David is fussing round me, giving me more salad and more wine. It's all warm and cozy and David has taken off his tie and unbuttoned his shirt a bit. It's a shirt I bought him, I notice.

"So the glamour puss is just a work colleague, is she?"

I promised myself that I wasn't going to mention the bitch from Rome. That I was going to rise above it and just worry about the disk. But the more I look at David, the more I need him to reassure me one more time.

"Georgie, she's my partner," David says with a sigh. "On a case. Honestly, I never thought you'd be the jealous type. I'm rather flattered actually." He grins, obviously in an attempt to diffuse the situation, but I'm not ready to stop—not yet.

"What case?" I'm playing with fire here, but I can't help myself.

"Darling, it's work—just a boring fraud case," he says dismissively, as if he wants to move the conversation on.

I blink. For some strange reason I am close to tears. Why won't David tell me the truth? Doesn't he trust me? If only he would tell me everything, then we could straighten everything out without all the secrecy.

"Georgie, I love you," David says seriously, taking my hand. "I know I've been working too hard and I know I haven't been giving you enough attention. But in a couple of weeks I'm going to have a lot more time on my hands. I thought maybe we could go away somewhere properly. What do you say?"

"I'd love to," I smile. Maybe it's too much to expect David to confide in me. Maybe I've got to earn his trust and convince him that Mike and me are really history. The important thing is that David loves me. And when this is all over we can go away somewhere and everything will be okay.

David leans over and kisses me. I love the smell of him. I

put my arms around his neck and he kisses me again. Tender, sweet kisses turn into urgent, passionate kisses.

"Now, get your kit off," he murmurs as he takes off my top. I lean my head against his broad shoulders as he kisses my neck, kisses my breasts. I wrap myself around him and he lays me down on the kitchen floor. And then, in a seamless movement he takes his coat off the back of the chair and puts it under me. That's so like David—even in the heat of passion, he thinks about the cold limestone on my bare bottom. We make love for a long time. Urgent one minute, gentle the next. All I want to do is to hold on to David, hold him so tight he'll never get away. I know absolutely that I belong in these arms. And I totally understand why David hates Mike so much. If I thought the bitch from Rome was making a play for David, I'd happily try to get her fired.

When it's all over we lie in silence for a few minutes. I stretch contentedly and try to shift myself a bit to the left because something is digging into my back, but David's weight is preventing me from moving. I reach down to move the coat a bit, and find my hand inside David's pocket.

Absentmindedly, my hand closes around something that I assume is his wallet. And then I take a sharp intake of breath. It isn't a wallet at all. In fact, it feels exactly like a Zip disk.

17

David drives me to work. It isn't really on his way, but he drives me anyway. He plays an Oasis album on the way, and we sing along loudly. David used to always listen to the "Today Programme" on Radio 4, but I once told him he was old before his time and since then he's been buying albums at random so he can show off to me that he knows all about pop music. He actually introduced me to the White Stripes, which I find really impressive, even if he still calls them the White Strips.

Usually I would love David driving me to work. I love his fantastic big car that purrs along, and the heated leather seats that you can adjust to perfectly suit you. I love the fact that he's bought me coffee and a croissant and doesn't seem to mind that crumbs are going everywhere. It's just that I have a disk in my bag that doesn't belong to me. Not that it belongs to David either, but I don't feel good about going into his pockets and stealing something, even if my intentions are honorable. And they are honorable. I'm going to give the disk to Mike but only so that this whole sorry tale can come to an end. David will just have to drop the whole thing, and everything will be okay. But I still feel very uneasy. Would David ever forgive me if he found out? The very thought makes me sick to my stomach. Not so sick that I can't finish my croissant, but still pretty bad.

David pulls up outside Leary and I kiss him good-bye. He gives me a big hug. "You have a great day. I'll give you a call later."

I don't say anything. I'm so close to telling him everything, and if I say one word I don't think I'll be able to stop myself, so I just give him a smile and get out.

As I walk into Leary, I pass Guy, who is on his way out.

"Hi Georgie," he grins, winking at me.

I smile back and keep walking. And then I freeze. Guy is on his way out . . . he's probably on his way to New York. I didn't think they'd have sent him away so quickly. I've got to do something! If Guy goes to New York before Nigel can tell him what's really going on, the merger will go ahead and Leary will be shut down and Nigel will lose his job. I can't let it happen.

I think quickly. What I need is a diversion so I can tell him what I heard last night. Unfortunately there are no diversions on hand, and Guy is nearly at the door.

"Guy! Don't go!" He turns round and a couple of people who are waiting in reception look up interestedly.

"I mean it. You can't go. Not until . . . until we've talked properly."

The receptionist looks at me strangely, and Guy looks embarrassed. Oh great. Now everyone's going to be told that Guy and I are having an affair.

"I've got to go," says Guy kindly, as if he's talking to a child. "I'm really late and there's a taxi outside waiting for me. Look, have a word with Nigel."

"No!" I grab his arm and he tries to shake me off. This is not the measured conversation I had hoped for.

"Guy, I need to talk to you," I hiss. Honestly, you'd think he would listen to me. I mean, I am one of his personal researchers, a trusted face in a cold, corporate world and all that.

"Look, I'm sure it can wait." Guy is staring at me. The two men waiting in reception are also staring now. I realize that one of them is the guy I saw last night with Robin. Maybe they've been sent to make sure Guy never makes it to New York. Maybe they are waiting for me to go, and then they're going to follow him out to the cab and do something terrible . . . or maybe they are waiting for him to leave so they can sort out the merger and keep the Learys out of it.

The receptionist calls out to Guy that his taxi won't wait much longer and then she gives me a meaningful look. I'm sure it's along the lines of "have some self-respect." She has a point—I am holding Guy's arm very tightly.

Guy starts walking and I go with him. He'll be grateful eventually, I reason.

Once outside, I usher Guy into his waiting taxicab and get in after him.

"So you're coming, too, are you Georgie? Fine. The Bolton's, please. Now, Georgie, what exactly can I do for you?"

"You can't go to New York." I'm looking out of the back of the cab to see if we're being followed. "They're just trying to get you out of the way. Robin said so . . . you've been asking too many questions. And Duncan Mailor is behind it all. He's the chairman at Tryton, which is involved in all the HG acquisitions and he was on the board at that company in America where they went to prison and he's going to close us all down and you've got to stop them . . ."

Guy is grinning broadly.

"Georgie, did you hear where I told this cab to go?"

I shake my head.

"Chelsea. I'm going to see the Learys. And a couple of the other investors. They are all voting against the merger."

"You mean . . ."

"I mean, you have done some very valuable work, but maybe you want to watch a bit less television."

"But last night . . ."

"Yes, Nigel told me what you heard last night. And I'm glad you told him. It seems the announcement of the merger was a little premature. One or two of our board members seem to have taken the view that if the merger plans were announced, the deal would become inevitable. Unfortunately for them, our investors did not take kindly to being told about the strategic direction of the company by worried employees, and so the merger talks have been suspended."

"Duncan Mailor!"

"Taylor," Guy corrects me. "Well, Taylor was one of them. But the real force behind the merger was Robin. He owns quite a bit of stock—insisted on it when he was appointed, and it appears he wanted to cash in. Which he could only do if the company floated, or was sold. Luckily the majority of the other investors are more long term in their ambitions."

"So . . . so it's all off?"

"Well, it is for the time being. And I can't imagine the shareholders are going to be very keen on the idea when they know the facts. I'm sure we will merge with another company at some point, just not HG, and not now."

I breathe a sigh of relief. "But what about that man in reception?"

"I think he was waiting for Robin."

"Waiting for Robin?"

"Yes, I think he was going to take him home."

"You mean . . ."

"I mean that you are talking to the new chief executive of Leary. The chairman was meeting with Robin first thing this morning, and I'm on my way to see the Learys now.

They always like to meet the chief exec formally on appointment."

"So you're not going to New York, then," I say slowly. I'm silent for a while. We saved the day. Nigel and I really did it! It nearly makes up for my embarrassment over the little episode in reception. Why do I always have my most excruciating moments in front of Guy?

"No, not New York."

Guy stops the taxi.

"You're going to be very late for work."

"Mmmm."

"But thank you for trying to save me from a free trip to New York."

Guy grins and takes a crisp £10 note out of his wallet. "This should cover your taxi back to the office. Tell Nigel we have been having a strategic planning meeting and that's why you're late."

I get out of the cab and shut the door.

Guy winds down the window. "One more thing." I look up expectantly.

"Thanks. Really. And tell Nigel that I'd never have guessed it was him if he hadn't labeled the documents 'Information Pertaining to the Strategic Combination of HG and Leary Publishing.' "

My mouth opens but nothing comes out. Does he mean . . . did he know about the envelope? When we came in for the meeting, did he already know? But before I can ask Guy anything, the taxi has driven off.

I walk into the office triumphantly. As I step out of the lift I look around the first floor proudly and walk over to Nigel's desk, grinning ear to ear and giving him a little wave. But Nigel doesn't wave back. He doesn't even smile. His desk is back to normal—all neat piles and color-coded

ost-it notes. He walks over to my desk as soon as I've sat
own.

"Nigel! Have you heard about Robin?" I whisper excit-
dly.

"Georgie, you're late for work," Nigel says simply. "I
ill not tolerate tardiness in this department. I assume you
ill be working an extra half an hour after work today.
Now, I think we both have work to be getting on with. The
ensions Bulletin questionnaire you submitted has a num-
er of questions relating to investment managers, which I
on't think are at all relevant to the Bulletin, so would you
indly make sure the revised questionnaire is with me by
he end of play today."

So that's it then. No celebrations, no more investigative
ork. It's just boring old crappy research. But underneath
Nigel's stern expression I'm sure his eyes are twinkling.

In a way I'm relieved everything is back to normal here.
could do with something going right in my life. I turn on
y computer and the phone rings.

"Georgie? Thank God! I've been trying you all morning.
o, did you get it?"

"Hi, Mike," I say unenthusiastically. "I, um, yes, I got it.
ll bring it round later, shall I?"

"You are a total gem. Yes, bring it round tonight. I'm
ere till seven. Maybe we can get a drink afterward? See
ou later, sexy."

"Okay."

I put down the phone. I don't really feel like going out for
drink with Mike later. Maybe I could send him the disk
nstead. Yes, that's a much better idea.

I dig out a piece of paper and start writing: "Mike. Here
s the disk. I hope it means we can end this whole stupid
aga. G."

I fold it in half and put it in an envelope along with the

Zip disk. I carefully write Mike's name and the address of his St. John's Wood flat on it, and take it down to the post room.

If I pull this off, I muse as I walk back upstairs, I will have saved Leary, and saved David's career. I think I might start a diary, so that my children can read it and be impressed. Or better still, a video diary. That way I might end up on TV.

I could get famous, and then I might become an executive coach or something, teaching people how to grab opportunities and be masters of their own destiny. I could have a slot on day-time television for people who've lost their jobs. ("Oh, Bill. We have all lived through the threat of redundancy. Why, when I was working at Leary, I came very close to losing *my* job. But instead of accepting the inevitable, I fought the merger. I may have been just a researcher, but I wasn't afraid of my Goliath . . .") I'm just working out whether my pink dress from Gucci would work well on TV when Nigel interrupts my reverie.

"Georgie, that is a further ten minutes that I will be adding to the clock tonight. Will you please sit down and do some work? And no more personal calls today."

Fine. If I can't make calls, there's always e-mail. I've got to tell Mike I'm not coming round tonight. Short and to the point.

GEORGIE BEAUCHAMP: Hi Mike. Afraid I can't come round later after all—lots going on at work. Have put the disk in the post; you should get it tomorrow. Georgie.

I turn back to the Pensions questionnaire. I can't believe I've still got this stupid thing to do. Is it really important in the big scale of things? I actually think we should have an amnesty from normal work and have a day off or something to celebrate the company not being torn apart by that nasty HG company.

Ping! Ooh, it's an e-mail. Maybe it's David? No, it's Mike.

MIKE MARSHALL: You're putting it in the post? Georgie, do you realize how important this is? Put in on a fucking bike, at least. In fact, sod that—I'll come and pick it up myself. Where are your offices? M

Mike come and pick it up? I don't think so—Nigel would go ballistic, and anyway, I don't want to see him. Sending it on a bike is possible, but that would mean going back down to the post room and then convincing reception that sending a bike to Big Base Records is a genuine business necessity. And somehow I don't think they'll fall for it. Not to mention the fact that I am too embarrassed to talk to anyone in reception since they witnessed me hanging on to Guy's arm earlier.

I hit Reply.

GEORGIE BEAUCHAMP: Sorry, the post has already left. You'll get it tomorrow though, and I put it in a padded envelope. G

Well, it's half true. The envelope was definitely padded.

18

I don't get home until eight. I seem to be turning into someone who works late on a regular basis. The thing is, once I started looking at the Pensions questionnaire properly, I realized that actually a lot of it needed changing. I mean, there were questions like "Pensions Bulletin has recently undergone a design revamp. Would you say, on balance, that you prefer the current illustrative design, or the previous photograph-led design?"

Investment Analysis magazine has a whole team of designers working on it, but Pensions Bulletin is just a two-page newsletter, so that question had to be taken out completely, along with all the questions on individual writers and columns. By the time I had a questionnaire that actually seemed to refer to Pensions Bulletin it was nearly seven-thirty. Even Nigel looked like he wanted to go home, but he stayed as long as I did. And then, as we were walking out, he said, "Thanks for your work on the merger situation. It has been resolved, as I believe Guy has already informed you. I believe that in the circumstances it would be beneficial for the organization if the subject and events surrounding it were not mentioned again." And that was that.

I look around the kitchen for something to eat. With all these impromptu dinner invitations and trips to Rome I haven't done any shopping for ages and all I can find is toast. Still, it's something. I was hoping to see David tonight, but he's working late.

I put on the television and sit with a cup of tea and hot buttered toast watching "EastEnders." Pat's looking a bit worse for wear, but I can really sympathize. I mean, life can be quite exhausting sometimes.

Just as the credits start to roll, the phone rings. I lean over to see the caller ID, half hoping it's David, but it's Candy. I could leave it to ring, I think. I mean, I could easily be out. And I really don't have the energy to talk to Candy. But then again she is David's friend. And I don't want to be rude.

"Hello?"

"Georgie?" Who else does she think it's going to be?

"Yes. Candy?"

"Oh thank God you're in."

"Candy, are you okay?"

She sounds dreadful, like she's been crying.

"Oh yes, oh, everything's fine. Just, you know, ringing to see how you are."

"Oh I'm fine. Really fine."

"How's everything with David?"

"Oh, fine. We're fine," I say wearily, unable to think of anything else to say. Then I hear a muffled sob.

"Candy, what's wrong?"

She sniffs. "Nothing."

"You're sure about that?"

"Georgie, remember when you said that Mike was calling you and stuff, and that you thought he wanted you back? You didn't mean it, did you? I mean, he wasn't really asking you out and stuff, was he?"

I pause. On the one hand, I would still love to tell Candy just how much Mike wanted me back. She was always so dismissing of our relationship, so convinced that Mike would leave me, and I want to be able to tell her that the only reason he left me was because he didn't feel good enough. But on the other hand, I can't risk it. Candy might get it into her head to tell David and that could be disastrous. No, I'm going to have to swallow my pride and pretend that I totally misread the Mike thing. For the second time.

"No, not really. We just saw each other once and, well, nothing really. No, nothing going on there."

"Oh I'm so relieved. I was so worried."

"Worried? Candy, you don't have to worry about me. I'm perfectly capable of looking after myself."

"It's not you I'm worried about."

"What, you're worried about David? Look Candy, I love David. I would never do anything to hurt him, you know that." I blush as I speak. Wouldn't do anything apart from going on holiday with his worst enemy. Stealing disks from his coat pocket. You know, nothing *really* bad.

"It's not David I'm worried about either," Candy says, sniffing again.

"Surely you're not worried about Mike?" It suddenly occurs to me that Candy must know about the whole David–Mike thing. Didn't Mike say that Candy was the one who had told David how well Mike's business was doing? Maybe David has also confided in her?

"So what's the matter then?"

"I'm worried about me. Me and Mike."

Candy and Mike. What on earth is she talking about?

"Candy, what are you talking about?" I say sharply. Honestly, I've been dealing with dodgy mergers and jealous boyfriends, and all Candy is worried about is her friendship with Mike!

"Georgie, don't you know that Mike's the father of my baby?" Candy says very softly.

"Sorry, Candy, I think I missed that. I thought you said that Mike is the father of your baby . . ."

Candy is silent for a while. "We're getting married just as soon as we can," she continues slowly. "He's going to meet my parents and everything. Only he's been acting oddly for the past few weeks and hasn't come home quite a few nights, and I think he might be having an affair."

Mike and Candy. I feel like I've been winded. Mike and Candy. How? When?

"Candy, what do you mean? Are you serious? Is this your idea of a joke, because if so it really isn't funny."

"I'm not joking." Candy is hardly audible.

"But . . . how long? I mean how long have you two . . ."

"Two years."

Two years. So that means . . . But that's impossible. That's when Mike left me for the . . . Oh my God. Candy is the stick insect.

"You . . . you . . ." I am at a loss for words. I am beyond words. All those times she'd told me to leave him, to give him up, she'd wanted him for herself.

"How could you do that to me? I thought you were my friend."

I'm having problems remembering to breathe in and out. All this time I thought Mike left me for some bimbo, and it was Candy. Candy whose shoulder I used to cry on—or lean on anyway. She'd get me off before I started crying in case I smeared whatever she was wearing.

"Georgie, you wouldn't understand. I love Mike. I always have. We were meant to be getting together that night you met him—I had the bloody dinner party so I could seduce him. You stole him, and I just took him back, that's all. And now we're going to get married and we're going to be really happy. I just . . . I just don't know where he is right now . . ." Candy starts sobbing down the phone.

"Why didn't you tell me before?" I'm playing for time. I'm not ready to decide how I feel about all this yet.

"David said not to. He didn't want you to be upset. He's never really forgiven Mike for what he did to you, and when he found out I was pregnant, he got really funny. Kept asking if it was definitely Mike's and stuff. Anyway, he made me promise not to tell you until he'd spoken to you himself. But I thought you might be . . . I thought Mike might be having an affair with you."

So David *knew*? Was he trying to protect me, or was he just pissed off because his plans for Mike would now affect Candy, too? I try desperately to organize my thoughts. So, Mike ran off with Candy. Well, that doesn't sound like the "fling" he told me about. He also told me that he left me because I was too successful and he wanted to prove himself. And I'm supposed to think that Candy, with her great job and flat in Notting Hill is *less* successful than me? Less intimidating? The total and utter lying bastard. It was all a complete load of bollocks to convince me to help him out. And I fell for it. I actually believed him.

"Candy, I'm sure Mike isn't having an affair," I manage to say eventually. "Why don't you talk to him later?"

"That's the point. I don't know if there's going to be a later. I've been looking through his wardrobe and half his clothes are gone."

Gone?

"Are you at his flat now?" There's a pause.

"His flat? He doesn't have a flat. He lives with me."

"But what about his flat in St. John's Wood?"

"Georgie, what are you talking about," says Candy, sounding exasperated. "Why would Mike have a flat in St. John's Wood? He lives in my flat in Notting Hill."

Why would he indeed? Something tells me not to press the point on the flat. If Candy doesn't know about it, there's probably a good reason for it. And I'm not sure Candy is in any state to find out about it from me.

"Sorry Candy, I thought he said something about having a flat. I must have made a mistake. Look, I'm sure everything's fine. Why would Mike have an affair?"

"I know, you're right," says Candy, her voice still breaking up every so often. "It's just that he's out all the time at the moment, and today there was a message on our phone confirming his flight to Malaga tomorrow, and he hasn't said anything about us going on holiday. And anyway, he's meant to be coming down to Hampshire this weekend to see Mummy and Daddy. To talk about the wedding and stuff. And Daddy keeps asking me about his stupid business and about his money and . . ." she breaks into sobs again.

"His money?"

"His investments. He's one of the investors in Mike's company."

Of course he is. All Mike's talk about how difficult it was to raise the money. How could I have believed that he'd be capable of getting investment on his own?

Much as I hate Candy for lying to me, I can't help feeling sorry for her. And to be honest, I'm almost relieved that she and Mike are together. It means that our little trip to Rome is unlikely ever to get out—Mike would have too much to lose.

"Candy, I'm sure it's a business trip, or they've got the dates wrong or something. Look, everything will be fine." I want to end this conversation now. I can't take in any more information, can't issue any more platitudes.

"Georgie?"

"Yes?"

"You promise nothing happened between you and Mike?"

I pause. I could tell her that Mike was all over me like a rash, that her scheming to get him off me in the first place has backfired. But it wouldn't make either of us feel much better.

"God no, nothing. We met for a couple of drinks, that's all. Actually, we didn't have much to say to each other."

"Thanks."

"Okay, look, I've got to go now. I'll talk to you soon, okay?" I hang up, take the phone off the hook, and lie back down on the sofa. Poor stupid Candy. And poor stupid me.

I want to speak to David. I want some reassuring words about how everything is going to be fine. I want him to tell me about the whole Mike fiasco so we can laugh about it and put it behind us. I want to bury my head in his shoulder.

I dial his office number and he picks up immediately.

"David Bradley."

"Hi darling, it's me. Still at work at this time?"

"Oh, Georgie, hi." He sounds strained.

"Why didn't you tell me about Mike and Candy?"

David sighs audibly. "How did you find out?"

"Candy just told me. I can't believe you didn't tell me."

"I thought you'd be upset," he says in a low voice. "I didn't think you were still in touch with Candy, so I thought it didn't matter."

"Did you know that Candy's father invested in Mike's company?" As I say the words I realize how stupid I'm being; of course David will know. He probably knows everything about Mike's company.

"He's not the only one. Mike convinced half of our old schoolmasters to invest their pensions in his stupid company," he says bitterly. "Look, I'm sorry Georgie, but I'm going to have to call you back, okay?"

"Okay, but I still can't believe you didn't tell me about Candy and M—"

"Georgie," David interrupts. "I'm in the middle of something here." His voice sounds strangled. "I'm sorry, I've got to go. Look, I need to talk to you, but not now. Can you meet me for lunch tomorrow? Langhan's at one?"

I agree and he puts the phone down. David sounded terrible.

Usually he's so calm and collected. I wonder what could have got him so rattled. He has never spoken so sharply to me; it's as if he's cross with me or something. Which is silly—I mean, why would he be? Unless . . . oh God, he must have just found out about me and Mike. Why else would he be so short with me? He probably thought it was a complete coincidence that I was in Rome when he was, and now Mike must have told him after all. Probably because I sent the disk instead of taking it round. My heart pounding, I turn on the television, scan a few channels, and then turn it off again. I need to concentrate. I pour myself a large glass of wine and try to focus. Somehow I've got to figure out what to say to David before one P.M. tomorrow to make everything okay again. But how can I explain away a trip to Rome? How can I admit I've been lying to him?

❧ 19

The menu is in front of David, but his eyes are darting around unable to focus on any one thing. I take his hand. I look around the packed West End restaurant, which is full of men in pin-striped suits talking loudly.

"Is everything okay?"

David looks at me, distracted. I am waiting for him to tell me that he knows all about Rome, all about my flirtation with Mike. I am waiting for him to ask why, so that I can answer and tell him how stupid I was and that I'll never do it again, ever.

But instead we're just sitting here in silence, his eyes darting around the room like he thinks he's being followed or something. I want to reassure him, but what can I say?

"David, look, about the whole Candy and Mike thing. It's really not a big deal. I know why you didn't tell me: you were trying to protect me. But I'm so over Mike . . ."

David is looking at me as if I'm completely mad.

"Right, right, of course."

Is he trying to make me suffer?

"David, what's the matter?" I've never seen him like this. He walks everywhere purposefully, knows exactly what he thinks about everything. He doesn't do stress or anxiety; he's always the one who tells other people that everything will be okay.

He focuses on the menu for a minute, as if he's trying to collect his thoughts, then looks up at me.

"I think I'm about to lose my job," he says flatly. I'm filled with relief. So that's all! David doesn't know about me and Mike; it's just a work thing. Maybe they've found out about the Mike saga being made up. Which is also bad, but not as bad as him finding out about Mike and me. I mean, there are other jobs.

I try to look concerned and surprised. "David, I'm sure it's not that bad, is it?"

His eyes are darting around again.

"Georgie, if I tell you something, will you promise, and I mean really promise, not to tell another living soul?"

I nod. This is going to be great. David will confide in me, I can be all understanding and supportive and we'll get through it together. It'll just make us stronger as a couple. And one day we'll look back and laugh at how serious it all seemed at the time.

"I'm working on a case that's, well, a bit close to home. I didn't want to do it, but I couldn't get out of it."

I'm not sure where he is going, but I squeeze his hand and wait for him to continue.

"It's about Mike . . ." David looks up at me, as if he needs to check my reaction.

Here we go. I nod again, but inside I'm feeling quite excited. Just wait till I tell him that I know all about it and have totally saved his bacon!

"What about Mike?"

"He has been under surveillance for several months."

David looks down and then up again. Like he can't focus on anything, even me, for too long.

"He's been defrauding his company's investors and the bands he's signed."

I can't help feeling disappointed. I thought David was going to tell me the truth, and instead he's telling me the false story. Why can't he just admit that he was jealous and that he screwed up?

"His investors," I say with a sigh. "You mean Candy's father?" I ask.

"And the rest. At least Candy's father can probably afford it. Mike got people to invest their last penny in his bloody record label. He got people who should have known better investing their pensions—their *pensions*, for crying out loud. He managed to get about a million together by convincing friends of his parents, friends of my parents, and people we both knew when we were growing up, to give him their last bit of cash."

"But they'll get their money back, won't they? I mean the business is doing really well, isn't it?" I'm a bit unsettled. This conversation isn't going the way I thought it would.

"Get it back?" David laughs sarcastically. "Get what back? There's nothing left. Mike took every last penny out of the company to buy himself a flat, and has been faking invoices to sell to a factoring company. He even got into some sort of money laundering for a gang in Rome. He is in very deep trouble. But not as much trouble as he's going to be in with me for ripping off my parents' friends. I am never going to let him get away with that."

I'm really confused now. And maybe a little bit scared.

"We got a tip-off from one of his employees who gave us this disk with a lot of incriminating evidence on it," continues David. "Apparently their salary checks have been bouncing, and none of the bands or DJs have been paid for the past four months. The employee in question got sacked soon after. Since then I've been gathering evidence . . ."

He looks at me and I can see his forehead twitch with tension. "That's why I had to go to Rome—I was following Mike. He's been moving funds into Spain via Italy and

Switzerland. He took a whole load of money in with him to Rome, but we don't know how; his bags were checked at the airport and nothing was found."

David sighs, and carries on in a deadpan voice. "My contacts there confirmed his links with an organized crime group in Italy. He's a fucking liability.

"Anyway," he continues with a sigh, "we had enough evidence to swoop today. We've been working with the police and they were all ready to arrest him. Except that I was looking after the vital piece of evidence. And now it's gone missing."

Okay, this is not the way it was meant to go. I'm getting a really nasty feeling here. When is David going to admit that the whole thing was made up because he was jealous?

"It went missing?" I ask in as casual a manner as I can muster.

"Yes. I just can't understand it. I had it, and now it's gone. But it's worse than that. I think someone's trying to set me up. Someone has actually been searching through my files—when I started to boot up my computer this morning, it had already been turned on and not shut down properly. And now my firm suspects that I'm trying to bury evidence. They got a tip yesterday that I'd been blackmailing Mike and demanding money in return for "losing" the disk. And money's been appearing in my account. I didn't even notice. My firm thinks I'm a criminal, Georgie. This morning they had the police in."

He looks like he's going to cry. "It's looking really bad. I'm not sure how I'm going to get out of this."

The waiter comes over to take our order and David stops talking. He stares out of the window, trying to compose himself. I ask if we can have a few more minutes. Seeing the state David's in, the waiter backs away quickly.

Everything has gone hideously pear-shaped. If what

David says is true, then Mike has been lying to me. Which would be nothing particularly new. But if Mike has been lying to me, then what I have done is . . . more terrible than anything in the world. Suddenly I start to feel sick and now I'm the one who's sweating as I piece together the events of the past month.

"How . . . how long did you say you've been following Mike?" I'm trying to sound perfectly normal, but my voice is cracking.

"About six months in all, I think. I've been on the case for about a month."

"So, what, you joined the case about the time we bumped into Mike?"

"A couple of weeks before."

"And he would have known, he would have been aware, that you were on to him when we bumped into each other."

"Yes, yes. Look, that isn't important. The thing is, I think someone I know may be trying to frame me. Someone must be working with Mike. I just can't work it out."

I think I might be about to faint. All I can think about is the package Mike gave me to carry to Rome; the disk I stole from David; the phone call in Italy from Mike's "family." Everything is going black. But I'm not fainting. I'm just realizing how stupid, how utterly stupid and horrible I've been. I want the ground to swallow me up.

"It was me."

I say it quietly. All my muscles are tense as I wait for David's reaction.

He looks at me strangely.

"What do you mean, it was you?"

I am very hot and uncomfortable.

"It was me who took the disk." I'll leave the money issue

to one side for now. I mean, David doesn't need to know that, right?

David's face is deathly white. I can feel my skin go all prickly and I feel like I'm somewhere else watching this episode played out by a body double. It's far too awful to be really happening.

"Don't be ridiculous," he says in a strangled voice. "How could it be you?"

"Mike told me you were trying to frame him because you were jealous. I thought you might get into trouble. Mike told me that you'd do anything to stop him being a success, and I didn't want your firm to find out . . ."

David takes in a sharp breath and doesn't say anything for a couple of minutes. Then his eyes narrow. He looks up at the ceiling as if he's trying to count to ten before saying anything.

"You took the disk?"

I nod glumly.

"And you still have it?"

I shake my head, even more glumly.

"Where the fuck is it?

"I sent it to him."

"You sent it to him." I don't think it's a question, so I don't answer. It's like when I used to be bollocked by a teacher at school. Saying anything just works against you. Better to stay silent and stare at the floor. I look up quickly to see David's expression. His face has blackened. I don't think I've ever seen him so angry.

"You stupid, stupid girl."

He is almost shuddering with rage. My nails are digging into my palms as I fight to remain calm.

"You do realize what you've done?"

I look back down at my plate.

"Mike said you were fabricating evidence against him,

said you were jealous of him . . ." I trail off. It all sounds so implausible now. I can't believe I was stupid enough to believe him.

"He said I was jealous of him."

I almost think David is going to start laughing, that we can start joking about how stupid I've been, but then I see that his eyes are still flashing with anger.

"I told you not to talk to him. I asked you not to have any contact with him. And instead, you merrily let him feed you a whole load of bullshit, which you believed. You believed that fucking prick and thought that you would wreck the bloody case, wreck my career, and probably wreck my entire life. Just who the fuck do you think you are, Georgie?"

I fight hard to keep tears from pricking my eyes.

"It'll be okay, though, won't it?" I look beseechingly at David, desperately hoping that there will be a solution, a way out. "I'll tell your employers what I did. They'll understand, won't they?"

David's eyes are cold and hard.

"You do realize what you've done, don't you? It's called aiding and abetting. It's illegal, you know. If you tell the police that you stole a disk from me, they probably won't believe you, and if they do, you'll be the one with a criminal record."

He puts his head in his hands.

"Of all the people. I just can't believe it was you."

A huge lump has been developing in my throat for the past ten minutes and I know that within about thirty seconds big fat tears will be cascading down my cheeks. I can't bear to cry in front of David, can't bear for him to see how utterly pathetic I am. I have doubted and betrayed him and he might even go to prison, and it is all completely my fault. Everything.

Grabbing my bag, I stand up and run out of the restaurant. Outside, I crumple on the pavement, ignoring concerned passersby as I bawl my eyes out. My throat is hurting, my eyes are red and raw, and still the tears come. David is right. I am a stupid, stupid girl and I don't deserve him. I suppose there is some justice in the world after all—after what I've done, he'll never want to see me again.

I manage to stand up and start walking down the street toward Green Park Tube station. The last thing I want now is for David to leave the restaurant and find me wailing on the pavement. I can barely walk straight, but I need to get home and work out a plan. Somehow I have got to get David out of trouble. And somehow I have got to make sure that Mike pays for what he has done. My mind racing, I hail a cab. Once I'm sitting down, I have another thought, and I reach for my mobile phone.

My mother is waiting for me at the door as the cab pulls up. "You look a mess," she says matter-of-factly as she gives me a perfunctory hug and leads me into the kitchen where a hot cup of tea is waiting. "I would have preferred wine, but I know what you and David are like when it comes to tea," she explains.

At the mention of his name I nearly start crying again, but I don't seem to have any tears left. I sit down, and wait for her to join me. And then I tell her everything.

I tell her about Rome, about seeing David with his colleague and how I thought he might have been having an affair. I tell her about Mike, about Candy and the baby. I tell her about David at the restaurant, about the police. It takes about an hour, and by the end I feel almost purged.

I take a sip of tea and look up expectantly. This is where my mother always comes into her own—ask her for advice and she manages to sort your life out and anyone else who happens to be around. She will be able to tell me exactly what to do. She always has done in the past. But now, right when I need her, she seems to have nothing to say.

For a good five minutes she just sits and looks at me. And then she says "Georgie, David is right, you know. You are very stupid."

Great. I mean, I knew that already. I have enough people telling me how stupid I am. What I'm looking for here is someone to tell me how I can get out of this god-awful mess. If I can't turn to my mother in my hour of need, who can I turn to?

"You know," my mother continues, "you have to grow up and realize what you have. If you keep letting yourself get sidetracked, you're going to lose everything that matters and you'll be left with absolutely nothing."

"I am grown-up," I mutter.

"If you're so grown-up, then why are you here telling me about how terrible everything is instead of focusing on the real issue?"

"But this is the real issue," I shout. "I love David, he hates me, and I want to get him back."

"No, Georgie." My mother stares at me the way she used to when I was little and had done something really bad. I feel about five again. "The real issue is that a really good man, who has only ever been wonderful to you, is in real trouble, and it's your fault. And another man, who has only ever been a complete time waster, is going to get away with a great deal of money that belongs to other people. And that is also partly your fault. If you can stop, for just one moment, thinking about yourself, then there may be a chance that you can do something about this terrible state of affairs. So stop trying to work out how you can get David to like you again, and instead try to work out a way to get him out of the mess that you have got him into."

She's right. Of course she's right. It's just that right now I don't want to know that she's right. I want her to give me a hug and put me to bed and tell me that everything will be okay. I was hoping she'd just be able to make a few phone calls—to the police, to David's bosses, telling them that it was all a bit of a mix-up, and probably best not to mention it again, particularly in front of me. I have a sinking feeling, however, that this particular mess is going to take more than a couple of phone calls to make things right again. I swallow my pride, and look up at my mother beseechingly. "Will you help me?"

ॐ 20

We're sitting outside Mike's flat in my mother's battered Mini. Well, not exactly outside his flat, more opposite and along a bit, so as not to draw attention to ourselves. My mother is dressed as a cleaning lady. (I'm not convinced that white linen trousers and an apron with red poppies all over it constitutes typical cleaning lady dress, but my mother is in no mood for questions.) James, who has driven us there, is looking extremely uncomfortable. My mother refused to let him bring the Jag because it would stand out, but I can't help thinking that James looks so wrong in a Mini that anyone looking at us would be convinced we were up to something. And a Jag would hardly stand out in St. John's Wood, whereas a Mini looks completely out of place. But what do I know?

"Call him," instructs my mother, and I take out my mobile. As expected, Mike's home phone rings until the answerphone picks up.

"I told you. He's in the office waiting for the disk to arrive. He won't be coming round here for ages, if at all." I wish Mum would just take my word for it sometimes.

"Right, I'm going in."

Mum lets herself out of the car and walks purposefully down the road. She takes a bunch of keys out of her apron pocket and lets herself into Mike's house, taking a quick look around her before going in.

"And Mike's not going to notice that his keys are missing?" James asks me.

"No! He's in a meeting."

It wasn't too difficult getting Mike's keys. I popped into his office to assure him that the disk would be arriving "any minute" and just accidentally on purpose picked his keys up off his desk on my way out. He's always losing things so he'll never notice. If all goes according to plan he will be sitting at his trendy round desk for the next few hours wondering when the postman is going to arrive with the envelope. Which gives us plenty of time. All we need to do is to pick up the disk from his flat, where I actually sent it, and then I can get the keys back to Mike. Easy peasy.

The Mini is getting increasingly uncomfortable. I'm charged with adrenaline, and being cooped up is torture. James and I don't have a great deal to say to one another, so we sit, waiting.

Suddenly my mobile rings. It's my mother.

"You're going to have to come in," she tells me. "There are lots of letters here and his desk is covered with papers and I don't know which ones to take."

"What do you mean?" I ask. "You don't need papers, just the disk."

"Darling, I am not going to leave with just a disk. Mike has all sorts of papers here. I'm sure we can find something more interesting than just the disk."

I can't decide whether to be terrified that my mother seems intent on searching Mike's flat, or delighted to have a reason to leave the car. Either way, I have to go in. I give James a quick peck on the cheek and cross the road, looking around me. I know there won't be anyone looking, but . . . I can't help feeling like I'm starring in a "Starsky and Hutch" episode as I approach Mike's building. As soon as I reach the main door, the buzzer goes to let me in. And when I get upstairs Mike's door opens almost immediately. My package is lying on the floor and I pick it up gratefully, putting it straight in my pocket. I then follow my mother into his study, where piles of paper are all over the floor.

"What a mess!"

"We can tidy up afterward," says my mother. "Just find what you need."

I stare at her. "You mean these papers weren't all over the floor when you arrived?"

"We do not have time to sift through files," my mother says slowly but firmly. "Now kindly get on with it."

I start sifting through the papers, but I can't make head or tail of them. There are investment agreements, letters from banks, business plans, all in piles on the floor. But I have no idea what I need. Banking information must be a good place to start, though, if Mike has been stealing money. I pick up a few credit card statements, but other than proving that Mike eats out a lot, they don't tell me very much.

"Hurry up!" hisses my mother. "Come on, darling, you work in the City. You must know what these things mean."

"I do not work in the City," I say pointedly. "I work in the West End. And I am not a financier. I research stuff."

"Then do some research! Come on!"

I knew it was a mistake letting my mother come. I sift through a few more papers. And then I see something interesting. It's a bank statement in Mike's name, but it isn't a U.K. bank. It's a Spanish one. And a lot of money has been deposited in the past month. Like hundreds of thousands of pounds.

And it hasn't come from Big Base Records, it's from Proud Promotions. I've never even heard of Proud Promotions.

"Proud Promotions," I mutter to myself as I continue to sift through papers. "Who the fuck are Proud Promotions?"

My mother looks up. "Don't swear, darling, it's so unbecoming," she chides me. "Now, did you say Proud Promotions? There's an invoice here to Proud Promotions for £100K. And look, another one for £50K. And another . . . and another . . . is this what you need? Will this get that Mike what he deserves?"

I want to say yes, that we've cracked it, but to tell the truth I have no idea whether these invoices are important or not. I need more information and I have no idea how to get it.

Unless . . . oh, but I couldn't, could I?

I suppose desperate times call for desperate measures. I take out my phone and dial a number.

"Nigel Lymes."

"Nigel! You're there!"

"Of course I'm here. Which you patently aren't, Georgie. And unless you are ringing to tell me about a serious illness, I am going to be filing a report for HR this very afternoon."

"Yes, look, I'm sorry I haven't been at work, but there's been a bit of an emergency."

"I see. And would you like to elaborate any further?"

"Nigel, look, forget about this for a minute will you? I need your help."

Nigel pauses.

"And why would you need my help?"

"I'm in trouble, Nigel. A friend is, too. I need to find out some information about a company—who runs it and stuff. It's called Proud Promotions. Could you do a quick search for me?"

"You could go to Company's House, you know." Nigel doesn't appear to want to play ball.

"I know that. I haven't got the time though. Please, can you just see what you can dig out?"

Nigel acquiesces and I hear him typing furiously.

Mum is scrabbling around on the floor piecing together balance sheets, letters, and bank statements covered in scribbles.

I can't believe that just a couple of days ago I was in this flat being impressed by Mike's decor. How convinced I'd been that Mike had turned his life around just for me. How could I be so naive? I shudder to think of it.

I can hear Nigel's computer whirring. "Okay," he says, "we're getting somewhere now. Not much information, I'm afraid."

My eyes are scanning the floor for something, anything, that might make some sense of all of this. I wish David was here—he'd know exactly what to take. Except if David was here, the police would probably turn up and then he'd be done for trespassing, too—again, all my fault. And then I see it. It is a statement of revenues from Proud Promotions, which has a company address in Switzerland. I pull it out from under a pile of press releases about the enormous success enjoyed by BB Records and the recent successful round of investment that had netted the company £1.2 million.

The revenue statement shows that over the past year and a half, Proud Promotion's revenues have totaled over a million pounds. All the revenue has come from Big Base Records.

"Nigel, are you still there?" I am breathless with excitement. "The company isn't a U.K. one—it's based in—"

"Geneva," interrupts Nigel. It's a holding company, owned and set up by a Mr. Geoffrey Proud."

Geoffrey Proud. The name is sort of familiar, but I can't place it.

"Just Geoffrey Proud, or is there a partner?"

"No, just Geoffrey."

"Nigel, you are so my favorite person, thank you," I gush.

"Is that all, then? I'd hardly call that an emergency."

"No, there's one more thing. Nigel, how easy do you think it would be to break into an airline's reservation system?"

"You are joking, I presume?"

"No. I need to know the details of a flight to Malaga. I know that it's leaving tonight sometime; I just need to know which airport it's going from and whether a Mike Marshall is booked on it."

"You just need restricted flight information? Oh, well, that's easy," Nigel says sarcastically.

"Please. I know you can do it. Look, I will do anything if you help me out, I promise."

"Anything?"

I hesitate. What could Nigel ask me to do? What am I saying? I quickly remind myself that I am doing this to save David.

"Anything."

"Don't call me 'Nigel' anymore."

"I'm sorry? What?"

"Everywhere else I'm known as Steve. Steve is my middle name. I tried telling personnel when I joined but they didn't remember. I want to be called Steve."

I take a long, deep breath. I can't believe it! I am so close to laughter, but I know I have to suppress it. It's just the idea of Nigel knowing how awful his name is and not saying anything for . . . how long can it be? He's been at Leary much longer than me—it's probably near to fifteen years. Poor old Nigel. Sorry, Steve.

"Steve, consider it done. And I'll make sure everyone else does, too."

"And you'll say you found out by accident? You won't tell them I asked you to?"

"Of course. You know, if you don't tell anyone about this."

Honestly, who needs colleagues you can go out to lunch with when I've got a pal like Nigel? Maybe when this is all over I'll make him a cake with "Steve" written on it. Then again, maybe not . . .

Suddenly Mike's phone rings. Mum and I look at each other, not sure what to do. I mean, of course we're sure what to do (not answer it, obviously), it's just, you know, unexpected. We stare at the phone as it rings and then the answerphone kicks in.

"Please leave a message after the tone." Short and to the point, I guess.

"Geoff, it's Rob here from Foxtons. Your buyers are wondering when your keys are going to be delivered. I've had confirmation from your solicitors that the money has been transferred to the PP account, so if you could give me a call I'd appreciate it. I'll try you on your mobile now."

Keys? Geoff? So that would make this Geoff Proud's flat. But then why did Mike pretend it was his? Why is Mike's stuff in it?

And then it hits me. Mike Geoffrey Marshall. The second name he professes to hate. I would bet my bottom dollar that his mother's maiden name is Proud—it's the oldest trick in the book. Mike has set up another company under a false name, and transferred all the investment money from Big Base Records to his fake one in Geneva. And now he's sold "Geoffrey's" flat, and is planning to bugger off to Spain with all the money. Not if I can help it, he's not.

"Got them!" My mother holds up a cluster of bank statements triumphantly. There are a number of payments to solicitors, and some withdrawals from a Swiss bank account.

This is all the evidence David needs, surely. My heart is beating so loudly I'm convinced Nigel will be able to hear it down the phone. David will be okay. Everything's going to be fine. If only we can stop Mike getting to Malaga.

"Nigel, sorry, Steve, are you still there?"

"Yes." He sounds annoyed. "Mike Marshall, you said?"

"That's right. Traveling to Malaga tonight."

There's a pause. And then I hear Nigel's breathing get quicker.

"I'm sorry, Georgie, I just can't get through. Their security measures are too complex. I'm . . . I'm only a first stager, you might say. I haven't really got on to the advanced stuff yet. I'm really sorry . . ."

He sounds distraught. I want to tell him that it doesn't matter, we'll find out another way, but I can't think of another way.

"Are you sure? Can't you send someone an e-mail or something?"

"Georgie, these systems are just out of my league. I've tried everything. I just can't get in. Is there anything else I can do?"

"No, no, don't worry. Look, thanks . . . Steve."

"Yes, well. Be back at work tomorrow morning."

I quickly hang up and grab the statements. I've got to get this information to David. He'll know what to do. And even if they can't catch Mike, at least David will be in the clear. He probably won't ever talk to me again, but at least I won't be responsible for ruining his life.

"Mum, help me clear up this stuff so Mike doesn't suspect anything when he gets back."

My mother reluctantly tears herself away from Mike's bank statements and starts to put them in neat piles.

My mobile phone rings. It's James. He is breathing fast. "There's someone at the door," he says. "There's someone at the sodding door, and if your description of Mike is anything to go by, it looks like him."

My heart leaps into my mouth. "He can't be here!" I whisper. "He's at the office waiting for the disk."

"No he bloody isn't," says James. "Get out of there quickly!"

The phone goes dead and I look at my mother with alarm. "He's here. James says he's outside!" Mum looks up with alarm. I sneak up to the window to have a peek, and sure enough a cross-looking Mike is reaching for his keys. Only he can't find them. Of course he can't, I realize with relief. I have his keys.

He walks away from the door and I think we're safe. But then he kneels down, and starts digging into a flower bed. He can't have hidden a spare set of keys there, surely? He has. Oh my God. He's coming in!

This is not looking good. If Mike comes in, it isn't going to be easy to explain ourselves. We have broken into his house, and are stealing his papers. Mike will be in his rights to call the police, they will lock us up, and David will go to prison because he never got the information and . . .

Suddenly I hear a terrible crashing noise. Mike hears it, too, and turns away from the house. "Quick! Hide!" I hiss, and my mother and I dive behind the sofa next to the window. On the floor I see a postcard with a flamenco dancer on the front. I pick it up. The postmark is just two days ago, from London. "Can't wait to dance the night away in Spain. See you in Malaga! Vanessa x."

Malaga? Vanessa? So Mike isn't going on his own? I rack my brain to think of a Vanessa Mike has mentioned, but I draw a blank.

And then I hear a familiar voice.

"I'm dreadfully sorry, but I think I may have driven into your car. Terrible shame. Probably going to cost the pair of us a fortune!"

It's James! Out of the window I see the Mini crumpled into the back of Mike's BMW, and James is bumbling around pretending to look for his insurance details while Mike stares at the damage, aghast.

My mother looks furious. "He's been looking for an excuse to get rid of that car for ages," she says crossly. "It's a perfectly good run-around."

"Mum," I hiss, "he did it to help us out. For God's sake!"

"Us?" Mike is shouting. "I am not paying for any fucking damage. You stupid fat bastard!"

"How dare he!" exclaims Mum. "James is not fat. He is just carrying a little excess weight, and if that insolent young man thinks he can shout abuse at James, at my husband, well, he's got another think coming."

She gets up as if to jump to James's defense and I have to pull her back.

"He'll recognize you," I hiss. "Come on, let's get out of here."

Stuffing the papers under my shirt, we creep out the front door and down the stairs. As James demonstrates to Mike that the damage to his car is not significant by showing how easy it is to dislodge his number plate ("See? These BMWs just don't have the craftsmanship of other cars. Your bumper would have fallen off on its own."), we quickly slip out the back door.

* * *

I need to get to David quickly. I kiss my mother and jump in a cab. I have never been to David's offices before and as the taxi draws up in front of a huge building that seems to take up an entire road, I check the address again. "Are you sure this is the right place?"

I know that David works for one of the "Big" accounting firms, but I hadn't really expected the offices to be this big. The firm has offices all over the country, and all over the world, so I thought each one would be pretty small really.

The taxi driver grunts at me, and drives off, leaving me at the main door. The reception itself is as big as a nightclub, with paintings everywhere and clusters of leather chairs and sofas where people are sitting and having intense conversations. I walk hesitantly up to the reception desk.

"Is David Bradley here?"

One of the receptionists looks up. "Do you have an appointment with Mr. Bradley?"

"Um, no, not really," I reply. "But if you tell him Georgie is here, I'm sure he won't mind."

The girl looks uncertain, but she dials a number anyway.

"Hello, this is reception. We have a Georgie downstairs for David Bradley." There is a long pause. "I see. Okay, thank you."

She smiles at me. "Mr. Bradley can't see you, I'm afraid."

"No, you don't understand. I'm his girlfriend, Georgie Beauchamp, I really have to see him very urgently. Please call him again."

The receptionist calls again. "Oh hello, it's reception here again. We have a Georgie Beauchamp down here very keen to see Mr. Bradley. Ah. Okay, well, thank you."

She looks up at me sympathetically. "I'm afraid he doesn't want to see you," she says softly.

My eyes start to well up. I can't believe this. I'm being dumped by a receptionist. David hates me so much he can't even bear to set eyes on me.

I go over to one of the leather chairs and sit down, unsure what to do next. I can't just go, not until David has the disk. But if he won't see me, I'm scuppered. I decide to wait. At some point David will have to leave the building, and when he does I will grab him and make him listen to me. I look at my watch. It's two-thirty. I pick up a copy of the *FT* from a table in front of me and begin to read.

I'm in the middle of the TV review section when I sense someone coming toward me. I look up to see David's glamorous partner from Rome approaching.

"Hi!" she says with a big smile. "I work with David, and I understand you wanted to see him? I'm afraid he's a bit tied up at the moment but I could give him a message for you if you want?"

At last, someone who can actually help me!

"The thing is," I say, "I've got some information here that I need to get to him. I'd really appreciate it if you'd make sure he gets it."

"Of course," she says smoothly. "Why don't you give it to me now?"

I start rummaging around in my bag. All the bits of paper are crumpled up and in a mess. But before I can organize the statements one of the receptionists interrupts us.

"Vanessa, I've got a call for you. Shall I put them through to your voicemail or would you like to take it here?"

The woman looks up. "Who is it?"

"Didn't say, but he says it's important. I wouldn't ask, but he sounded quite determined to talk to you."

"Fine, I'll take it down here." She turns back to me. "I'm sorry, the papers you were talking about—shall I take them now?"

Vanessa . . . It couldn't be her, could it? Mike did say he had a friend at David's firm, some woman who used to work for the police, but surely this can't be the same Vanessa who sent the postcard, the one who's going to Malaga with him? Vanessa is standing over me and when I look up she must notice the recognition in my eye because she flinches slightly.

It is her! At least it could easily be, and I can't risk it. I have to think quickly—thank God I haven't given her the disk yet.

"Actually," trying to sound as normal as possible even though I can feel myself shaking, "why don't you take the call? I've got to sort through all these papers anyway."

"Oh, it's no trouble. I'll just wait while you go through them. I'm sure the call can wait."

There is no warmth in her smile and I'm running out of excuses.

I delve back into my bag and have a brain wave. I quickly find "ring tone" on my mobile phone display and within a couple of seconds it springs into action with a piercing rendition of a Bach fugue.

"Sorry, I'm going to have to take this," I say apologetically and seize the opportunity to move away from Vanessa.

She walks over to the reception desk reluctantly to take her call. I quickly dial David's number on my mobile.

"Good afternoon, David Bradley's office."

It's Jane. Thank God.

"Jane," I whisper. "It's Georgie. Look, I need to talk to David."

"Don't we all," says Jane mournfully. "He's in with the senior partner. I can't get in to see him. No one can. Except his new partner Vanessa. And I don't like her much either. Only passed her exams last year apparently and already she's a partner. Georgie, what's all this trouble he's in? I knew I shouldn't have gone on holiday—"

"I'm downstairs with Vanessa now," I interrupt. "Or rather, I'm trying to get out of her clutches. I've got some stuff for David and I don't trust her with it. Is there a cafe or somewhere you can meet me in five minutes?"

Vanessa is putting the phone down and turning back toward me.

"Well, there's a Starbucks round the corner," says Jane.

"Perfect. I'll be there."

"Vanessa," I say loudly. "I'm really sorry but it looks like I've brought the wrong stuff. I thought I had some work-related papers that David had left at my flat, but it turns out they're ... um ... other stuff, so I'll just ... give them to him later, okay?"

Before she can answer, I slide my phone into my pocket and make a dash for the door.

I order a hot chocolate with extra cream. I feel like I need something comforting and warm. As I pick up the cup I realize my hands are trembling.

I can't believe that Mike is about to run off to Spain with Vanessa, the bitch brunette from Rome. She must have been keeping Mike posted on exactly what information David had all along.

There are people all around me drinking coffee, talking idly with friends. In the corner is a group of three boys who look like they're bunking off school. They are sharing one coffee between them and smoking furtively. I long for the days when bunking off school was about the worst thing I could do. Unlike, say, being naive enough to believe my stupid ex-boyfriend and nearly getting David arrested.

My resentment of Mike grows as I stir my chocolate. What bloody right does he have to care so little about the feelings of everyone else? But really my resentment is directed at myself. I was so easily flattered by Mike I didn't think to question his motives.

"Are you all right, Georgie?"

Jane wakes me from my reverie. Jane has been David's PA for, well, forever really. As long as I've known him, anyway. She's a formidable woman somewhere in her early fifties, with a very no-nonsense approach to life—David and the other partners are actually quite scared of her. If she thinks David is working too hard, she won't put calls through to him and she knows more about his firm than any of the partners combined. And if she disagrees with you, well, you don't often win an argument with Jane. But she is absolutely loyal. And right now I could do with a familiar face.

"Not really," I say glumly, cupping the hot chocolate between my hands and taking a sip.

"Jane, you don't think David would do anything wrong, do you?"

"David? Of course not. Best partner that firm's got if you ask me. They work him too hard, of course, but that's another matter. I've never seen someone so drained and tired. He needs to go on holiday, you know. Somewhere hot."

"Yes, yes, you're right." A holiday. God, if only.

"Now what's all this about? And why did Vanessa tell me not to put through any calls from you?"

I breathe a sigh of relief—at least it was Vanessa and not David refusing to talk to me. But it confirms my suspicions: it's definitely the same Vanessa.

"David's in trouble, big trouble," I say wearily. "It's partly my fault, but mainly Vanessa's." This may not be the absolute truth, but there's no point in making Jane cross with me now, is there? And it is more Vanessa's fault than mine. I mean, she actually meant to be bad, whereas I was duped into it.

"Go on." Jane looks at me expectantly.

"I've got some stuff here—a disk and some papers—that will make everything okay, but he needs to get it soon. Like now, in the next hour. And Vanessa can't know about it. If she does, she'll ruin everything. She's totally betrayed him."

I add this last piece of information with a flourish, knowing that it will get Jane fired up. If she didn't like Vanessa before, now she positively hates her.

"Georgie, are you telling me that one of the partners in the firm is acting unprofessionally? These are very serious allegations."

"I know. But she is. She's running off to Spain this evening. She's a complete cow."

For a minute I'm scared that Jane is going to tell me to stop wasting her time. That she doesn't believe me. But then she looks up at me and opens her handbag.

"Is that the information there?" Jane looks at the envelope I'm clutching.

"Yes. Look, you've got to get this to David safely."

"Of course. Now, Georgie, I recommend you go home now and have a bath. You look dreadful."

"Do you think David will be okay?"

"If what you say is true and the information here is what you say it is, then I'm sure he'll be fine."

I nod silently. I need some words of reassurance. I can take David hating me, but I can't take the possibility of his career being ruined. It would just be too unfair.

Jane picks up the envelope and puts it in her handbag. "Look, my dear, he'll come round. They always do, just you see."

She thinks this is still about me and David, I realize. She

thinks I'm worried he won't love me anymore. Of course I am worried about that—I could well have messed things up completely on the romantic front. But something tells me that we couldn't have carried on as we were anyway. There were too many secrets. Candy, Mike, David—they all knew more about what was going on than I did. Well, I don't want to be protected anymore. I don't want to be the naive, trusting Georgie. If David had been open with me from the start with the whole Mike business, I'd never have believed Mike's lies. If Candy had been honest about her feelings for Mike, I'd have left them to it and saved myself a whole load of heartache. I do love David, but I'm not sure that's enough right now.

"Just you remember what I said about a holiday," Jane is saying. "Looks like you could do with one, too."

She nods at me and leaves. I look at the time—it's still early, and I've got an idea. I do some mental calculations, and walk quickly toward the Tube.

"You really want it all off?"

"Yes, really."

My hairdresser, Adrian, looks at me uncertainly. "How about a bob?" he suggests, but I shake my head.

"I want a crop," I tell him matter-of-factly. "I want to look utterly and completely different."

At this, Adrian's face breaks into a smile. "One of those transformation cuts, you mean? Well, in that case, I'd say we need to do a bit of color, too, don't you think?"

I nod gratefully and let him lead me to the basin to have my hair washed. David may have liked my hair long, but I'm not doing this for David. I'm doing this for me. I want a new start.

As Adrian talks to me about the flat he's just bought with his boyfriend and the cost of furniture, I watch my appearance change. First, he divides my hair into sections, paints them with dye, and wraps each one up in tin foil. Next, when the foils have been taken out, he cuts away at my hair with scissors, inches of hair cascading onto the floor. There's no going back now, I think to myself, and a big grin appears on my face.

An hour and a half after I first sat down, I am staring at myself appraisingly. I have short hair, with a teeny tiny fringe that virtually disappears when I put it to one side, and beautiful golden highlights that seem to make my skin glow.

I suddenly understand what Audrey Hepburn was doing in *Roman Holiday*. The film wasn't about romance or about driving around in Vespas. It was about someone growing up. She needed to cut her hair to say good-bye to the girl who took orders and did what she was told. She didn't turn her back on her responsibilities, but she changed the way she accepted them. After her weekend in Rome she was an adult who did things on her terms.

The girl looking back at me in the mirror isn't the same Georgie who thought having Mike fancy her again would solve everything. Who expected Mike or David to provide her with everything, from a social life to financial status. No, the Georgie I'm looking at now is the same one I saw in Gucci. Except this time the transformation wasn't quite so expensive.

I wince slightly when I think about my credit card bill, but then think what the hell—a few less cab rides and a ban on cappuccinos, and I'll pay it off. The point is that in spite of everything, I feel good about myself. I finally feel like I'm in charge.

Adrian brings a mirror over so I can see the back.

"You know, I thought it'd be a mistake you going short,"

he says. "But you look gorgeous. Like a little urchin. Now you go and show him what he's missing, whoever he is."

I want to tell him that there's no "he" to miss anything anymore, but there doesn't seem any point really. I like my hair. And that's enough.

I stand for a moment looking at my reflection in the mirror, then I take out my mobile phone. There is one more thing I have to do.

"Candy? Hi, it's Georgie. Can I come round and see you?"

21

The reception to International Magazines Inc. is nearly as glamorous as David's, but where David's reception has lots of important-looking people in suits buzzing around and talking about the latest low-cost airline merger and the likelihood of further consolidation in the construction industry, this place is full of women with sharp haircuts discussing Marc Jacobs waiting lists and whether the Laura Ashley revival is just a flash in the pan.

But having felt so out of place in David's offices, I now feel right at home. A woman tells me that she loves my hair and rather than do my usual "Really? You like it? I'm not sure it's really me actually. Your hair is much nicer," I smile graciously and accept the compliment.

I am thankful, however, that I had the insight to change my clothes before I came—this morning I resorted to borrowing clothes from my mother's wardrobe and they didn't fit me at all, but after my haircut I nipped into Top Shop and bought a simple black linen shift dress and a pair of ballerina pumps. My legs may not be particularly tanned, but still, I'm sure the pale and interesting look is in right now. I glance at myself in the mirrored walls of International Magazines' reception and think to myself that *InStyle* was right, you can make cheap clothes look expensive if you know what you're looking for. I actually look quite sophisticated.

The doors of the lift open, and Candy emerges. She is still amazingly thin, considering she's pregnant. She's dressed all in black and her blond hair is tied back neatly in a ponytail. She looks at me and then does a double take.

"George! God, you look amazing. What happened to you?"

I give a halfhearted smile. "Oh, you know. Shall we . . . can we go and get a coffee or something?"

"Great!" I can see her taking surreptitious looks at me as we walk down the street. And she hasn't made one comment about how I need accessories, or a different pair of shoes.

There is a small cafe on the corner and when we sit down I notice that "Stand by Your Man" is playing on the radio. I don't know whether to laugh or cry.

Candy looks tired. She tells me about her hectic schedule and a nightmare fashion shoot she's trying to set up, but while her voice is bright and breezy, I can see real tension in her face. I think this is the first time I've ever seen Candy look stressed.

Maybe it's the pregnancy, I think.

"So . . . ?" she says expectantly when we make it to a free table with our frothy cappuccinos. She looks at me, and then at the clock on the wall. I'm guessing I haven't got much of her time.

"It's about Mike," I begin.

"Ah. Yes." Candy looks thoughtful. "Don't tell me. He's leaving me for you. You've finally got your revenge. I suppose that's your victory haircut. Am I right?" Her face is smiling but her eyes are thunderous.

"No!" I exclaim. "Candy, Mike has lied to both of us. I

didn't want you to find out from anyone else: he is going to Malaga, you were right. Only, I'm not sure he's coming back. He's got David into a whole load of trouble and he's buggering off tonight. I just . . . I thought you should know."

Candy stares at me and doesn't say anything. Somehow this isn't going as expected. There is none of the bonding, none of the hugs and tears that this sort of revelation usually brings about in films. Candy is sitting quite still, tight-lipped, and is now gazing into the distance.

"I was the one who told you about the tickets to Malaga," Candy says sharply. "I don't see why you had to drag me out of a meeting to tell me something I knew already."

"I . . . I didn't know if you knew that . . . he isn't coming back."

I look at Candy worriedly. Is she going to have one of those delayed reactions and get incredibly emotional in a minute or two? But her eyes don't convey any emotion at all.

"Right," she says crisply, standing up to go. "Is that everything?"

I can't work out what's going on. Didn't I explain myself properly? Doesn't Candy realize what I'm saying?

"Candy, look, I know this is bad news, and I'm sorry to be the one telling you, but how can you be so calm? Aren't you worried about the baby and stuff? Don't you care what an utter shithead Mike has been? What he's done to David?"

I'm so angry I feel myself wanting to take out my frustrations on Candy, to make her react, to make her cry. Not exactly mature, I know, but it's been a tough day.

Candy stares at me long and hard and then looks down.

"There is no baby," she says flatly.

No baby?

"Since when? Candy, what happened?"

"What happened," she says slowly, "is that I wasn't pregnant after all. Wasn't ever pregnant, actually. I thought I was—I missed two periods and felt really bloated. And when I found out that I wasn't, I couldn't bear it. I thought that if I could just keep everyone thinking I was pregnant, then everything would be fine. Mike would marry me . . ."

A small tear is wending its way down Candy's cheek. I try not to feel pleased that she's finally upset.

"It looks like even a real baby wouldn't have done the trick anyway," she says.

"You're well shot of him," I say quietly.

Candy nods. "And you're welcome to him."

Me? She still thinks that I'm going to Spain with him?

"Candy, he's not going to Malaga with me. This is not about me and Mike. There's someone else."

Candy looks up sharply.

"Someone else? That's impossible. Who?"

"I don't know. Some bitch that David works with. She's stitched up David and now she's running away with Mike."

Candy looks me up and down as if she's trying to work out whether to believe me or not. Evidently she does, because after a few seconds she looks down and smiles.

"I shouldn't think he'll get very far."

"What do you mean?"

"I mean," she says, looking me straight in the eye, "that I rang the airline this afternoon and canceled the ticket. The eight-thirty flight to Malaga will be leaving without him. And without this . . ." Candy reaches into her bag and brings out Mike's passport. "Without this, I don't think he's really going anywhere. Do you?"

Her smile breaks into a real grin. Tears are still rolling

down her cheeks, but she has a glint in her eye. "I've been pretty stupid, haven't I?"

"You and me both," I agree.

"I can't believe I fell for him," Candy sniffs. "After all those evenings telling you he wasn't worth it."

"I thought you had just told me that so you could have him to yourself," I say, half joking and half accusingly.

"No! Oh my God, Georgie, I would never do that! I mean, I did fancy the pants off him, but I really didn't mean to be so two-faced. I only let him move in with me because he said if he could just move in with me for a little bit he'd get himself together . . . he said that you two needed a clean break, you know, so that you could get over him properly. . . ."

We both start laughing. It sounds so ridiculous now.

"So he didn't leave me for you?"

"I resisted him for at least two weeks," Candy smirks. "And then, when I finally gave in, I was so guilt-ridden I couldn't call you or see you or anything. I only called you the other week because Mike said he'd seen you and I wanted to make sure there wasn't anything else to it. David adores you and I couldn't bear the idea of you letting Mike screw things up, except that I couldn't say anything because David had said not to say anything about me and Mike. And then when I told you I was pregnant, and you kept talking about Mike, I just lost it."

"Candy, I'm so sorry. God, we're both total suckers aren't we. And Mike isn't even a good kisser."

"Mike? God, he's awful! And you know he's started to dye his hair?"

We both convulse in giggles, then Candy puts her coffee down.

"Georgie, I haven't had a drink, a proper drink, in an awfully long time. You don't fancy one, do you?"

"I would love that. Let's drink a toast to our abysmal taste in men and to us being proper friends again," I suggest.

Candy smiles and stands up.

"Not abysmal," she says. "David's one of the few good ones."

I feel a lump in my throat appear as I follow her out into the street.

ꕥ 22

It's 10:30 P.M. My answerphone is flashing. Ready for the worst, I press Play on the machine and sit on the edge of the sofa.

"Georgie, are you there? It's Mike. Pick up the bloody phone. I need to talk to you.

"Georgie, what the fuck is going on? Oh, for fuck's sake.

"Fucking call me.

"Georgie? Do you think this is funny? Don't be an idiot—pick up the phone. I know you're there; they said you weren't in work today . . ."

I turn up the volume of the television and go to the kitchen to get a bottle of wine. I'm already pretty drunk, but getting drunker seems like a pretty good idea right now. Candy and I made our way through about five gin and tonics earlier and nearly got kicked out of the pub for being so rowdy—very unlike Candy. But now I'm back and I've got to face the music.

I don't know how much Mike knows—it depends how much Vanessa has pieced together really. To be honest, I was hoping that he'd have been arrested or something by now, but it seems he's still very much around. At least he won't be able to go to Spain and David will be okay. I just never want to see him again.

I open a bottle of red, and notice that it's Bulgarian. I

can't help checking the vintage to see if it's a 1999. I realize that I have never asked David whether he made that whole thing up about the Bulgarian wine to save me, or whether it's really true. I wonder if I'll get the chance to ask him.

The phone rings, startling me. I'm tempted to answer—what if it's David—but decide that it's more likely to be Mike, and leave it to be answered by the machine. Sure enough, Mike's voice soon comes ringing out of my answerphone. He's trying to sound all friendly, but I can hear the bitterness in his voice. "Georgie, if you're there, please answer the phone. I didn't get that package you were sending me. You know I'm relying on you, don't you? Look, give me a call, okay?"

I decide enough is enough and pull the telephone out of its socket. Then I turn off my mobile for good measure. Frankly, they can all go hang, I decide. What I want right now is a nice hot bath.

I wake up to a loud ringing noise. I open my eyes slowly and try to get my bearings. Okay, so I'm not in my bed, I'm in a lukewarm bath and my skin is all wrinkly. As for the noise, well, obviously that's the doorbell. Dammit, can't a girl get just a little peace and quiet?

I stagger to my feet and my head starts throbbing as I pull on a robe. That'll teach me to drink gin and wine in the same evening. What was I thinking?

The door buzzes again and I hear Mike's voice call my name. Anger wells up inside me—just who the hell does he think he is? Without thinking, I pick up the intercom. "Sod off and leave me alone," I say loudly. "Just leave me bloody well alone. You are a pathetic bastard."

I want to add "and me and Candy both hate you, so there," but figure that I don't really want to sound like a fifteen-year-old.

"Georgie. Where's the fucking disk, Georgie?"

Mike's voice is slurring—evidently he's been drinking too. He's also shouting, all his sentences peppered with expletives. I'm not usually too worried about what my neighbors think of me, but I'm going to have to lay low for a while after this.

Mike moves away from the intercom. "Open the fucking door," he shouts.

I run to the window and open it wide. Looking down I can see Mike two floors below, sitting on the pavement, a bottle in his hand.

"They're all wankers, Georgie, you know that don't you. You think you can trust someone, and what do they do? Take your passport, that's what. She took my fucking passport!" He starts to laugh maniacally.

"Mike, just go away, will you? I don't want to see you again. Ever."

I start to put the window down again but am jolted by the noise of glass smashing. Mike has thrown his bottle against the wall.

"Fine. You don't want to give me the disk? I'm going to come up and get it."

He starts making an attempt to climb the wall up to my flat. I grab a large ceramic vase my mother gave me for Christmas last year in case I need something to defend myself. Okay, so a ceramic vase may not be the most fearsome of weapons, but there's nothing else at hand.

"You do know how much I hate you, don't you?" I shout down at Mike as he feebly attempts to climb up the drainpipe leading up to my window. "You are the most pathetic creature that ever lived. I know all about you stealing money from people, and about Vanessa, too. You even got me to carry your money in through customs for you, you total bastard."

Mike's attempts to climb the wall are coming to nothing. He jumps up several times and clings on to the drainpipe only to slide straight down again.

"Oh come on, you'd have done anything to get in my trousers," he shouts, giving up on the climb. "You've never stopped fancying me, have you? Never got over the fact that I just couldn't give a fuck, did you? Well, I hope you're happy with David. Boring bastard David who wouldn't know how to seduce a fucking prostitute."

I throw the ceramic vase down toward Mike. Not near enough to hit him, but near enough to make myself feel a bit better.

"David, boring?" I shout. "Mike, you obviously have no idea how utterly sleep inducing you are. And if you think that I fancy you, well, you can bloody well think again. Why do you think I faked feeling sick in Rome? It was so I didn't have to kiss you, let alone sleep with you, you pathetic shit!"

I am getting into my stride with this insult hurling, and look around for another object to throw out of the window.

Mike looks very agitated. "Are you fucking throwing things at me? You don't want to throw things at me, Georgie." His voice is menacing now. "Bad things happen to people who really piss me off. The prick who nicked my Zip disk for instance—know what happened to him? No, well, you wouldn't, would you. But he won't be bothering me or anyone else again. Got friends, you see. They *deal* with things like that." Mike has given up attempting to climb up the drainpipe and has sat back down on the pavement again.

"You mean your Italian friends?" I say sarcastically, picking up a bowl full of potpourri.

"Family," Mike corrects me. "Italian *family*." He laughs.

"Now, let me into your flat or I am going to break your fucking door down . . ."

But before he can finish his sentence, we are both blinded by lights. I put my hands over my eyes, and as they adjust to the brightness I see ten, maybe twelve men in police uniform appear out of nowhere and surround Mike. He tries to kick out at one of them but fails miserably and is led away into one of three black cars that I hadn't even noticed were there. A young man looks up at me.

"Sorry to trouble you like this. There won't be any more bother this evening," he says brightly, then nods and gets into one of the cars.

I stand at the window, dazed, and watch the cars drive off. Were the police there all the time? How did they know Mike was here? God, what did they hear me say?

Within a few minutes the road is quiet again. I would think that I'd imagined the whole thing if it wasn't for the smashed bottle and the broken ceramic vase, which I'm now going to have to replace so that my mother doesn't give me a lecture about being clumsy. But just as I'm about to shut the window, I hear a noise below. I look down and my heart skips a beat when I see that it's David approaching.

He stops a few yards away from my front door and surveys the scene. He looks at the broken vase and the smashed bottle, then slowly looks up to my window. Our eyes meet and we stare at each other for a moment or two. I can hear a cat yowl in the distance, but otherwise there is complete silence.

"Thank you," he says. "For the disk. For getting it back."

"You're welcome," I reply. It's a cool, still night, but I can feel that my face is red and hot. I want to ask David up, but something stops me. I feel awkward, like someone at the end of a first date, not sure whether the other person really likes them or not.

"They got Mike then," I say, not sure whether or not this will be news to David.

He nods.

"And Vanessa?"

"Oh yes," says David. "We had serious doubts about Vanessa and were waiting for her to trip up. Quite tidy, the way it all finished."

"Is that . . . is that why you didn't want to introduce us in Rome?" I ask tentatively.

"Exactly," says David, and then there is silence again.

I want so much for David to come in, to take me in his arms and tell me everything is okay. But it's not as simple as that, I remind myself. And anyway, he doesn't seem to want to come up.

There's a long pause before David speaks again.

"Georgie, I need to know whether you still have feelings for Mike," he says slowly. "I need to be able to trust you."

"Trust me?" I say incredulously. "After everything I've done today, you need to know if you can trust me? David, I've had Mike here this evening threatening me with his bloody Mafia friends because I gave Jane that Zip disk. My mother and I broke into his flat to get it and my stepfather wrote off a car so that we didn't get caught. Of course you can trust me."

"That was very sweet of you, Georgie," he smiles. "I'm sorry. But you must admit, you have caused me a bit of strife in the past few days."

I take a deep breath in. It would be so easy now to make up with David, to give him my usual cheeky grin and say I'm sorry. To admit that I've been a bit silly and that I should just listen to him in the future and not be so impetuous. But I'm not going to do it.

"David, do you know why I took the disk?"

David sighs. "You thought you were helping me, I know. But come on Georgie, you believed Mike—the very person I told you not to see."

"Exactly! David, just listen to yourself, will you? You *told* me not to see Mike? I'm your girlfriend, not a child. Why didn't you just tell me what he was up to instead? You even told Candy not to tell me about her and Mike, so I had no idea what a liar he was. David, you are a wonderful boyfriend in so many ways and you are truly a great lover. But you can't treat me like a little girl! Are you really surprised that I end up doing stupid things when you don't ever let me know what's really going on?"

David looks up, dumbfounded.

"Are you trying to say it's all my fault?" he says incredulously.

"No, of course not," I sigh. "What happened is all my fault. But you do need to take a bit of responsibility. What I'm talking about is us. If there is an us, that is. If there's going to be an us . . ." I pause for dramatic effect. "I just think that you need to change the way you see me. To tell me what's going on instead of treating me like a child and shielding me from everything. I need you to take me seriously . . ."

My voice trails off as I look at David's face. He looks shocked. Oh God, he probably can't believe that having put him through hell I'm now having a go at him for not trusting me. Am I being unfair?

Suddenly gripped by fear that I could be screwing up yet again, I decide to shout down to David that I was completely in the wrong and that he probably had really good reasons not to tell me about Mike. But before I can open my mouth, I notice his face changing. He still looks serious, but now he's looking at me as if he's seeing something he hasn't seen before. I couldn't be sure, but I almost think he looks a bit proud.

"You're saying there may not be an us?" he says softly, so softly that I can only just hear him through the night air.

"Well, no, not really," I shrug. "But it got you to listen, didn't it?"

"I'm sorry, Georgie. Really and truly sorry. I thought, well, I thought it was up to me to protect you. I didn't realize I was shutting you out. I just . . . I didn't want you to know about the horrible stuff I get involved in. Could I . . . could I maybe come in so that we can talk about this with some, well, privacy?"

I nod and walk over to press the intercom buzzer. I push it several times, but I can't hear David opening the door.

"It's open," I call, walking back to the window, but David isn't on the street anymore. I lean out of the window to see where he's got to, and to my amazement I find that he's climbing up the wall. He is shinnying up the very same drainpipe that floored Mike.

"David, what are you doing?" I call excitedly. "You're insane!"

"Not insane, Georgie, but perhaps a bit stupid," David replies, grabbing onto the wall for a better grip. "I thought I was doing the right thing keeping the truth from you. I didn't want you to worry, and if I'm absolutely honest, I probably didn't know you really cared about it. But Georgie, the last thing I wanted was to lie to you. I just didn't want to worry you unnecessarily. Plus, I knew you had feelings for Mike and I thought you might think I was making the whole thing up." He swings his legs onto the top of the first-floor window.

"And you're right. I mean, about me," he says thoughtfully, pausing to change his grip. "I've been thinking that I need to make some changes in my life."

"Changes? You don't need to change," I say gently. "You're pretty much perfect as you are. Just, you know, tell me stuff. Don't keep secrets from me. David, be careful won't you . . ."

I'm half hanging out of the window now, terrified that he's going to fall.

"No, I do need to change," says David through gritted teeth—his head is now level with my windowsill. I hurriedly move my planters into the flat. "I don't want to spend so much time at the office anymore. Jane has booked me on a course in 'delegation' and I'm going to really try."

I grin. I can just imagine Jane telling David exactly what she thinks of his delegation skills.

"You see," David says, pulling himself into my sitting room, "I haven't had a holiday for a very long time. Rome made me realize what I'm missing—what we're missing. And if I'm going to take a long holiday, well, I need to be able to delegate. To trust the people working for me."

"Except Vanessa," I point out, as David's feet touch the floor.

"Yes, except Vanessa." He's standing in front of me now, sweat glistening on his forehead, brick dust staining his city coat. Noting my shocked expression, he shrugs and grins. "Jane also said I should try a romantic gesture. The florists were shut, so I thought climbing up to your window might do the trick . . . it's all about balance, you know . . ."

I raise my eyebrows at him. I have a sneaky suspicion he might have seen Mike attempt, and fail, to climb up to my window and was determined to outdo him. But that's absolutely fine by me.

"Anyway," David continues, "the point is that I need to

get to a place where I can take a few weeks off without worrying that everything's going to fall apart."

He puts his hands on my shoulders. "Honeymoons can't be short, can they? You would want to go away for at least two weeks, wouldn't you? If you . . . I mean, were you to do me that honor . . ."

He trails off and looks at me beseechingly. Is David . . . did he just . . . is this what I think it is? I don't want to say anything, in case I misheard. In case he was joking or something.

"Two weeks is generally considered about right," I manage. The corners of David's mouth start to edge upward.

"You mean, you might think about it? Even though I can be an arrogant prick sometimes?"

I grin. "David, you're not arrogant. Just misguided. And a bit too protective sometimes."

"All valid criticisms," David admits with a smile. "Now, what about you? Am I allowed to tell you what your faults are yet, or are we still focusing on me?"

"Definitely still focusing on you," I say firmly. "Probably will be for quite a while yet."

"I see. I suspected as much," murmurs David, kissing my neck. "Your hair is beautiful, by the way. It suits you short."

"I didn't know if you'd like it."

"You look like a sassy chick," he says appraisingly. "Far too gorgeous for a boring accountant like me."

"There you go again," I say crossly, pulling away. "Don't say that when you know very well that you're not a boring accountant. You climb up drainpipes, dance like Fred Astaire, and bust organized crime rings. That is definitely not boring, and I think you are obviously not *just* an accountant."

"Okay," grins David. "But maybe I should spice things

WHEN IN ROME . . .   263

up just a little bit. You know, become a little less depend-able, keep you on your toes?"

I punch him in the arm. "I wouldn't say you're exactly dependable at the moment, actually."

David looks up, hurt. "I thought we'd been through all that?" he says quietly. "It's been a really difficult time, Georgie, but I really think that you—"

"The curtain rail," I interrupt, and see relief sweep across his face. "David, that curtain rail has been leaning against the kitchen wall ever since we bought it. Now, if you were really dependable, I'd have curtains up over there instead of two large windows through which my neighbors can see everything."

"Everything?" asks David with a cheeky smile, and he starts to undo my robe. "Well, I think the least we can do is give them something really good to look at . . ."

"David!" I yelp, looking at him in horror. "You can't be serious! There is no way I'm going to let my neighbors see—"

But before I can finish my sentence, David leans down and hoists me over his shoulder.

"I wouldn't dream of letting them see you naked, my darling," he says. "I meant *this*." With a deft movement, he bends down again, picks up my copy of *Roman Holiday* and throws it out of the window. I hear it land with a thud below and wonder what my neighbors will make of the smashed vase, broken bottle, and used video tomorrow morning.

David puts me down on the bed and throws my robe on the floor before turning back and kissing me. As his hands move expertly around my body, he whispers in my ear, "I think we've had enough of *Roman Holiday*, don't you?"

Pulling off his trousers, I agree with a smile. Now that

we've had our own Roman Holiday, I'm determined to spend less time watching TV and more time going out and experiencing things firsthand. Less time dreaming and more time doing. It's going to be great. And anyway, I can always buy the DVD. . . .

Did you love *When in Rome. . . ?*

Don't miss Gemma Townley's new novel,
Little White Lies,
available in bookstores everywhere.

Pretending to be someone else seemed to be the per-
fect answer for Natalie: She could get the guy, have
the clothes, and live the life she always wanted. But
the deception can't last forever. Will Natalie pull it all
together and figure out who she really is before it's
too late? Will everyone understand that she was only
telling Little White Lies *and meant no harm?*

For a sneak peek, read on. . . .

Published by Ballantine Books

Let me ask you a question. A theoretical one, if you'll bear with me. Would you ever open someone else's mail? No? Of course not, I knew that.

Okay, but supposing there was this special letter. A really enticing-looking letter in a thick creamy envelope, handwritten, with no return address on it. And let's suppose that this letter was sent to you. Kind of by mistake. And that you had no way of forwarding it on.

Still not tempted?

Fine. Well, let's also say that the person to whom the letter is addressed was a member of one of the most exclusive private-member clubs in London and had a fabulous social life. While you were really bored, having just moved to a new city where your social life hadn't exactly blossomed yet. And suppose you had to look at the letter day after day just sitting there on your mantelpiece.

Imagine, if you will, that this person had a stack of mail piling up in your flat and that you were looking after it for her, even though it was very doubtful she'd ever come and claim it.

And let's just say that the intended recipient of the letter had moved out of your apartment over a month ago and she still got more phone calls than you did.

Now would you be tempted? Just a little bit?

No? No, of course not. Me neither.

Boom Boom. Huh, huh, yeah.

The ceiling is shaking, which would suggest that Alistair, the guy who lives upstairs from me, is having yet another party. I've been trying to read *Vanity Fair*—my mum's favorite book—for the past hour, but each time I get to the end of a paragraph, I realize I haven't taken any of it in and I have to go back and start over again. Which is a shame because it's a great book, and I want to find out what happens next. So far, clever but wicked social-climbing Becky Sharp is manipulating everyone around her, and everything seems to hinge on money and virtue—the more a character has of either, the better off they are, although money without virtue is preferable to virtue without money. It's fascinating, but I can't help feeling lucky I live in a more enlightened age.

I try reading again, but it's no use—Becky Sharp cannot compete for my attention when hip-hop is booming through my head. Maybe a magazine is a better idea.

Trying to ignore the loud music and laughter coming from his flat, I pick up a copy of *Elle* and alight upon an article on de-cluttering. "Clear out your wardrobe and create a new you!" it says. Now, there's an idea. That would be a constructive way to spend an hour or so.

Although it isn't quite how I imagined spending a Saturday night in London when I decided to move here. I felt delirious with excitement when I handed in my notice a month ago telling my boss that I was moving to London and there was nothing he could do about it. It felt so good, marching into his office with this little smile creeping over my face. I almost expected a standing ovation and film music to play when I told him—or possibly for Richard Gere to turn up and sweep me off my feet and out of the office. You see, I'm not the sort of person who ups sticks and moves. I've always been good, straightforward, and predictable. No one saw this coming—least of all me. But life has a funny way of changing on you, doesn't it? Things weren't going so well back in Bath, where I was working and living at home, and when I mentioned to my mum that I was thinking about moving to London, she was so excited, I just had to go through with it. Even if I was scared as hell.

But like my mum said, you only get one chance at life, so you've got to take every opportunity open to you. Even if it meant leaving my friends, my family, my job . . . And anyway, I owed it to my mum to give it a go. She's always wanted to move to London and live the life of "high society," as she puts it, ever since she was a little girl. But she didn't ever do it—she got married, had children, and before she knew it, she'd missed her chance. And since Dad hates being anywhere you can't see a field, she doesn't even get to visit London very often. I do know what he means, though—cities can be scary places.

Anyway, the point is I'm doing it now. And I can't just sit around listening to music being played at a party I'm not at. I've got to make a go of things. Mum would be so disappointed if she knew I'd spent a month staying in every night. I've got to at least try and let her enjoy a little bit of London life through me.

It did feel good walking out of my job at Shannon's, the advertising and marketing agency where I was working, knowing there'd be no more sitting in the pub every Friday night after work bitching about the new Brand Director who called everyone "sweetness" in this really irritating, patronizing tone. No more having to wear short skirts every time we did a pitch. And no more wondering whether a job in Bath that I didn't really like was the best I could hope for. No, I was taking control of my life. I was getting out of the West Country and its super-relaxed-but-actually-pretty-small-minded-if-you-bother-to-dig-beneath-the-surface-a-little-bit attitude. And I was on top of the world.

Maybe I should have sorted out a few more practical details before I just moved here, but I got a bit carried away by the momentum and the romance of arriving in a big city with nothing but a suitcase. I was the heroine of my own little story. I wasn't going to settle for "not quite what I was hoping for." And I was going to prove to Mum that I could do it—she's only got one daughter, so it was up to me to make her proud. Of course it does mean that I don't really have much of a job right now—I do have a job, it's just not quite what I anticipated. But working in a shop isn't so bad. And I have been reading *The Guardian* and looking for suitable openings in advertising. At least I've been meaning to. I just need to deal with the little voice inside me that keeps reminding me that I never really wanted to work in advertising, anyway.

I look at the article more closely. Closets are a window to the soul apparently. If yours isn't in pristine condition, the author writes, how can you expect your life to be? Hmmm. I hope that's not true. My wardrobe is in a terrible way. It's small, cramped, and full of nasty wire hangers.

Wandering into the bedroom, it strikes me that chucking out everything and starting again might not be such a bad idea. I can really clear the place out—new life, new wardrobe. And once it's all sorted out, maybe the rest of my life will start to fall into place a bit more.

Although . . . I stare at the wardrobe, wondering where to start. Maybe it isn't such a great idea, after all. I have no money for new clothes, and what's the point of clearing everything out if you can't go shopping straightaway to get beautiful new clothes that miraculously reduce your waist and make your legs look longer?

After a few moments' hesitation I wander back to the sofa. There's no urgency—now is probably not the best time to be going through my wardrobe, anyway. It's Saturday night, for heaven's sake. I should be doing something fun.

Boom boom, huh huh huh, uh huh, huh, yeah.

I ditch the magazine—the music's way too loud, and there's no way I can concentrate. Maybe I should cook something. I could try out a great new recipe or something. I'm always saying I have no time to cook properly, and now's my chance.

Having said that, my kitchen isn't really the easiest place to cook in. I say kitchen—but what I really mean is a little area kind of adjoining my sitting room that has a sink, a fridge, and a cooker. Then there's a little table that sits between the kitchen "area" and the sitting room "area" and . . . well, that's about it, actually. There's no cupboard space and I've had to line cereal boxes up on my bookshelves because there's nowhere else to put them.

That's the thing with London. You see a flat description in an estate agent's window ("Hip Ladbroke Grove flat, one bedroom, perfect for entertaining"), and you think you're going to get something like the place Monica has in *Friends*. And then you get there and the "perfect for entertaining" actually translates as "the kitchen is in the sitting room, so it's only one step."

I suppose I could do more with the place—it's a bit bare, I know. But the thing is, I haven't really got anything to "do more" with—I came up from Bath on the train, and I could barely carry any of my clothes, let alone anything like pictures or books. And anyway, I didn't want to bring all my baggage—physical and metaphorical. Moving to a new city is the start of a new life, and bringing reminders of Bath would rather defeat the point. My old pieces of furniture are just that—old. They're part of my old life with Pete. Pete's my boyfriend. Ex-boyfriend, rather. He's part of the reason I moved here. Like I said, I'm not ready to settle for "not quite what I was hoping for."

Still, that's no excuse for not making the place look more lived in, more personal—I've been here a month now, after all. The trouble is, I can never seem to decide what look constitutes "personal." Do I go for modern and clean with leather sofas and furry rugs? Pete would have sold his grandmother (or me, if I'm honest) for a modern, light apartment complete with leather sofa, huge plasma-screen television, and one of those showers with glass bricks. At one point we even set up a savings account, thinking we could buy somewhere. But we never saved much—there were always more important things like football season tickets (him) and shoes (me). Maybe neither of us actually wanted the flat. Not really.

So anyway, there's modern, but I'm not sure that's really me. Then there's the whole shabby-chic look, which, let's get real here, is probably more suited to my budget, anyway. Since I moved here what savings I had managed to claw together have been dwindling rapidly. Vintage would certainly work in this flat. Plus, I'm living on my own for the first time in a long while, and I rather like the idea of going incredibly girly, just because I can. There's no PlayStation to find room for, no one insisting that anything with flowers on it belongs in an old people's home. I could create a pretty haven, all of my own.

But am I actually a girly sort of girl? I'm not entirely convinced. I never wear pink, and never really did the whole cashmere sweater thing at school. I was more of a tomboy, always a complete mess. Actually, I only really twigged about the whole grooming thing in my first term at university. It was so simple I don't know why I didn't get it before—spend an hour on your hair and put some makeup on, and boys take more notice of you. It also helps if you laugh at their jokes rather than take the piss out of them— I learned that in my second term. Duh! By the time I came back home I knew all the tricks of the trade. And that's when Pete finally noticed me. For the first time ever, he actually came over to talk to me as a girl, rather than as "one of the lads." All my life pretty much (well, since I was about thirteen), I had been crazy in love with him and he'd never seen me as more than a mate. And all along, all I needed to do to get his attention was put on some lip gloss and get my hair to do that glossy swingy thing. I'd have been unbelievably pissed off if I hadn't been so happy I was finally getting him to notice me.

Of course the other decorating option is that whole Indian/ethnic look—teak tables, deep red patterned rugs, and incense stick. Again, I don't know if it's me, but I've got to start somewhere, haven't I? There's a shop on the Portobello Road that sells loads of little tables and rugs and they aren't even too expensive.

I suppose I'll make up my mind eventually. And until then, I'll just have to make do with what I've got.

I look around the room for inspiration. There are two books on the arm of the sofa. My stereo, which has seen better days, is on the floor, surrounded by CDs and tapes. A dodgy mirror the landlord left is hanging desolately on the wall, reflecting the empty wall opposite with its cracking paint and holes suggesting where pictures might go. And then there's a pile of letters cluttering up my mantelpiece, none of which are even for me. When I took this place for a six-month lease, the landlord asked mc to keep hold of any mail for Cressida, the previous tenant, "just in case she comes back." Which was a little disconcerting really—it feels like it isn't quite my flat, like I'm just looking after it for the previous incumbent. But what's worse is that she gets way more mail than I do.

Maybe what I need are some photographs on the wall. Some throws over the sofa. Then I could take up the carpets and sand the floor. Or I could buy a huge big rug and make it really cozy . . .

I really don't know how people make big decisions about things like decorating so easily. It's like they have this incredible confidence that there is one way of doing things and that their way is it. Take my parents. Dad likes classical music and can't stand loud bars or pubs. He likes going on holiday but only if he can drive—he hates planes. He likes traditional English food and reads biographies rather than fiction. Mum, on the other hand, likes Italian food, glamorous restaurants, chintzy furniture and fabrics, holidays in Europe, and films with Michael Caine in them. I know if they'll like something because they are so clear-cut, so decided. Mum always says, "I know what I like and I like what I know," and it's true, she does. But I always want to ask her "How? How do you know? How can you be so sure?"

You see, I like Italian food, too, but I also like Chinese, Japanese, English, and French. I've been vegetarian and vegan, and also done the Atkins diet (with lots and lots of steak). I like romantic comedies with Meg Ryan, but I also like French films and thrillers. I like going out clubbing, but I also like staying in. I like cozy meals à deux and I like rowdy parties. Sometimes I'll dress top to toe in neutral beige and camel; other times I'm as colorful as the rainbow. And I can never decide which I prefer.

And then there's Pete. I mean, I thought I liked him. Thought I loved him. But I was never really sure. Or was I just never sure that he loved me?

So anyway, back to the cooking. Let's see . . . I open the fridge door. Two eggs, some celery (very detoxifying apparently; I just wish it didn't taste so awful), and a loaf of bread. Is that really all I have? I open the freezer compartment and see the pizza I bought from Fresh'n'Wild the other day. Immediately my head fills with arguments against the "cooking a fancy recipe" idea—cooking for one is a waste of time; I don't have anything to cook with; I can't be arsed . . .

God, this is crazy. I'm at home on Saturday night. No big deal, right? So why am I so on edge? And why am I getting little knots in my stomach over Alistair's music? I mean, sure it's loud, but this is Notting Hill. People do have parties, don't they? What's so wrong with that?

I guess there's just a little voice inside me that won't go away, telling me it's my fault I'm on my own on a Saturday night. That if my mother were here now (and, you know, twenty years younger), she'd have wangled herself an invitation to the party rather than sit all alone listening to it. That I'm never really going to make it here and as soon as my money's run out, I'll be going home, tail between my legs.

Uh huh, boom boom, huh huh, yeah.

We do say hello to each other from time to time. But that's it. And even that isn't strictly true—I'm always the one who says hello, and Alistair just kind of smiles back.

He's very sexy, though. Not really my type—I mean he's far too trendy, for a start. He wears these dark-rimmed Buddy Holly–style glasses and wears a uniform of dark denim, and I think he's a designer or artist because he always carries round this portfolio. He's so "London"—you'd never see someone like that in Bath.

I probably should stop being intimidated by all things London. Everyone else here just seems to get on with it, instead of getting excited about something stupid like the tube. I guess I'll get used to it eventually, but you have to understand I grew up in a little village, and every night my mother would tell me stories about the bright lights, danger, and excitement of the city. By the time I was a teenager, I thought that life began and ended in London and that being stuck out in the West Country was the worst thing that could have happened to me. People talk about "community" as if it's a great thing, and it is, really it is. But can you imagine living in a place where everyone knows what book you're reading; where your neighbor congratulates you on the very day you get your first period; where everyone on your street knows what you got in every single exam at school? Believe me, it gets suffocating. When I got a bit older I was at least able to go to Bath, the nearest town. But it's hardly exciting, is it? It's full of tourists mostly, and everyone thinks it's really "pretty." Well I'm sick of pretty. I want gritty, exhilarating, and wild.

There's also the problem that Bath is a very small town when you've just split up with someone. Particularly when the reason you split up is because you knew they were cheating on you, and now you can't go to a bar or restaurant without looking around furtively to see if he's there with someone new.

I look through my CDs and tapes—everything from Stan Getz to the White Stripes. Hmmm. Bjork. . . . haven't heard that in a while . . . but probably too intense. Air . . . ? No, too mellow. That's the trouble with albums, I find—you have to commit to one specific mood. I know it's terribly uncool, but I secretly love compilations. I love the variety, and also it means I don't have to make up my mind to listen to one artist or another. My fingers hesitate over an old compilation tape I made when I was at school and I pull it out. I spent my life making tapes for my friends when I was at school—it was probably my favorite method of communication. The right mixture of songs can say "You're better off without him" or "You're such a great friend, and I'm really sorry I ruined your favorite top" so much better than words can. This tape is a typical compilation of its time—a couple of weepies like "Unbreak My Heart," some tracks by the Breeders and PJ Harvey that captured my teenage angst perfectly, a few dance tracks, and the odd retro song from an obscure band that I put in to demonstrate how cool I was. CDs may utilize wonderful technology, but the flip side is that no one spends as much time on compilation tapes anymore. Downloading tracks in seconds is just not the same as having to record manually, listening to each song and hitting the *stop* button just in time at the end of each song. Maybe tapes aren't so bad after all, even if they do get chewed up on a regular basis.

Pleased to have made a decision so quickly, I put the tape on and lie back down on the sofa, determined to chill out and make the most of the evening. This is just a short-term blip, I remind myself. How long have I been in London? One month. Just over four weeks. I can't expect to have a social life already. These things take time to cultivate. I lived in the village for twenty-six years, so no wonder I never had a night in.

I find myself thinking longingly of the little flat I shared with Pete in Bath, with a roaring fire that kept me warm when he was out doing whatever it was he was doing (or rather, *whoever* it was he was doing). But, I remind myself, I wasn't happy really. I was surrounded by friends and family, but I was still lonely. And sure, I got invited to all the parties, but it was always the same people talking about the same old things. Everyone knew everybody—hell, everyone had been out with everybody at some point. There was no excitement, no intrigue, and no one who didn't know me as "Nat'n'Pete"—I could never be anonymous, never rebuild my identity. Whereas here . . . well, there's certainly no problem where anonymity is concerned. And if the scales have tipped a little far the other way, I'm sure they'll balance eventually. I turn up the stereo a bit more. It's the Indians singing, "Life ain't no bed of roses." Don't remind me, I think ruefully. Still, look on the bright side. I made the move. I am no longer living in Bath, town of Jane Austen, ancient ruins, weird-tasting "spa" water, and endless fields. I am no longer Natalie from Bath—I'm Natalie from Notting Hill.

The phone rings and I leap off the sofa to get it. There's only a handful of people it could be. My mother—but I spoke to her last night and she doesn't tend to ring two nights on the trot; Chloe, my best friend, but that's unlikely, too—she'll be out somewhere, I'm sure; or . . . Pete. We've spoken probably once a week since I moved here, and our phone calls are generally pretty much identical. We start off telling each other how brilliantly we're doing and how happy we are; then we talk about work, our families—any neutral ground we can find—and then he always says, "I still don't get why you moved away. Come back, won't you? We used to have fun." And I say something like "No, you used to have fun and most of the time it wasn't actually with me," and then he starts telling me I'm paranoid, and I get all defensive and accuse him of sleeping with other people, and before we know it, we're having the same argument we've had for about three years over and over again. After a while, I usually end up in tears. I am over him; I just get upset when I think about the time I wasted with him. Thinking that he felt the same as me.

"Hello?" I say hopefully. So we argue. Doesn't mean I don't want to hear from him.

"Hello. Is that Cressida Langton?" says a smart-sounding woman.

My heart sinks. Okay, so the other possibility is that the phone call won't even be for me. Which is pretty irritating, considering that I'm the only one who lives here. I wish now that I'd had the number changed, but it cost £40 and at the time I thought it wouldn't be a problem keeping the old number when I moved in. And it isn't. Apart from the irritating fact that bloody Cressida gets more phone calls than I do and she doesn't even live here anymore. Still, it's probably a good thing. If it had been Pete, I might have admitted that I'm feeling a bit low. And that would have been disastrous.

"No," I say, trying to keep the disappointment out of my voice. "She moved out a month ago."

"Oh. Do you have a forwarding number?"

"No, I'm sorry," I say for the tenth time this week. Has Cressida not considered telling her friends her new number?

"Well, that's a shame," the woman says, sounding very irritated. "This is Nobu. She booked a table here tonight, and I need to know whether to hold it."

"Nobu?" That's only the most expensive restaurant in the whole of London. Cressida was meant to be there tonight? Wow. She's suddenly gone right up in my estimations.

"Yes," says the woman.

"Right," I say after a slight pause. I can't believe I'm on the phone to Nobu! "Well, I'm sorry I can't really help."

"No, well, there we are."

And with that, she hangs up.

* * *

Huh huh, huh huh. Boom, yeah.

I stare at the phone for a few seconds, trying to imagine going out to dinner at Nobu. Cressida's probably a super-glamorous urbanite. Glamorous and rich. I wonder who she was meant to be having dinner with.

My eyes rest on the pile of letters addressed to Cressida. Suddenly they seem rather more interesting. I wonder what sort of mail someone who eats at Nobu gets.

I wander over and pick them up. Most of them look pretty dull. But there's a big brown envelope that looks kind of interesting, and a smaller creamy one that's hand-written. Then there's a catalog, which I can see through the clear plastic wrapper. I leave the rest of the letters where they are, and take the two interesting-looking ones and the catalog back to the sofa with me.

I suppose I could open the catalog. I mean that's just junk mail, isn't it? It won't have anything personal in it.

But as I'm about to rip it open, I stop myself and roll my eyes at my ridiculous behavior. I cannot believe it's got to the point where I am actually thinking about opening other people's junk mail for entertainment.

Although, having stooped this low, I do kind of want to open it. I guess if I'm going to be pathetic, I might as well do it properly.

Looking around furtively as if worried that someone's going to see me, I quickly pull open the plastic cover and open the catalog up. I know it's just a catalog, but it still feels a bit weird opening someone else's mail.

But I suppress my doubts and turn my attentions to the catalog. If you can call it a catalog, that is—somehow this seems too beautiful for such a plain description. I've never seen mail order like it! For one thing, the paper it's printed on is luscious, and for another, it's full of the most amazing things, all of which are incredibly expensive—stone lamps and velvet gowns and other things that no one needs at all but that look so beautiful you'd probably remortgage your house just to have them. If you had a mortgage in the first place, that is. I think I'll keep this for Mum—it's the sort of thing she'd love.

I imagine my sitting room full of beautiful "objets." Did Cressida order from this catalog? When she lived here, was this room full of opulent throws and cushions? I bet she did. She probably had candles burning, too. I half close my eyes and imagine deep velvet curtains at the window, leather and suede cushions on the floor, and a fake fur throw on the sofa. Okay, as soon as I've got some money saved, I'm going shopping.

I put the catalog down and stare at the other letters. My appetite is whetted now, and I want another little peek into Cressida's life. It wouldn't be so bad if I had my own little stack of letters to open, but I don't have a single one. I got a bank statement this morning (never a nice thing to see at the beginning of the weekend), and I got a postcard from my parents two weeks ago—and that's it since I've been here. Do people not write anymore? Evidently they do; it's just that they write to Cressida, not me.

After a few minutes' hesitation, I pick the big brown letter up, ostensibly to take it back to the main pile of letters, but secretly to look for a sign that it's also junk mail so that I can justify opening it. Instead, I get a shock. There's a discreet stamp on the left-hand corner that says "Soho House." How did I not see that before? Surely it's not from the Soho House? The private members club that everyone who's anyone goes to? The one that opened up a New York club and got featured right away in *Sex and the City*? Don't tell me Cressida was a member?

My heart starts beating a bit faster. If you want to talk

"high society," this must be as close as it gets these days. Suddenly London doesn't feel quite so impenetrable, after all. I actually have a letter from Soho House. Correction—Cressida has a letter from Soho House. But she's not here, is she? And I have no idea where she is, either. For all I know she could have moved to Australia and she's hardly going to care about a few letters back here, is she?

I give the envelope a good feel—there isn't much in there. A few sheets of paper at most. Then I put it down again. This is unbearable. I can't go looking at someone else's mail. But come on, this is Soho House! When else am I going to have this kind of opportunity again?

I turn to the other letter, which looks equally enticing. The envelope is thick and creamy, and the handwriting is elegant, written with a proper fountain pen.

Cressida Langton, Flat 3, 127 Ladbroke Grove, Notting Hill, London W11.

It just sounds so smart, doesn't it? And it's my address now. I live here. Screw Pete, and screw the party upstairs—I don't need either of them.

I wonder what Cressida looks like. Beautiful, probably. I can't imagine anyone unattractive going to Soho House. I stand up to look in the mirror, hold my head up and straighten my posture, imagining that I'm her. "Dahling, you look divine," I say to my reflection, pretending it's Catherine Zeta-Jones or someone. Okay, so maybe the accent's a bit much—I'm sounding more like the Queen than Liz Hurley—but I can work on that. "Just dashing out for drinks at Soho House." I tell an imaginary Pete. "Oh, Alistair, I'm sorry; I can't stay long—I've got dinner at Nobu in an hour . . ."

As I speak, my hands are irresistibly drawn toward the letters again and I pick them up, fanning myself with them, completing the picture. It wouldn't hurt to just have a little eency-weency sneaky peek, would it? I mean, no one will ever know, will they? I'm sure Cressida's never going to come back and claim them, so having a little look won't make any difference at all. Except that she might come back, mightn't she . . . and then what would I do? It wouldn't exactly look good to hand them over already opened, would it? Damn, and they look so irresistible, too.

Almost reflexively, I pull my hand away as if the tips of my fingers have been singed.

"Natalie Raglan, what on earth do you think you're doing?" I say to myself under my breath, pulling myself out of this "Cressida Langton" reverie.

That was close. I smile at my reflection as I hear "Tempted by the fruit of another" coming out of my stereo. I'm not sure this is what Squeeze meant when they wrote the song, but the words are pretty apt. I will resist my temptation. These letters are someone else's private correspondence, and I am not the sort of person to open them. Period.

I flick on the television, but before I can start seriously channel-hopping, the phone rings again.

"Rescued!" I cry, reaching for the phone.

"Natalie?" asks a familiar voice. "You sound a bit out of breath."

"Chloe! Yeah, well, I just ran across the flat. Or, rather, dived across the sofa."

Chloe and I have lived next door to each other since we were about five, and until I came to London, we did pretty much everything together. My brother, James, died when I was six, and my parents took a long while to get over it, so I used to be round at Chloe's house more than I was at mine for a couple of years. We were inseparable—we went everywhere together, read the same books, saw the same films . . . God, we even had our first kiss on the same night. Not kissing each other, obviously, but kissing boys. It was with James and Steve from school and we were both fourteen. We even insisted on standing about ten feet from each other in case anything went wrong, and then we ended up giggling so much James and Steve got completely paranoid and walked off as if we were a pair of demented morons. I was quite relieved actually—James was a really crap kisser and I was worried Pete would find out. Not that it would have mattered in any significant way—it's not like Pete ever asked me out at that stage, but at the time I had this idea I was saving myself for him.

Anyway, since then Chloe and I have done pretty much everything together—college, university, even work; we joined Shannon's agency in Bath on the same day. I took a scattergun approach to getting a job after university—I didn't know what I wanted to do, so applied for pretty much everything, while Chloe was quite prepared to slum it for a while and try to figure out what she wanted to do with her life. But I persuaded her to send in a CV with mine to a few companies, and we both got a job at Shannon's. In the event, Chloe turned out to be a natural, whereas I never really felt in my heart of hearts that it was what I wanted to do. But if I hadn't decided to quit and move down to London, we'd still be working side by side.

To be honest, though, since I've been in London I've actually been avoiding Chloe's calls. It's not that I don't want to talk to her—of course I do—it's just that I wanted to leave it until I had more to tell her. She's my best friend, after all. The last thing I want is for her to think I'm sitting on my ass every night. I want to impress her with fantastic stories of my wonderful social whirl—my glamour-filled days and hedonistic nights. And also, I can't tell her the truth because she'd end up telling my mum. And I can't bear the idea of Mum's dreams of moving to London going pear-shaped for the second time in her life.

"Well, at least you're in!" says Chloe in her familiar cheerful tones. "I wasn't sure this was the best time to call."

I pause. I want to tell Chloe about being a bit lonely, a bit scared that I've jumped in at the deep end and can't quite remember how to swim. Chloe's always been the one I tell my problems to (believe me, there have been a lot of them). We always used to love spending Saturday night watching old movies and discussing our (usually disastrous) love lives, and I know she'll be expecting me to confide in her as usual.

But somehow I can't do it.

As Chloe tells me about her week, I think about how surprised she was when I actually went through with my promise to move to London. Actually, I surprised myself, too. I only said it for effect one night when Pete got back at midnight with no explanation as to where he'd been. So I told him I was sick and tired of it, and that I was leaving him and moving to London. And when he told me to stop being ridiculous, I dug my heels in and refused to admit that I hadn't really been planning to move—not in any serious way. And then when my mother heard . . . well, she was so excited, I couldn't tell her that I wasn't sure I'd really meant it. Well, it's done now—all I need now is to think of a way to make my life sound a little more glamorous than it actually is.

My eyes are drawn to the letters again. I suppose I could always tell a few white lies, couldn't I? You know, just spice things up a bit. I mean it's not like Chloe's here or anything. She'll never know.

I look away. God, Natalie, I chastize myself. You're actually thinking about hiding the truth from your best friend?

Just because you don't want everyone to think you're a failure?

"Natalie? Are you okay?" Chloe whispers into the phone. I haven't said anything for several minutes, which is not like me at all—we usually both talk so much that it can be a struggle to get a word in. "Look, if things aren't working out, you can tell me, you know. There's no shame in admitting you were wrong . . ."

I feel myself redden. Admit I was wrong? I don't think so. If the alternative is disappointing Mum and having Pete crow over me, then I'd rather make up a whole new life than admit I'm alone for the fourth Saturday in a row. And anyway, doesn't Chloe realize where I am? I'm in Notting Hill. I live at 127 Ladbroke Grove. Of course things are working out.

My eyes rest back on the letters.

"Am I okay?" I hear myself say in a slightly strangled voice. "God, I couldn't be better!"

Shocked at what I've just said, I redden again.

"Really? It's just that your mum said you sounded a bit down when she called—that maybe you were finding it harder than you expected. I mean it's a huge place, London . . ."

Mum? Oh, God, was it that obvious? I thought I'd done a great job of telling her it was just like she thought it would be when she called the other night. Evidently I need to work on sounding more convincing. And what better time to practice than the present?

I take a deep breath. "Huge and fabulous!" I say to Chloe, trying to smile as I talk. "Actually, you're lucky to catch me in at this time. I was just heading out for the evening."

I cringe as I talk, but try to convince myself everything's

okay. I feel kind of empty inside as I talk, but I guess that doesn't really matter.

"Oh, I'm so pleased," says Chloe, sounding relieved, and I get a pang of guilt. She actually cares, and I'm making up ridiculous stories about having a great social life. "So where are you going?" she asks.

"Going?" I desperately try to think of somewhere. And then it comes to me. Or rather, the left-hand corner of one of Cressida's letters draws my eyes over.

"Oh, Soho House, actually," I say before I can stop myself, then wince. I can't believe I said that.

"You're not!" exclaims Chloe. "God, Natalie—that's the hottest club in London. Who are you going with?"

Who am I going with? Shit—who on earth could I be going to bloody Soho House with?

"With . . ." I start to say, then pause. This is ridiculous. I've got to tell Chloe the truth. Just say it: *I'm not really going. I made it up.* But I know I can't do that.

"Some . . . people?" I say hesitantly

"Just some people? God, I wish I knew people who go to Soho House. So what's it like—in London, I mean?"

What's it like? How should I know? I want to say. I've been in pretty much every night since I got here. The view from my window is wonderful, and on my way to and from work I walk right through Portobello market, with all its great bars and restaurants, but I haven't been into a single one.

But I don't tell her that. Instead I take a deep breath, cross my fingers, and tell her about all the great bars on Portobello Road that I've passed and longed to go into, using my imagination when it comes to what the insides are like; about all the great clothes stalls at the market where you can buy vintage shoes and cool T-shirts for £5; about the Spanish area at the top of Portobello, just where it joins

Golborne Road, where you can get the best olive oil and custard tarts in the world.

"Then there's Tom's, the deli/café, which is the best place for breakfast, and Beach Blanket Babylon, which does the best cocktails ever," I enthuse, not mentioning that I gleaned this information from *Heat Magazine* rather than personal experience. As I speak, I think to myself that this is what London should be like. What London probably is like for people like Cressida. What I hope London will eventually turn out to be like for me.

"It's great," I conclude at the end of my description of this great mythical-for-me City where anything can happen, and where nothing has yet happened to me. "Really great."

"It sounds amazing," sighs Chloe. "I'm so pleased. Pete was saying just the other day that he thinks you'll be back in a month, so it just shows how little he knows. And now you're going to Soho House! Everyone's going to be so impressed."

Pete said what? God, the arrogance of that man. Well, I'll show him. I'm going to make a success of things down here. In spite of the guilt that is flooding my veins, I feel a little rush of excitement at the thought of everyone back home thinking I'm having a great time. I know I've told some white lies. Maybe some not-so-white ones. But at least now everyone's going to think my life is fabulous. That's some consolation for the fact that the reality is rather different. Anyway, why shouldn't I be going to Soho House? Cressida did, and she lived in the same flat as me. Anything's possible.

"So," I say, changing the subject before I get too carried away. "What about you, what are you up to tonight?"

"Well, everyone's at The George, so I'll probably go there

for last orders. And Rebecca Williams is having a party, so we'll probably end up there later."

"Great—sounds really good," I manage to say, trying to sound enthusiastic. Rebecca Williams is one of those teeny tiny passive-aggressive types with perfect hair and nails, and she's always been a prime suspect where Pete's late nights were concerned.

"And what about the shop?"

"Shop?" I haven't told anyone back home that I'm working in a shop. I mean, I used to work in advertising. I was in line for a promotion. I'm hardly going to admit that I'm the one who has to fold and refold jumpers now, even if I do work in one of the most glamorous shops in Notting Hill. So I sort of fudged it, and told everyone back home that I was doing a similar sort of thing to the job I had before, and left it at that. I mean, I'm working in fashion, aren't I? And I used to have some fashion clients at Shannon's. So it's sort of the same thing. Isn't it?

"You know, your own little shop? Don't tell me—you've changed your mind. I guess it wouldn't be the first time . . ." Chloe's giggling. I suddenly remember the drunken evening we spent together the day before I came down to London. I admitted to her that my real ambition in life was to have my own little shop full of beautiful things. Actually, when I told her about it, I was thinking about a shop with nice soaps and maybe a few clothes in it, but having looked at Cressida's Found catalog, I've rather upped my expectations.

"No, I haven't changed my mind," I say indignantly. Chloe always teases me about never being able to make my mind up. And it's really not true. Not about the big things, anyway. At least, not always.

"So you're going to do it?" Chloe asks interestedly.

"Yeah right. Like I'm just going to open my own little

shop. Somehow I don't think it's going to be that easy," I say with a sigh. "I think it should probably be classed as 'dream' rather than 'ambition,' if you know what I mean. You haven't told anyone, have you?"

" 'Course not," says Chloe. "I mean, I said my ambition was to beat Charles Saatchi at a pitch, so I'm hardly one to talk, am I? So, with all your glamorous antics in London is there any news on the romantic front?"

I pause. I mean, the obvious answer is no. No, I haven't. So why am I thinking this and not saying it out loud? Why is the thought of Chloe going to Rebecca's party and telling everyone I'm still single so difficult for me to handle?

"Natalie?" Chloe asks curiously when I fail to speak for a few seconds. "You have, haven't you? Oh, my God, you've got a boyfriend!"

She sounds so excited. Would it really be so wrong to let her think that I'm going out with someone?

Bloody hell, what's happening to me? Of course it would be wrong. And also incredibly sad. I stopped making up boyfriends when I was fifteen, and Chloe never believed in any of them, anyway.

But my mouth seems to have taken on a life of its own.

"Um . . . well, maybe," I say coyly. I wish I could see myself, because the look of indignation on my face would surely stop this storytelling in its tracks.

I move over to the mirror to frown at myself. Actually, I can look pretty scary when I want to.

"I knew it!" Chloe squeals. "Who is he? What's his name?"

Shit. His name. *See?* I tell myself crossly. *See what happens? Now what are you going to do?*

I look around the room desperately for inspiration. Somehow I don't think Cressida's letters can help me here. My eyes travel upward toward the ceiling.

"Alistair," I say weakly. "He . . . um, lives upstairs from me." Okay, good, so we're moving back to reality. I accept that it may be a slight exaggeration to say that we're sleeping with each other, but he does at least live upstairs. That's got to count for something, surely?

"Your neighbor!" exclaims Chloe. "Natalie, you're wicked!"

"You have no idea just how wicked," I say glumly. The worst thing is that telling Chloe I've got a boyfriend actually feels quite good—it's like those dressing room mirrors they have in shops that make you look about two sizes smaller than you actually are. You know it isn't true, but you enjoy it all the same.

"That's really cool," continues Chloe wistfully. "So when are you going to invite me up to visit?"

"What, here?" I get a sudden jolt of alarm. She can't come here. She'll find out I've been, well, perhaps elaborating on the truth just a little bit. . . .

"Don't you want me to come and stay?" Chloe sounds defensive.

"Of course. Oh, God, I'd love you to come and stay. Can we just make it in a few weeks time? I'm . . ." I quickly try to think of an excuse. ". . . I'm going away with Alistair next weekend and I'm going to be working the weekend after that," I hear myself say. "But I'll call you, okay?"

"You're already going away for the weekend with him?" Chloe asks. "Wow. Does he have any eligible friends?"

I try to remember if I've seen Alistair with anyone good-looking, then remind myself that it doesn't really matter, since Alistair is little more than an imaginary boyfriend, so whether or not he has eligible friends is really rather academic.

"I'm sure I can dig one out for you," I promise.

"Fantastic! Well, let me know when and I'll be down."

"Okay. Have fun tonight!"

"And you . . . Bye!"

I put the phone down and sit still for a moment. I feel strangely elated.

It's true that the facts are not good.

Fact number one: I have a pretty shit job, really.

Fact number two: I haven't got any friends down here.

Fact number three: It's Saturday night and I am in watching TV.

Fact number four: I have just lied to my best friend and felt good about it.

But maybe it's like they say—appearances are what counts. What started out as a little white lie to stop my mum from being upset has turned into a made-up life complete with boyfriend. And the worst thing is, it feels really good. Chloe thinks I'm going to Soho House, and that I'm going out with Alistair. Which means Mum will be over the moon, and Pete . . . well, hopefully he'll be less than happy. Maybe he'll realize that I'm perfectly able to live my life without him. Now all I need to do is find a way to move from appearances to reality.

Trying not to think too hard about what I've just done, I flick on the telly and feel a wave of pleasure wash over me when I see Hugh Grant offering Julia Roberts some apricots with honey. Channel 4 is showing *Notting Hill*. I feel a swell of pride as I see him walk down Portobello Road— my new home! I love this film. I watched it with Chloe when it first came out, and that's when I decided I was going to move to Ladbroke Grove. I told everyone, and they all just went "yeah, yeah," and no one really believed me. And now I'm here. Hah! I quickly put my Fresh'n'Wild pizza in the oven and pour myself a glass of wine.

* * *

I stare at the film credits. My bottle of wine is empty, and to tell the truth, I'm not feeling quite as buoyant as I did before. I mean, I always cry at the bit where the guy whose wife is in a wheelchair refuses to leave her behind when they go chasing after Julia Roberts. But I don't usually cry this much. The film ended about ten minutes ago, and I'm still feeling weepy. The thing is, they're all so incredibly sorted in that film. I mean, Hugh Grant meets Julia Roberts because she just walks into his shop. And they're all really good friends. Maybe I was stupid to think I could start again. I certainly never thought I'd be lonely in a city that's got so many people in it.

After mulling for a while I get up to get myself a drink of water. When I see my reflection in the mirror, I nearly start crying again—I look really dreadful, with makeup all down my face and the diamanté clip I bought today from Portobello market hanging desolately from a few strands of hair.

But of course this is just the red wine talking—or, you know, crying. I'm fine, really. I should just go to bed.

I start to clear up, picking up the empty pizza box and chocolate wrapper and shoving them in a bin bag; then I go round the rest of the flat chucking out all the debris. I have to admit it's not particularly impressive—empty meal-for-one boxes, empty bottles of wine, copies of *Heat* and *Hello!*. I'm going to get rid of all this crap, and I am going to sort my life out, I think determinedly. I'm going to do what the magazine article said—clear out my life, and create a new me. And that includes chucking out Cressida's letters—to hell with the landlord. This is my flat now, and I don't see why I should let her letters clutter it up. Maybe I'll even get my number changed, after all.

But instead of picking up the letters I pause briefly.

Chucking them out is certainly an option. But what if Cressida does come back? Or what if the landlord comes round to collect them?

I stare at them for a while, trying to work out whether keeping them would demonstrate strength or weakness. In my heart of hearts, I wonder if the reason I don't want to throw them away is that I'm secretly desperate to know what's inside.

But that's ridiculous. There's no way I'm going to open them. I've been bad enough this evening, telling Chloe that I have a super-glamorous social life when all I'm doing is sitting around eating pizza. There is no way I'm going to open someone else's mail, as well.

I guess I could give them to the estate agent. He could probably redirect them to Cressida, wherever she lives now. But in reality he'd probably just throw them away—I mean, why would he care whether Cressida gets her letters or not?

I pick up the thick, creamy, handwritten envelope and hold it up against the light, but I can't glean any more information from it. You're only doing this because you're bored, I remind myself. It'll be some boring letter with nothing of interest inside. And anyway, opening someone else's mail is just plain wrong. Like stealing. Or spying on someone. It could even be breaking the law.

Unless . . . unless by opening it I was able to find out who it came from, so I could return it with an explanatory note. The Post Office opens mail sometimes to return it to the sender, doesn't it? So I could just do it for them. You know, save them the time . . .

No. Stupid idea.

Not wanting to give in to temptation, I look at the Soho House letter again instead. Okay, well, this one is more like business correspondence. It's not like it's from a friend, or a hospital or a bank or anything. It's not personal.

Who am I kidding?—of course it's personal. It's got Cressida's personal name on it.

But if I don't open it, I'll never know what's inside. My mother dreamt all her life of being a Cressida-type who goes to all the best parties. You never know, if I open it I might even find out how to become like her myself. And if Cressida's can't be bothered to let people know she's moved, that's hardly my fault, is it?

Quickly, before my conscience can get the better of me, I rip open the envelope. Then I put it down again. What is happening to me? Why do I even care what's inside the envelope? So it's from Soho House—so what?

Although, now that I've opened it, I suppose I may as well look. The harm's already done.

Right?

Slowly, my fingers close over the contents of the envelope, and I draw them out. Trying to convince myself this is an absolutely okay thing to be doing, I turn over the pages to find a Soho House program with a letter addressed to Cressida from someone called Podge inviting her to the private view of a film next week and a special dinner the week after that in honor of some film director I've never heard of before. So that's what people do at Soho House.

I stare at the letter for a few minutes, trying to imagine what it would feel like to be Cressida, getting a letter like this for real. To be a member of Soho House, in with the in crowd. I glance at the program again, imagining I'm her. Hmmm, a couple of films I might go to. Not sure about the dinner . . .

Then I notice a boxed item announcing that there's a festival down at Soho House's country outpost, Babington

House. That's where the glitterati go for weekend breaks in the country. Although it isn't the country I know; the rooms have baths in them and huge entertainment systems, and the Cow Shed is actually a spa where you can have treatments like Raw Hide (exfoliation).

I stare at the other letter. My curiosity is aroused now and I'm desperate to open it. But I'm not going to. I may not be rich and fabulous like Cressida, but I have integrity. Kind of. I wonder if Alistair knew her. I bet she'd have been invited to his party—the difference is, she probably would have been too busy to go. Still, no matter. I live here now. And I'm going to have a great time, even if I don't become a member of some private members club.

I pin the Soho House program to my notice board, and put the Found catalog on my coffee table—they somehow brighten the place up and make me feel more sophisticated. Then, frustrated with myself, I pick them both up again and put them in a drawer. I wish I was more like Mum— she was so beautiful and sophisticated when she was younger. I've seen photos of her in her sixties minidress looking like a model. I bet if she'd moved to London when she was younger, she'd have ended up working on *Vogue* or something. Whereas I'm like Dad—I play it safe and like being with people I know well. Mum can flit round a party and meet everyone there, whereas I'll always find my group of friends and stick with them. But I'm going to have to change if I'm going to make things work here. For one thing, I don't have a group of friends to hang out with, which means I'm going to have to bite the bullet and make some new ones, however scary the prospect seems. I'm not going to be a failure.

And in the meantime, there's no point trying to be Cressida, wondering whether to buy a new cashmere blanket and which private views to go to with my celebrity friends, because I'm patently not her. Anyway, it's gone midnight, I'm tired, and I'm going to bed.

As I get up to go to the bedroom, I pause slightly, then pick up the second letter. Without questioning my intentions, I take it with me to the bedroom, propping it up on my bedside table.

Not that I'm going to open it.

No way.